Vengeance

Vengeance

A Valentine Shepherd Novel

SHANA FIGUEROA

FOREVER
YOURS

New York   Boston

Copyright © 2016 by Shana S. Figueroa
Excerpt from *Retribution* © 2016 by Shana S. Figueroa
Cover illustration by Craig White
Cover design by Scott Silvestro

Cover copyright © 2016 by Hachette Book Group, Inc.

Forever Yours
Hachette Book Group
1290 Avenue of the Americas, New York, NY 10104
forever-romance.com
twitter.com/foreverromance

First published as an ebook and as a print on demand: September 2016

Forever Yours is an imprint of Grand Central Publishing. The Forever Yours name and logo are trademarks of Hachette Book Group, Inc.

The publisher is not responsible for websites (or their content) that are not owned by the publisher.

The Hachette Speakers Bureau provides a wide range of authors for speaking events. To find out more, go to www.hachettespeakersbureau.com or call (866) 376-6591.

ISBN: 978-1-4555-6749-2 (print on demand, paperback)

To my best friend Kendall, who spit-balled crazy "What If?" scenarios with me that led to the genesis of this story, as well as the "hot dog truck/taco stand" line I'm very proud of.

Chapter One

Valentine Shepherd slid her fingers down her fiancé's bare chest, over his hard nipples and across the soft slopes of his abs. Robby had never been a hard body—the only exercise he got came from yard work or running from their neighbor's rottweiler when it escaped from the backyard—but he was naked and all hers. A fuckable man of integrity. He cupped her ass in his hands as she straddled him, face in a cockeyed grin, eyes hungry like they hadn't done this hundreds of times.

"What was his name again?" Val asked. She rocked on top of him, rubbing herself against his hardness.

"Chet," Robby said. "He didn't—" His breath caught when Val sat back and he slid into her. "He didn't give his last name."

Val rolled her hips against his, gliding him in and out. "What else?"

"He wants to meet at Union Station tomorrow." Robby moved his hands up her back. "Says he's got information that proves Max Carressa didn't murder his father." His back arched up and down in time with her cadence. "He didn't say anything about money. Makes me nervous about what he really wants."

She leaned down and kissed him, letting her tongue linger against his lips, then cross the night's stubble to flick his ear. "Don't be nervous, baby. I'll protect you."

He laughed at their little joke—he was the "fragile" defense lawyer with a big brain, while she was the "tough" ex-military private investigator with a big gun. She sat up again and flipped her strawberry red hair over her shoulders, then laced her fingers behind her head as she rode him.

He grabbed a breast in each hand, rolled her nipples between his fingertips. "But I don't want to meet at Union Station. It's…too public…Not safe…" He struggled with his words as his breath turned quick and rough.

Val's mouth watered. She was close. This moment was the best, right before. If only she could pull herself from the brink and savor the feeling. But biological imperative thrust her forward, a runaway train controlled by her reptilian brain. Her hips quickened.

"I want to meet Chet today instead." Robby gripped her breasts tight, the flesh bulging between his fingers. "I need to know where he'll be…this…evening. Come on, baby, tell me what you see—" A guttural moan forced its way out of his chest. His whole body tensed as he came. He pushed himself deep into her. White-hot lightning raced up Val's spine as she came with him. Her eyes closed and her mind slipped into the future—

I'm on a street with light traffic. Rain falls from a patchwork of scattered clouds. I see Puget Sound behind me, roiling as choppy waves mar its surface. The red October sun sets behind dirty brick buildings tattooed with graffiti of crooked words I don't understand. A man in a blue hooded sweatshirt pulls a pair of bolt cutters from his backpack, snaps the lock off a bike chained to a rack, and rides away with it. A moment later a young, thin Hispanic man wearing a slicker and lots of lip gloss bounces out the door, discovers his bike has been stolen. He stomps his foot, swings his helmet in the air, and swears. He sighs and begins to walk down the street in the rain. He walks a few blocks, turns left. Walks more. He stops between two buildings. Painted on one of the walls is a naked female torso with a clown head grafted on top and misshapen words spilling out of its mouth. The man leans down to remove a rock from his shoe. Traffic parts. Pedestrians disappear. For a moment the man is alone. Robby runs across the street and approaches him.

"Chet? I'm Robby Price. You called me."

Chet looks around, sees they're alone. "What the…How did you find me?"

Robby cocks his head between the buildings. "Let's talk over here." They disappear into the alley.

The scene faded from Val's vision like cigarette smoke drifting up and away. She looked down and saw Robby lying still beneath her, eyes closed, enjoying the afterglow. How nice it must feel, like licking cheesecake off a fork and rolling it around in your mouth after a rich meal. She felt only the sensation of having eaten without remembering the taste.

She caressed his cheek. He opened his eyes and looked up at her. "So? Anything?"

"You'll have a chance to intercept Chet this evening," Val told him. "He'll be somewhere in downtown Seattle. A guy will steal his bike so he'll be forced to walk. Then he'll stop to get a rock out of his shoe, and no one will be around. That'll be your opening to approach him unnoticed."

He smiled, grabbed her hands, and kissed them. "You're the best, babe." He looked at the clock and cringed. "Aw, shit, my dad will kill me if I'm late to work again."

She slid off him, and he hopped up and ran to the bathroom. Morning sun poured into their bedroom through bay windows that faced a patch of evergreen Pacific Northwest forest. Val back-flopped onto the bed and let the sun warm her bare skin. She heard the tinkle of water from the sink, then the scratch of Robby's toothbrush.

"What did he look like?" Robby asked between brushes.

Propping her knees up and crossing one leg on top of the other, Val bounced her foot in the air. "He looked Latino, effeminate. He's either gay, or he ate a stick of lip gloss." Her finger traced idle circles around her nipple, a hard outcrop atop a mountain of softness. "Could he be Max Carressa's lover? Like maybe Chet knows Max is innocent because Max was with him on the night of the murder?"

She heard Robby chuckle, then the tap of his toothbrush against the sink rim followed by the clink of it dropping back into its holder. "Could be," he said. Shaving gel sprayed, then a razor wisped. "Max is a pretty odd guy. He's got this rich playboy I-don't-give-a-fuck thing going on, but I get these weird vibes from him like he's got major skeletons in the closet."

"I thought all rich people had skeletons in their closets." She propped an arm behind her head. "Do you think he killed his father?"

"As one of his lawyers, I think he's completely innocent. As a normal person, I have no idea. Like I said, weird vibes. He's definitely not too torn up about it. But rich people hating their parents is pretty common, too, right?"

Val heard running water, then face splashing.

"What street in Seattle did you see Chet on?" he asked.

"I don't know," she said with a frown. "I didn't see a street sign in my vision. But I know that the building where he stops has a creepy naked clown painted on the side. I can figure it out from there."

Robby turned on the shower and poked his head out of the bathroom. "Won't that be like looking for a needle in a haystack?"

She rolled her eyes at him. "It's a private investigator's job to find hard-to-find things. I'll track down the clown and drive you there this evening, don't worry."

He smiled and disappeared behind the door.

Sighing, Val stretched out on the bed. She listened to the water plink against the shower walls and let her fingers trace a lazy path down the valley between her breasts and across her flat stomach. Since she'd never experienced a real orgasm, she was never fully satisfied after sex—like eating and never feeling full. The side effect was a sexual appetite and stamina that outpaced

most other women. Robby loved it, but he had a job to go to unfortunately. Her hand drifted between her legs, still ripe and wet
with him. She slipped a finger inside herself—her magic vagina,
or curious oddity, or mistake of nature, whatever it was. Her belly
warmed as she rubbed the sensitive sides, the nub of flesh in the
center. She moaned as she stroked deeper down and imagined
what it would be like to feel this times a thousand, or whatever
an orgasm was supposed to be like. All she'd ever experienced was
the sweet edge of climax, the desperate contractions before and
after her mind slipped into a jumbled, banal, or horrific vision of
the future.

Val felt her hips move in time with her strokes as if possessed
by their own will, heat rising in her cheeks. So badly she wanted
to feel what other people felt—the toe-curling ecstasy, the con-
sumption of her body by another, the *connection*. She forced herself to stop. Having an orgasm while her mind wandered often
resulted in visions of fire and death. She wasn't horny enough to
risk it.

Instead, she rolled to the side of the bed and pulled a pencil
and notebook out of her nightstand drawer, then flipped to an
empty page and started drawing the clown she'd seen in her vision. The notebook was filled with similar pencil illustrations of
random objects or scenes: a willow tree in front of a decrepit
barn, half a billboard sign, a pair of leopard-print stilettos. Sometimes, though rarely, a crude face. She wasn't great at sketching
faces, avoiding the practice required to get good at it. Since she
usually saw them in the throes of their deaths, she preferred to
forget them. Not every vision she had of the future came true, but

most did. Why her mind—or vagina—insisted on showing her people's often-gruesome demises was a mystery to her. It'd just always been that way, since her first sexual experience in junior high school, fumbling around with her best friend Stacey.

Val traced the naked clown, its head thrown back and mouth agape in a silent cackle. A word spilled forth from its throat and lodged in its maw. She tried to recall what the word said, but her mind's eye couldn't decipher the crooked letters that had been sprayed on the brick, cocked at strange angles in a style she couldn't quite read. It was something like "Diehards" or "Demons."

Robby emerged from the bathroom and put on a suit and tie. "So you'll pick me up at six?" he said as he shoved his wallet and keys into his pocket.

"Yep." She tapped her drawing. "Be prepared to meet Mrs. Chuckles."

He kissed her. "Love ya, babe," he said, then hustled out the door.

She had until the evening to figure out where the creepy nude clown was hiding. Val smiled—she loved a good puzzle.

* * *

Val heard her front door open and close as she scrolled through a lineup of clown images summoned by her computer's search engine. A moment later Stacey strolled into the spare room that served as the Valentine Investigations headquarters while clutching two cups of coffee.

"Morning, fellow hot bitch," Stacey said. She placed a venti latte next to Val's keyboard, then sat down and kicked her legs up on the leather sofa across from her friend, her tie-dyed skirt draping off the side of the couch. She sipped from her own giant cup. "The mom from the Brewer case called again this morning. She's got more ideas about who it could be that's stalking her daughter. She wants you to look into some guy from her daughter's science club."

"No need," Val said. She pulled a manila envelope off the top of a stack of papers on her desk and handed it to Stacey without taking her eyes off the computer screen. Nothing the Internet offered up looked like the clown in her vision.

Stacey opened the envelope and thumbed through a dozen photographs of a little boy hiding behind various objects as he ogled a teenaged girl in the background. "Who's this?"

"Connor Gleason, the Brewers' twelve-year-old neighbor. He's the one that's been leaving gifts and pictures and uploading creep-shot videos of her online. He's their daughter's stalker."

Thank goodness it had only been a misguided little kid obsessing over the poor girl, and not some violent psychopath. A nice break to a case that could've been much worse. Also a nice respite from the string of rapes and revenge porn jobs she was usually hired for, to help desperate clients get justice after the police proved useless. Something about the name "Valentine Investigations" attracted a large contingent of sex crime victims throughout the greater Seattle area, which was ironic on so many levels.

"Aw, the world's littlest stalker," Stacey said. "Maybe they'll issue him the world's littlest restraining order."

Val shrugged. "It's up to the Brewers if they want to press charges or just have a really awkward talk with Connor's parents. In any case, they still owe us our full fee. Don't let them talk you down."

Stacey saluted. "They will be charged the full fee, Sergeant."

Val cocked an eyebrow at the reference to her old military title.

Stacey slapped the envelope and pictures back onto the desk. "Thank God you turned me off boys. You don't see little girls pulling this shit."

Val rolled her eyes. Stacey liked to rag Val about turning her into a hippie lipstick lesbian, on account of being each other's first. Two awkward junior high girls, afraid of boys but comfortable with each other, curious to know what sex was all about, wanting to be prepared. After Val had a vision of her uncle's wide-eyed corpse draped over a smashed steering wheel instead of the spike of ecstasy she'd heard so much about, Stacey quickly confirmed that visions of dead people at sexual climax weren't normal. When Val's uncle died in a car accident three days later, she realized that whatever had happened to her during her very first orgasm went beyond abnormal. Stacey, of course, volunteered to help Val explore whatever this newfound ability was. Through her best friend's soft kisses and gentle caresses—and some impressive tongue work—Val pieced together the ground rules of her ability: the strength of the visions was directly proportional to the strength of her arousal; they were stronger when she had sex with another person rather than alone; she could sometimes control the subject of her vision if she concentrated at climax—otherwise, she saw random stuff, mostly death and destruction. Not all of it came to pass, but the vast majority of it did.

The revelations weren't totally about Val's odd ability, though. When all was said and done, Val realized she preferred men while Stacey preferred women. By high school the two had transitioned back to friends, and eventually business partners in Val's PI agency after she'd separated from the Army.

Stacey sat up from the sofa and craned her neck toward Val's computer screen. "What're you looking at?"

"Creepy-ass clowns," Val said. "I saw one in a vision, spray-painted on the side of a building somewhere in Seattle. I need to find out where it is and take Robby there tonight to meet an informant."

"Some kind of gang symbol?"

"Maybe." Val searched for "Seattle clowns," then "Seattle clown gangs," "clown gang symbols," "Seattle area gangs with clown symbols." Nothing.

"Dammit, the Internet has let me down." She sighed. "I'm going to have to ask Sten."

Stacey cringed. "Ew. Good luck."

Chapter Two

Val avoided making eye contact with the mayoral campaign volunteers lurking next to the Seattle Police Department entrance, but one waylaid her anyway on her way inside.

"Vote for Norman Barrister for mayor of Seattle!" A plump-faced college kid in a red T-shirt jumped in front of Val, waving a flyer and red plastic button in her face. "Change you can *believe* in!"

Another college kid in a blue T-shirt, wielding a blue button, appeared to Val's right. "Charles Brest is best! Don't mess with success!"

Sighing, Val took both their buttons, the penance she had to pay so they'd get out of her way. The college kids glared at each other but thankfully parted to let Val pass without any further harassment. Inside the station, she glanced at the buttons and winced at Norman Barrister's name emblazoned on the red one. What a sad coincidence that retired Colonel Norman Barrister, Val's old battalion commander, just happened to be from Seattle, and also had political aspirations. The idiot couldn't lead his units out of a paper bag, but while they died in one bloody Afghan skirmish after another, he racked up awards and medals that served well the myth of his "strong leadership abilities" that was the cornerstone of his campaign. He'd duped the district into electing him to the state's House of Representatives, so why not mayor? Hell, why not president? God knew if you had enough money, it wasn't that hard. Val dumped both buttons in the trash and walked into the heart of the station.

The place hummed with activity, a cacophony of voices talking, phones ringing, keyboards clacking. The police officers set up shop in a large open space, each manning an oak desk covered in paperwork. Val snaked her way through the desks, past Homicide and Special Victims, until she reached Vice. She spotted Detective Sten Ander in the far corner, leaning back in his chair, hands held casually behind his head as he conversed with a strung-out woman in a puffy leopard-print coat and ripped nylons underneath a black miniskirt. Val wasn't close enough to hear the details of their conversation, but after a minute of talking he waved a hand and two uniformed officers swooped in and cuffed the woman.

"I want my lawyer!" the woman shrieked as they led her past Val and through a door to the cells. Sten smirked at the woman's back until she disappeared, then cut his gaze to Val. He didn't bother sitting up as Val took the chair across from him.

"Ah, Shepherd," Sten said. "To what do I owe the pleasure?"

Val suppressed an eye roll at his use of her last name. They'd known each other since they'd both joined the Army right out of high school, even dated for a short time while stationed together at Joint Base Lewis-McChord. Now that he was a man of the law, he addressed her by her last name only, like he starred in a crime procedural TV show. He even looked a bit like a Scandinavian version of Jeremy Renner.

Sten sipped coffee as he eyed Val over the rim of a ceramic mug adorned with Norman Barrister's smiling face.

"I never pegged you for a Republican," Val said. "I would've thought you'd be more of a Guns and Dope Party kind of guy."

"Still waters run deep," he said. He licked coffee off the caterpillar attached to his face that he called a mustache, then propped his feet on his desk. "Let me guess—drunk sorority girl fucked some frat boy and is now pretending like her drink was spiked so her parents won't think she's a slut? Or someone sent dick pics to the PTA again?"

Val gritted her teeth. It'd been almost ten years since she'd broken up with Sten, but the asshole still held a grudge. He'd been cooperative enough when she'd first approached him for inside police information at the onset of her PI business. She'd assumed that he'd buried the hatchet in the name of justice, but soon realized his real motivation was the opportunity to play mind games with her. Val considered cutting him from her roster of contacts on many occasions, but just before her last straw, he'd cough up a piece of valuable info and buy himself a reprieve. At least he didn't demand money or sexual favors; apparently toying with her was payment enough.

"I am always amazed at what a big heart you have," Val said through a tight smile. "Always looking out for the"—she held up her thumb and forefinger, and narrowed the gap between them to an inch—"*little* guys."

Sten clanked his coffee mug down on a ceramic coaster. "What do you want, Shepherd? I've got places to be."

"Well, I wouldn't want to make you late for your men's rights rally." She pulled her notebook from her tote and flipped to the clown drawing. "Have you seen this picture before, maybe as gang graffiti?"

Sten leaned across his desk and eyed the illustration. A glimmer of recognition flickered in his gaze. "Why do you ask?"

"A client's daughter ran off with her gang member boyfriend. The mom says the boyfriend had this picture tattooed on his arm. She wants me to bring her daughter home."

Sten sat back again, picked up his mug, and took a long slurp. "Remember when you used to blow me in my dorm room before retreat?"

A trickle of bile rose up Val's throat. *Here we go with the mind games.* "I've repressed most of those memories, but yes."

"You were really good at sucking dick, did I ever tell you that? I guess practice makes perfect."

Val drummed her fingers on the side of her chair to occupy her hands. It was all she could do to keep from punching his smug face. She gave him a bored look and waited.

Sten took another long drink of coffee, relishing the moment. Finally, he said, "The Diamond Gang pride themselves on running 'high-class' hookers for low-class needs. Entrepreneurial sorts, despite their stupid clown logo. They hang out west of the I-5, around South Washington Street. Charge fifty dollars a pop."

He shoved a thumb in his mouth and jerked it out with a popping sound. "A small fortune for a junkie, but their girls are pros. *Practice makes perfect*." His thick mustache curled into a smile that didn't reach his eyes.

A shiver ran up Val's spine. She knew Sten had an edge when they'd dated—she'd always liked the edgy guys, though she knew she shouldn't—but only recently had she realized just how much he liked to see her squirm—like a sociopath. With a police badge. She forced out a "thanks" and stood to leave. In the end his words were harmless, and his idiosyncrasies worked to her benefit.

"Hey, Shepherd," Sten called after her as she walked away, "You find that poor girl and bring her home, to safety." He smiled again, and Val was struck with the image of a snake's mouth just before it swallowed its prey.

* * *

Val watched the rain smear the world through her windshield as she sat in her Corolla, idling in front of the Bombay and Price Law Offices sign outside Robby's work. After a few minutes of staring out the window, she saw him emerge from the glass building and trot through the puddles to her car. He tossed a gym bag with his suit shoved in it into the back, then hopped into the passenger's seat.

"Did you find Chuckles the Creepy Clown?" he asked, brushing water off his jeans.

"You know it," Val said. "I narrowed it down to South Washington Street, near the waterfront, then drove around the seediest areas until I found the graffiti with the right background that matched what I saw in the vision." She pulled away from the curb and began driving to Chet's future location.

"You're too good for me," Robby said.

Val knew the opposite was true. She needed him a lot more than he needed her. Robby's lawyer gig paid most of the bills, not to mention the stabilizing influence he had on her visions. They weren't as bad when she was with him, though she didn't know why. She'd have given up on love a long time ago if it hadn't been for Robby.

He looked at his watch. "How much time do we have to catch Chet?"

"The sun was setting in my vision, so we have about an hour, I think."

Val drove along the back streets through Seattle's underbelly to avoid highway traffic. She knew the streets well, explored every inch of them while growing up, looking for adventure, until her dad dragged her and her sister to the suburbs. They should've stayed in the city. Val loved her life with Robby in their two-story house with its white picket fence and stand-alone mailbox, but reminders of her sister's fate often bubbled at the edges of her suburban bliss, and she'd get the urge to burn it all down.

Her grip tightened on the steering wheel. She should let the past go, but then Valentine Investigations wouldn't exist, and she'd be another mindless peon floating through life, ignoring the rot that threatened to consume the world just outside of view from polite society. She'd rather have her sister's life back, but since that wasn't possible, punishing assholes who'd slipped through cracks in the justice system would have to do.

She parked the car along the curb of South Washington Street, on the opposite side of the road from the naked clown puking up the word she now recognized as "Diamonds." She killed the engine, and they watched the street where Chet was destined to appear at any moment as raindrops plinked against the roof.

"Talk to Max Carressa today?" she asked Robby.

"Yeah, we actually went to his house on Mercer Island," he said. "We walked him through the case as it stands now. It's all circumstantial. The police don't have enough to charge him with anything yet, but who knows when that'll change. He showed us where his dad fell over the balcony of the deck that extends off the study. It's got a gorgeous view of Lake Washington, and a sheer drop down a cliff. I almost got vertigo looking down, it was wild."

"Did you ask Max about Chet?"

"Not yet. I want to hear what Chet has to say before bringing it up. We've gotten fake information before. Guess that comes with working a local celebrity case." He grinned, then nudged Val. "My dad asked me about our wedding date again."

Val rolled her eyes. "God, what's his rush? It'll happen when it happens."

"He says if Mom was still alive, she'd want grandkids by now."

"I thought those little white fluffy dogs were supposed to be grandchildren substitutes."

"Why don't we just pick a date?"

"Because…" Val sighed. "I don't want to rush things—there's Chet!"

Thank God for Chet, loping down the street in his slicker and swinging his bike helmet at his side. She hated this conversation. Every time she imagined herself walking down the aisle, it'd be followed by an image of herself running away from the altar, out of the church and over the horizon. She needed Robby and loved him, but…she didn't know. Val guessed there was some sort of deep psychological reason for her reluctance that involved her superego and freak-of-nature status and past traumas and all that, but she preferred not to think too hard about it and hoped it would go away on its own.

They tracked Chet as he walked, oblivious to their presence. He stopped in front of the alley between two buildings, next to the clown graffiti. He leaned down to fish a rock out of his shoe. Traffic parted. They lost sight of any other pedestrians.

"Now!" Val said to Robby.

With his eyes locked on Chet, Robby jumped out of the car and began to jog across the street. Val heard the sedan's wheels screech before she saw it out of the corner of her eye, a blur of movement that seized her heart and crushed it before the rest of her brain could even register what she was seeing.

She had no time to react before the sedan slammed into Robby. He catapulted through the air like a ragdoll until he hit the pavement with a wet thud. Without slowing down, the car hung a hard right at the next intersection and disappeared. A piercing noise caught her attention; she realized it was her screams.

Val burst out of the car and ran to where Robby lay still on the ground. She knelt next to his broken body, unable to breathe, afraid to touch him.

"Holy shit," she heard Chet say, followed by his receding footfalls as he fled.

"Robby, oh God, Robby," she said, her voice shrill and panicked, willing for him to live with every part of her being.

His eyelids fluttered and he looked at her, then he looked through her at nothing. Rain wet his unblinking eyes.

A wail ripped from Val's chest as she sobbed over his body, only vaguely aware of the newly arrived traffic around her that stopped to gawk and offer useless assistance.

Chapter Three

Val gripped the sides of the police station chair until her knuckles turned white, but her body wouldn't stop shaking. She swept a continuous flow of tears from her eyes as a detective handed her a Styrofoam cup of water.

"We can't find another witness to the hit-and-run," the detective, Johnson, said. He sat down across from Val. "But we'll keep canvasing the neighborhood and see if any security cameras in the area picked something up."

"Chet saw it happen," Val said, her voice hoarse. With a trembling hand, she set the cup down on Johnson's desk, water untouched. "Chet can confirm that Robby was murdered. Find Chet."

"A first name and a vague physical description aren't enough to go on."

"Then get the phone records from his office! Chet called Robby's work phone two days ago to say he had information about the Carressa case. Robby works"—she swallowed hard—"*worked* at Bombay and Price. His father is one of the partners. Trace the call back to Chet's phone. Do I really have to tell you how to do your fucking job?" God, did Robby's father know yet? She couldn't imagine calling him with the news. She couldn't…

Sten ambled over from where he'd been watching off to the side. He leaned against the wall next to Johnson and looked down at Val. "Slow your roll, Shepherd. South Washington Street is crawling with junkies and gang bangers. People get shot and run over and stabbed there all the time. Robby Price was probably mowed down by some crack whore high off her ass. He wouldn't be the first. In fact, he wouldn't even be the first *this month*."

Val slammed her fist down on Johnson's desk, causing water to slop out of the foam cup. "Robby was murdered. There's no way it's a coincidence that Robby was run down right as he was about to talk to someone with important information about the death of Max Carressa's father. Someone didn't want that meeting to happen. Someone—"

Someone who knew exactly when and where Robby and Chet would meet that evening, something only Robby and Val knew. She'd told Sten about the clown—maybe he'd somehow pieced together what was happening and lain in wait for the right moment to run Robby down? But why? To Val's knowledge, Sten wasn't involved in the investigation into Lester Carressa's death. And Val had seen multiple images of the creepy clown spray painted on buildings around the Seattle waterfront. There was no way he could've known which specific image she was looking for.

And why hadn't she seen Robby die? She might have been able

to stop it if she'd known. Val put a hand over her mouth to stifle the sob that jumped up her throat.

"I'm very sorry for your loss," Johnson said. "We'll do everything we can to find who did this."

"You think Robby's death was a tragic accident, so excuse me if I think you're full of shit."

"We're all sorry your boyfriend died," Sten said, "but there's no reason to be rude."

Val fixed him with a glare that could have melted glass.

"Want me to give you a ride home?" he asked.

The thought of Sten knowing where Val lived turned her stomach. "Screw you," she said and shot up from her chair, knocking it over. She didn't know if Sten was involved in Robby's death, but she definitely didn't trust him.

"Call me if you want to talk about your feelings," Sten said to her as she stormed out of the police station.

She thought she heard him snicker.

* * *

Val drove home in a daze, exhausted from the effort to keep her brain functioning enough to make the trip. Hands still shaking, she fumbled with the lock on the front door until it clicked open, then she stumbled over the threshold and up the stairs to their bedroom—just Val's bedroom now. She collapsed onto the bed and sobbed into Robby's pillow, still ripe with his smell.

Why hadn't she seen him die in her vision? She'd seen hundreds of people die, some people she knew and some she didn't.

None of it she'd wanted to see, but she'd seen it nonetheless. The vast majority of it she couldn't change, but sometimes, very rarely, she could—she still felt a rush of anxiety every time Stacey mentioned getting on a boat for any reason. But like her poor sister's death, Val hadn't seen this coming. Maybe she hadn't wanted to see it. Maybe she hadn't seen him die because subconsciously she couldn't stand to know. Just like she'd done to her sister, she'd let him die because deep down she was a coward.

Val curled into a ball on her bed. She stayed there until the sky went dark and then light again, and didn't move even as her phone began to ring off the hook. At some point she heard a knock at the door, then a click as it opened, followed by Stacey's trembling voice.

"Val? Are you here?"

Val didn't answer. The stairs creaked as Stacey ascended them and appeared in the doorway to Val's bedroom.

"Oh my God, Val, I am so sorry."

Stacey lay next to Val and hugged her. Val cried into her friend's chest until it seemed all the liquid in her body had escaped through her tears. The sky grew dark again, and finally Val couldn't ignore the call of nature. With the effort of a person half dead, she dragged herself out of bed and into the bathroom. Stacey helped her undress and she took a long, hot shower, letting the water scald her skin as if it had the power to wash her guilt away. Afterward, she pulled on a pair of pajamas and fell into bed again. She heard Stacey talking on the phone to Val's father, then Robby's sister, then Stacey's girlfriend, until the house was once again cloaked in night.

Through a haze, Val awoke with the rising sun in her eyes. The gnaw of hunger pulled her out of bed, and she descended the staircase feeling like a popped balloon floating down through the clouds to the ground. Stacey sat at the kitchen table with a cup of coffee, playing with her cell phone. Her head snapped up when she heard movement at the kitchen's entrance.

"Val," Stacey said, and rose to hug her. "Are you hungry?"

"I don't know." Val's throat felt like she'd spent the night swallowing sand. "I think so."

"Sit down, I'll make you some toast."

Val slouched into a chair and watched her friend shove a couple pieces of bread into the toaster oven. Stacey's phone vibrated against the tabletop and she scowled at it.

"Goddamn Natasha's going nuts," Stacey said. "She doesn't understand this whole 'friend in need' thing. Thinks I'm cheating on her and keeps calling. If she weren't smoking hot, I'd have dumped her crazy ass by now."

Val's face twitched into a slight smile. "I am technically your ex."

"She doesn't need to know that. She's jealous enough as it is."

"And I thought your girlfriend's name was Kat."

"That's the *other* one."

"How am I supposed to keep track when their names change every couple months?"

"I use mnemonic devices. 'At the coffee shop for a chat is where I met Kat.'"

The toaster dinged, and Stacey buttered the warm bread, put it on a plate, and placed it in front of Val.

"How are you?" Stacey asked in a hushed voice. She took a seat next to Val.

"Still alive." Biting into a corner of the bread, she savored the melted butter that slid down her throat.

"What do you think happened?"

Val shook her head. "I don't know. In my vision, Robby crossed the street safely and talked to Chet. My visions don't always happen exactly like I see them, but I can't believe that of all the death I foretell, I didn't see his. Just like my sister." Her eyes blurred with tears.

"This isn't your fault," Stacey said, taking Val's hand.

"He wouldn't have been on South Washington Street if I didn't tell him to be there."

"You can't save everyone. Sometimes the universe just decides it's your time."

For a moment Val saw Stacey's face suspended in water, lifeless eyes wide open and mouth locked in a silent scream.

"No," Val said, wiping the image from her thoughts. "It wasn't random. Robby was murdered. I don't know how someone could have known exactly when and where he'd be in order to run him down, or why they'd want him dead, but I'm going to find out."

Val finished her toast and realized she was hungry for more. With food in her belly and a sense of purpose came a newfound energy. The fog lifted from her mind.

"I'd like some time alone, Stacey."

"Do you need help?" she asked with a hint of enthusiasm. Natasha would've flown into a rage if she knew Stacey meant the kind of help that might jumpstart a useful vision.

Val declined, and Stacey shrugged. "Okay, if you're sure," she said like it was no big deal, though Val saw a hint of disappointment in her eyes. Their old intimate relationship was long dead, but it was hard not to idolize your first romantic experience. They'd almost rekindled it once before, and now Stacey held a candle for what could have been. It was Val's fault. At the time, it had been the only way to save Stacey's life without ruining it. But changing the future came with a price, and the consequences lingered.

"I need time to think," Val said. "Thanks for everything you've done for me these last couple days. I don't think I'd be out of bed if it weren't for you."

"That's a lie. You were always the strong one. You'll get through this."

They hugged, and Stacey slipped out the door.

Val paced around the house for the rest of the day, watching TV and eating junk food, rebuilding her mental and physical energy. Finding Chet was her priority, but she had no leads on where he could be. She could try to backtrack from the clown graffiti to where Chet's bike had been stolen, ask around for him and hope someone was willing to talk, but that was a long shot. She knew what she had to do. She wasn't looking forward to it.

Val propped her laptop on her bedroom nightstand and stripped off her clothes. After rummaging through a box in the back of her closet, she found her old vibrator, confirmed the batteries still worked, and grabbed a tube of lube from the bathroom medicine cabinet. She worked hard to ignore Robby's toiletries, still propped next to the sink where he'd left them. Then she lay down on the bed and cued up a porno video on her computer, *Back Door Babes 3*—a little vulgar, but she wanted quick and dirty, to get it over with.

Val hit Play on the video, lubed up her vibrator, and turned it up to max. She touched the head to herself and rubbed it against her outer folds to the moans of the movie. Robby's caresses snuck into her thoughts, but she banished them. If she thought about Robby, she'd dissolve into a puddle of tears again, and she'd be no closer to finding his killer. No, she needed to pretend like she was someone else, one of the women in the video being rammed from behind by a hairy man with an eight-inch cock and loving every minute of it. She pushed the vibrator into herself and focused on the porn star's squeals of pleasure. She licked her lips and thrust the vibrator in time with the movie, imagining she was the one bent over, his thighs slapping into hers, rubbing her clitoris, begging him to fuck her harder in a relentless rush to the climax. Val writhed on the bed and felt herself at orgasm's sweet edge.

"Where are you, Chet?" she said with ragged breath as her body climaxed and her mind snapped away—

Chet sits at a table in a Chinese restaurant, a hole-in-the-wall with stained wallpaper and caterwauling music piped in through a scratchy sound system. He eats a dumpling with chopsticks and laughs with friends whose faces I can't see.

Blur.

Chet pees in a filthy toilet in a nightclub, ripped posters and graffiti covering black-painted walls, while two men grunt in a stall next to him as they have sex.

Blur.

Chet sputters as the life drains out of him and into a shag carpet, pools of blood blooming from underneath his back, pawing at the bullet holes in his chest until his hands go still.

Val gasped and her vision cleared, back in her bedroom again. Funk music played as the porno movie credits rolled. Chet might live somewhere near a Chinese restaurant—there were several dozen in the Seattle area. He might frequent a gay nightclub—also dozens in the Seattle area. She'd seen nothing of value in her vision, nothing to get her closer to finding Chet, nothing to help her bring Robby's murderer to justice.

"Goddammit!" Val threw her vibrator across the room. It crashed into a picture on the wall and fell to the ground amid shattered glass. A wave of hopelessness consumed her, and she burst into tears again. Why had she been given this horrible ability? It was a curse—a curse that killed a good person, a kind and decent soul, the man she loved.

She wallowed in her pain until a harsh voice from the back of her mind scolded her for giving in to despair. Moping around the house and crying all day wasn't getting her any closer to finding Robby's killer. She had to pull herself together, if only for Robby's sake.

Val sat up in bed and took deep breaths until her tears abated and her mind focused like a keen blade on the real task at hand. She was a crack private investigator, dammit. Her visions were a convenient tool, but she didn't need them to do her job, or to find Chet.

Val rose and bathed, threw on jeans and a long-sleeved V-neck shirt, then slipped on her vintage brown leather jacket on her way out the door. A glimpse of herself in the mirror confirmed her eyes were still ringed with red and her cheeks hollow, but her gaze was sharp enough to demand answers when she started asking questions. Her only connection between Robby and Chet was Maxwell Carressa. If she couldn't find Chet, then she'd go to the source himself.

Chapter Four

Val went to the Carressa mansion on Mercer Island first, figuring Max was most likely to be home in the early evening, but she was turned away at the gate that surrounded the property by a Mexican housekeeper over the intercom.

"Mr. Carressa is still at work," the woman said with a thick Spanish accent through the crackling speaker. "And he is not talking to reporters," she added, sounding personally annoyed for him. "So if that is who you are, then don't come back, please. Thank you."

Val half smiled—apparently Max had earned his staff's loyalty. Maybe he wasn't a stereotypical rich asshole with a penchant for murder after all.

She made the trip to the commercial district in Seattle, where Carressa Industries occupied the top half of the Thornton Building, a modest skyscraper. At the headquarters, Val exited the elevator and sidestepped a janitor sloughing a mop across the marble floor of the lobby. She approached a young woman in a pantsuit—either a secretary or an intern—manning the front desk. The woman looked up from a business textbook and greeted Val with a superficial smile.

She took in Val's casual clothing with a slight sneer. "Can I *help* you, ma'am?"

"I'm looking for Maxwell Carressa," Val said.

"He went home for the day."

"I was just at his house, and his housekeeper told me he was here."

"Well, he's not."

"Where else would he be, then?"

The woman frowned. "Are you the police?"

"Yes," Val said. "I'm investigating the murder of one of his lawyers, and I just need to ask him a few questions. If you know where he is, you should tell me. Obstruction of justice is a felony punishable by jail time."

The woman's lips tightened for a moment, then loosened with a sigh. She grabbed a sticky note, scribbled something on it, and peeled it from the pack.

"He's at this address," the woman said as she handed Val the note. "He goes there a lot after work to…blow off steam, I suppose. He owns the place, but it's not common knowledge. He likes to be discreet. I only know because I have a friend who works there, and she helped me get this job. I don't frequent the place or anything, really. Don't tell anyone I sent you."

Val lifted an eyebrow at the woman, then glanced down at the address. Another place in downtown Seattle, a much posher area than South Washington Street—though going by the woman's attempts to distance herself from Max's home-away-from-home, even the highest social elite couldn't bury all their dark secrets. Whatever he was hiding wouldn't stay hidden from her for long.

* * *

Val parked on Union Street, across the road from the address the woman at Carressa Industries had given her. She double-checked to make sure she was indeed at the right place. All that marked the existence of Max's hideaway was a single red door inlaid in a featureless commercial building, sandwiched between a jazz bar and a handbag store. No windows or signs gave a clue as to what the place might be. Tourists and locals alike walked by it without a second glance on their way to the waterfront.

Val approached the door, illuminated by one sole lightbulb, and knocked. A rectangular peephole slid open to reveal Asian eyes surrounded by thick eyeliner.

"Yes?" a no-nonsense voice asked.

"I'm here to see Maxwell Carressa."

"And who are you?"

"Seattle PD. I need to talk to him about the murder of one of his lawyers two days ago."

The peephole snapped shut.

"Shit," Val muttered. She considered whether kicking the door down would be enough to get Max's attention until about a minute later the entrance swung open. A gorgeous Asian woman in a strapless leather dress beckoned for Val to enter. Val followed her through a corridor so dark she could barely see the outline of the woman's lithe form three feet ahead. They rounded a corner and came to another door, this one all black, a red neon sign with the phrase "Red Raven in Moonlight" scrawled in cursive above it.

Val crossed the threshold into what seemed at first like a posh, mellow nightclub, all blacks and reds set in a dim glow to smooth electronic music. A few dozen people in expensive business suits sipped drinks and chatted with each other at black lacquer tables. Val did a double take when she realized at least half the crowd wore black bathrobes. What in the world was this place?

"Wait here," the Asian woman said before disappearing through one of three corridors that led away from the mingling room where Val stood. Val did as she was told for a couple minutes, trying not to stare at the weirdoes in black robes. They unabashedly stared at her, however, casting furtive glances at her comparatively cheap look, someone who clearly didn't belong at whatever this place was supposed to be.

She turned away from their judging eyes until she faced a corridor where darker, faster music wafted through. Out of curiosity she walked toward the music until she reached the source.

The hallway deposited Val into a lounge area with black leather couches surrounding a small stage. A beautiful man and woman performed a sensual dance for the benefit of a modest crowd. Val's mouth fell open when she realized the man and woman, writhing against each other in time to the music, weren't actually dancing—they were fucking. Her eyes cut to the spectators; she now noticed at least half a dozen of them masturbating while two couples performed oral sex on each other.

Holy shit—I'm in a high-end sex club.

Val had never been prudish, but this level of immodesty shocked even her. It was one thing to watch people screw each other on a computer screen; quite another to be in the same room with them. She felt herself blush and tried to look anywhere but at the people engaged in overt sex acts. Her eyes rested on a man in an expensive-looking suit, lounging on a sofa as he swirled liquor around in a tumbler glass and watched the show. In the dim light he looked like a twenty-years-older and thinner version of Robby, with close-cropped blond hair and a boyish face. His eyes wandered from the performance like he was bored until he noticed Val staring at him. He smiled and tipped his glass to her.

"Miss." The Asian woman's voice caught Val's attention. She stood in the threshold of the corridor Val had come through, arms on her hips and tapping her foot like she was dealing with a misbehaving child. "I told you to wait in the other room."

Val shrugged her shoulders.

The woman rolled her eyes. "Mr. Carressa will see you now."

She followed the Asian woman back through the mingling room, up a staircase, and into another dark corridor that ended at yet another black door. The woman opened the door and let Val enter Max's private office.

Val expected some kind of kinky setup with maybe a giant heart-shaped bed and chains dangling from the ceiling. Instead, bookshelves lined the entire periphery of the room, broken only by a ten-foot-tall Celtic-style tapestry depicting an ancient tree—Val guessed either the Tree of Knowledge or the Tree of Life—directly behind a huge mahogany desk piled with papers and more books. Through the cozy light that illuminated the study, she made out hundreds of tomes on advanced mathematics, interspersed with works by Shakespeare, Dickens, and many authors she'd never heard of, some in foreign languages.

A thin blonde in a skirt so short Val could almost see her vagina leaned against the desk. She regarded Val as if the disheveled PI were a new lab specimen. On the far end of the study a man in his late twenties stood next to a bookcase, head down as he leafed through a textbook. He wore the dark gray vest and slacks of a fine three-piece suit, the sleeves of his white dress shirt rolled up to his elbows. Thick, wavy black hair framed a Hollywood-quality face with a sharp jawline and rough-textured lips pressed together in concentration. Val heard the door close behind her as he lifted his gaze to meet hers. She'd seen him enough on the news that an introduction wasn't necessary, but he gave her one anyway.

"Hello," he said as he snapped his book shut, then put it back on the shelf. "I'm Max."

"Valentine Shepherd." The photos they used on television hadn't done him justice. He looked even handsomer in person, she couldn't help noticing.

Max gestured for her to sit down at a thick leather chair across from his desk. The movement exposed dragon tattoos inked in bright aquamarine colors across each of his inner forearms. As Val took a seat, she tried not to stare. They weren't dragons, she realized, but fractal patterns, like the intricate designs on folders she'd had as a kid.

He sat across from her at the head of the desk. "Kitty," he said to the blonde, "please bring Miss Shepherd a drink." He looked at Val. "What'll you have?"

"I'm fine, thanks. And call me Val."

"Sure thing, Val." The words rolled thick off his tongue as if he'd made a clever joke. He popped open a silver cigarette case, pulled out a joint, and held it up in front of him. Kitty sashayed over with a lighter and lit it. She went back to the periphery of the room while Max took a drag and then let out a long exhale, his hazel eyes watching the smoke drift away from him and disappear into the ceiling before snapping back to Val. His gaze pinned her down with an almost scary intelligence.

"You are not a cop," he said. "Impersonating a police officer is a crime."

"Yeah, but I don't really give a shit," Val said. "Somebody's got to do their job. Might as well be me."

He cracked a smile and took another puff from his joint. "I'm curious why you think Robert Price's death was murder. I heard he was hit by a drunk driver."

So that was why he'd let her into his inner sanctum instead of turning her away—curiosity.

"Robby was run down in broad daylight as he was about to meet an informant. That's not a coincidence. I was there when it happened."

"And what was he to you?"

"My fiancé."

"You?" Max raised an eyebrow. "I wouldn't have figured that."

"Why not?"

"Because Robby was a bit of a dough boy." He took another drag. "And you're not."

Val gritted her teeth at his backhanded compliment. Whatever Robby had lacked in the looks department compared to Max, he'd made up for in spades through compassion and warmth, something this pretty boy who might've murdered his own father probably wouldn't know anything about. She forced herself to stay objective and focus on what she came for.

"Robby was meeting someone named Chet, who said he had information that could exonerate you."

"No kidding," Max said, and looked lost in thought for a moment.

"Do you know anyone named Chet?" she asked.

"Got a last name?"

"No. Just Chet. Might be short for Chester. Effeminate Hispanic guy, early to mid-twenties. Probably lives somewhere around South Washington Street."

Max bit the tip of his thumb and squinted his eyes as if he were scrolling through a mental Rolodex. "Nope, I don't know anyone named Chet or Chester who fits your description." He looked at the blond woman. "Kitty, can you think of anyone?"

"No," she said in a voice like black velvet.

"What about the information that Chet said he had?" Val asked, a hint of desperation creeping into her tone. "What could an anonymous person know about you that might help your case?"

Max shrugged. "I have no idea. I would help you if I could. No one is more invested in proving my innocence than myself obviously."

Val deflated in her chair as the chances of finding Robby's killer went from slim to anorexic. She could search every gay bar and Chinese restaurant within a ten-mile radius of where Robby died, but even with Stacey's help, that could take weeks. The longer she went without any leads, the colder the case got. And that didn't include the planning she needed to do for Robby's funeral, boxing up his things, deciding what to give to whom—if she even had the option to choose since they weren't married—and figuring out what to do with the house she couldn't afford on her own.

Val realized she'd been staring at the tree tapestry behind Max at the same time she noticed he'd been staring at her. She blushed a little while his warm hazel eyes studied her, as if he could see into her and read her thoughts like one of his books.

"I'm sorry for your loss," Max said. "Maybe it was just an accident. The world is cruel that way. Sometimes bad things happen to good people for no reason."

She scoffed. "Like how your dad accidentally fell off his balcony?"

His gaze hardened but he smiled. "Yes," he said in a tone drier than the Mojave. "Like that."

Val stood. "I'm sorry for wasting your time. I'll see myself out."

He got up anyway and followed her to the door. As she approached the exit, he reached around her and grabbed the brass knob, turning it slowly before pulling the door open. Standing barely a couple inches away, she thought she felt heat radiating off him like he hid an inferno underneath his expensive suit.

She should have stepped back; she didn't. Whatever possessed him to suddenly enter her personal space, she wouldn't give him the satisfaction of being intimidated.

Well, not intimidated exactly. More like…intrigued. Dangerously. A moth drawn to his hidden flame. With him so close to her, she could see the five o'clock shadow spread across his jawbone, the slight chap of his lips, the light dancing off flecks of amber in his intelligent eyes. Intrigue turned to longing, a *want* for him so singular and intense it took her breath away. She eyed the buttons on his dress shirt and imagined slipping her hand between them, touching his flesh underneath—

"Nice meeting you, Val," he said as he held the door open for her, voice as cool and calm as winter snow.

She blinked as if snapping out of a trance. Stepping back, she sucked in a breath after realizing she'd been holding it. He smiled, but she recognized it as a practiced fake. Everything about his demeanor spoke of careful control—everything except the fire she felt in him just below the surface, one that threatened to consume her as well.

Chapter Five

Val stood in the lounge area of the Red Raven, thankful for a moment to collect herself without the Asian woman hassling her to leave.

What the *hell* happened back there? She'd never felt so intensely—*irrationally*—drawn to someone before. It was as if he'd flipped a switch deep inside her she never knew existed. But that was ridiculous. She'd only just met the man. And for God's sake, Robby's body was barely cold. What was wrong with her? She was a defective, weird, coldhearted bitch.

Goddammit, she needed to focus and stop being so selfish. She tried to piece together her next move, but the awful wave of despair returned to cloud her thoughts.

"Got what you came for?" a man said behind her.

She turned to find the Robby look-alike. "What makes you think I came for something different than what you came for?"

"No offense, but you don't look like you belong here."

Tears welled at the edges of her eyes. "I'm a freak. I don't belong anywhere."

"Don't say that. Everyone's got a kindred spirit. Hell, even those two weirdos found each other." He nodded toward the stage where the man and woman, still performing to the music, had moved into mirrored back bends conjoined at the groin. He lifted his hand to caress her face, but she grabbed his wrist before he could touch her. His eyes widened at the strength of her grip, similar to the look Robby got when she surprised him, something she could still do even after their three years together. Why hadn't she married him?

Val asked, "How does this place work?"

"People can stay out here, or there are private rooms in the back."

"Which do you prefer?"

"The back."

She released his wrist. "Show me."

He smiled. Val followed him through the only corridor she hadn't been down off the mingling area and along a passageway similar to a hotel hallway with rooms on each side. Lights above the door marked each room as available or not, though some had windows with the curtains drawn back to reveal occupants engaged in all sorts of fornication, from men masturbating while their partners watched to a woman getting busy with two guys. They came to a vacant room and stepped inside.

A queen-size bed sat in the center of the room, positioned underneath a mirrored ceiling. A glass table with a jar of condoms atop it was pushed up against the far wall opposite a shelf of sex toys. Though the smell of sex was strong, everything looked clean, as could be expected for the small fortune these people likely paid in membership dues.

"My name's John, by the way," he said as he pulled the window curtain shut.

Val tossed her jacket on the bed. "I'm Jane."

With his hands in his pockets, he stood so close to her, she could smell his aftershave underneath the musk of his day. "So, Jane, why are we here?"

Val hesitated. She could leave now, go home, and cry. That's what her heart told her to do. It was what she'd done after her sister died, when she was a helpless teenager with no other option except to hope other people would deliver justice. But she was an adult now, in charge of her own life and possessing an ability no one else in the world had. She'd be damned if she would give up now. Her glimpses of the future were always longer and more vivid with another person, and he looked enough like her fiancé to make the task almost palatable. She could get through it, for Robby.

Val grabbed one of the buttons on his thousand-dollar suit coat and yanked it off. He made a silent yelp.

"I've been bad," Val said. She ripped off another button. "I've hurt you."

She reached for his remaining button and he grabbed her wrist tight, pulling her flush to him. With his violent reaction and the uncomfortable squeeze of his hand, Val felt the kind of satisfaction she imagined a cutter experienced when the knife sliced their skin. In pain, but in command, substituting loss of control in one part of her life for the illusion of control in another. Her sister had been a cutter, right before the end.

"You've been a bad girl, huh?" he said through a wicked grin.

She used her free hand to grab his crotch, where his erection grew as she squeezed. "You have no idea how bad."

He leaned in to kiss her and she squeezed him harder until his body stiffened in pain. His lips stopped on their way to hers.

"Don't," she said. She could fool herself into believing she enjoyed this if it brought her closer to justice for Robby. But kissing was too intimate. "I have your life in my hands and I could crush it. I can't stop myself."

His breath was a furnace against hers as his chest heaved and his manhood throbbed against her palm. "Then you need to be punished until you learn your lesson," he said.

John spun her away from him, his fingers still biting into her wrist. With his other hand he loosened his tie, then she let him use it to bind both her wrists together behind her back. She wasn't normally the S&M type, but it fit her mood. She wanted to hurt someone, and be hurt back in equal measures. If the universe wouldn't dole out pain in fair amounts, then she would.

He jerked her around again so she faced him, then pushed her backward onto the table. Her feet still touched the ground, and if she looked up, she could see herself in the mirrored ceiling, red hair spread out in a halo around her head. He pushed up her shirt and ripped off her bra, slid his tongue over her breasts, and rubbed her nipples with his thumbs. Val shoved her knee into his groin and kneaded him there, so roughly he grunted in pain as she felt his erection harden into a steel rod.

"Naughty girl," he said with ragged breath. He cupped her breasts tight, fingers digging into her flesh, and sucked on her nipples. Val moaned as he bit them hard enough to leave a mark but not break the skin. Sweat bloomed across her body and she felt herself ache for release, in her sex and her soul.

I'm sorry, Robby.

John gave her breasts a final squeeze before he stood up and flipped her over so her bare chest pressed into the glass tabletop while her legs braced against the floor. Val blinked at herself in another mirror underneath the table, this one tilted at a forty-five-degree angle so both she and John had a clear view of the action from below. He pulled her shoes, pants, and panties off, then kicked her legs apart. He let his own pants fall to his ankles, cock ready to burst. He reached his arm between her legs and grabbed her pubic hair, then moved his fingers through her wetness and up to her rear, where he pushed a finger into her backside. Val threw her head back and gasped as he thrust his finger in and out while rubbing his erection between her spread legs.

Her body was edging toward climax when he stopped again, and she felt a moistness as he slid his tongue between her cheeks.

"You *are* a dirty girl," he said with a wide grin.

Val had to stifle a dry laugh. This weirdo was living his wet dream tonight.

He slapped her backside so hard, Val yelped, and again, she felt the satisfaction of swapping emotional for physical pain. "Dirty girl," he said. She heard the ripping of a condom package, saw him slip it on. He slapped her hard again. "Naughty." He whacked her ass again and again until her skin burned, then he slammed his cock into her and pumped like a man who hadn't tasted a woman in years. She imagined it was Robby behind her, back from a long business trip. *Babe, let's try something different.*

Stop me if you don't like it. Val's breasts bounced against the glass, lightning pulsing through her with every thrust, pushing her to climax.

"Robby, who killed you?" Val whispered as the tentacles of an orgasm seized her brain and pulled her under. "Robby—"

A Frisbee flies overhead, caught by a teenage girl who throws it back to her partner. I'm surrounded by families in a public park, the Seattle skyline glinting in a clear azure sky. A warm breeze tickles my skin. The grass around me is so green, I think someone's littered the ground with emeralds. A little boy runs up to me with blond hair like Robby's and gorgeous brown eyes with bursts of green at their centers.

"For you, Mommy," he says, and hands me a dandelion.

I reach for him as he runs away from me to gather more flowers. I feel kisses on the back of my neck, hands resting on my shoulders.

"Let him go," he whispers into my ear. "He'll be back."

The vision evaporated, and Val was disoriented for a moment when she realized she was on her back now, looking up at the ceiling. John stood over her, his condom removed, masturbating on her chest. He grunted as he came, white goop shooting between her breasts in spasms before oozing down her rib cage. He braced himself on the table with his free arm as he caught his breath.

When John saw the *What-the-fuck?* look on her face, he said, "You passed out for a minute. I didn't want to keep going if there was something wrong with you."

Val blinked away tears that had welled during her vision. "I'm fine. It's…a blood sugar thing."

She'd seen a vision of her and Robby's possible future, if he'd lived and she'd married him. Their beautiful son. A life that could have been, that she'd cut short. And *still* no useful information on where to find Chet, or Robby's killer.

A fresh lump grew in Val's throat as John asked, "Can we exchange phone numbers?"

Chapter Six

Max watched Val leave his office and let his face fall into its usual deep frown. His headache was finally beginning to ebb, letting the gears of his mind turn without pain gumming them up.

He didn't know what to make of her—a beautiful redhead dressed down and a bit haggard, with gray eyes the color of steel, who assumed he was somehow involved in her fiancé's death. Max had liked Robby; his junior lawyer had been a fun, easygoing guy, quick with a smile and possessing an infectious warmth—basically the opposite of Max. They might have been friends had they met under different circumstances.

Robby had mentioned his fiancée in passing, but Max hadn't pictured her as a woman like Val. He'd imagined a sweet, all-American girl, maybe a blond medical resident with dimples when she smiled. Not the tough-as-nails vision with the delicate face of a Rembrandt portrait come to life, a woman he was convinced could break him in half if she thought it would do any good—and also hair that smelled like apples.

He'd walked her to the door as an excuse to get close to her and take in her aroma. It was a very strange thing to do, he realized, something he'd never done before. Even as he'd leaned toward her and breathed her in, he didn't understand why he felt compelled to do so, only that he did. He expected strawberries, but that's wasn't what he got, and he liked it. A *lot*. The way she'd recoiled from him, though, she probably thought he was some kind of deviant. Which was true.

He had no doubt she wouldn't stop until she found Robby's killer, if Robby had in fact been murdered. Thank God she wasn't a real police officer investigating the death of Max's father. If she had been, Max guessed he'd probably be in jail by now.

What information could Val's source possibly have that would exonerate him of his father's death? Maybe it was a scam to blackmail Max out of his father's fortune, a fortune that hadn't truly belonged to Lester even before the old man died. If money was the ultimate goal, then whoever his blackmailers might be could have it, he didn't care. He just wanted to be left alone to rebuild his life.

Max extinguished his joint and returned what was left of it to the silver cigarette case. He walked to his tapestry, then flipped a switch behind the rough fabric. The tapestry rolled upward to expose a window overlooking the club's sex rooms. From his bird's-eye view, he surveyed the menagerie through the one-way mirrors that comprised the rooms' ceilings, his guests in the throes of passion, connecting with each other on the most basic level. Max could only imagine the burst of euphoria that drew them to this place—the orgasm, the climax. The best part of sex—so he'd heard. He'd read about it many times. At least they were capable of feeling such a miracle.

As his eyes drifted from room to room, he did a double take when he spotted the redhead being rammed from behind by a middle-aged businessman. Max believed Val's sorrow was genuine; why would she spontaneously fuck some random guy only days after her fiancé's death? Her eyes were closed and her face was pinched like she concentrated on something other than her own pleasure.

"Curiouser and curiouser," he muttered. He watched them for a while, the man jackhammering away while Val continued to look somewhat distracted, like she wasn't having much fun. A form of self-flagellation maybe. But whatever she felt, it was enough to get her off, because after a few minutes her body tensed in orgasm, then went limp. Odd, maybe she had a condition, or...or—

Max froze as raw excitement seized him. Could she be the one? The thing that had haunted his visions for as long as he could remember? Her hair was the same color as his raven, he now realized.

He watched as her partner stopped, jostled her for a response, then exited her and gently turned her over. She fluttered with the aftershocks of climax, but her eyes remained closed and her face placid.

Yes, she *could* be the one.

He looked at his assistant, standing at the ready like she always was. "Kitty, would you mind?" He unbuttoned his pants with trembling hands. "I need to check something."

Kitty's face lit up in an eager grin. Of course she didn't mind;

this was her favorite part of the job. Originally one of the club's performers, Max recruited Kitty to be his personal assistant after he'd discovered her impeccable organizational skills and work ethic—and love for no-strings-attached sex. She was so much easier than the roller-coaster ride of emotions and painful soul bearing that came with a real girlfriend.

Max pushed his trousers down to his knees and sat in his chair, his eyes fixed on Val. Kitty kneeled down in front of him, then wrapped her succulent lips around his penis and sucked like a pro. He slipped a hand into her halter top and ran his fingertips over her ample breast, feeling her nipple harden at his touch. Her mouth moved up and down the entirety of his shaft, lingering on his tip to run her tongue around its circumference. Below, Val stirred and her eyes popped open. She seemed upset now. Either she'd been turned off by her partner, or...

She'd seen something. She *was* the one.

Max usually had stamina in spades—his condition demanded it—but at that moment he was so excited Kitty could have breathed on his cock and he would have come. He closed his eyes as the climax hit him fast and hard, and his mind snapped away—

10292837736789098765678867572632780827646 52656
769178976276432787897897087567867829865542 3435
6467455678909001001982765414567881726572825 423
3256537475936374563848936426265444333144515 515
3456616561235711131719232831374143475359616 771
7379838997101103107

He resurfaced to the present. Hot damn, he'd been right. She was the one. The string of prime numbers on the end confirmed it, and the numbers were never wrong. Kitty wiped the corners of her mouth and gazed up at him expectantly, ready to help again if he said the word. He pushed away from her and shot up from his chair, yanked up his pants, grabbed a pen and paper, and wrote down every number he'd seen. Then, like a crazed college student, he pulled a slew of books off the shelf: *Fourier Analyses*, *Boundary Value Problems*, *Partial Differential Equations*, *Advanced Calculus*. He flipped to their appendices and circled chunks of numbers from his vision that coincided with the information in the books, adding arrows between the chunks to denote how he thought they connected, until the paper looked like a bizarre football diagram. Finally he consulted the Internet, and underneath his scribbling wrote down an address, a day, and a time.

"Clear my calendar for two days from now," Max told Kitty. "Make up some feasible lie if anyone asks where I am. And get me a pair of bolt cutters."

Chapter Seven

Val held the crude drawing of Chet's face up to the annoyed bartender. "You sure you don't recognize him? Young Hispanic guy, about five-foot-ten, goes by Chet. Loves lip gloss."

Mickey, the bartender, set his port-colored mouth in a pout and raised a penciled eyebrow. "I said I don't know him. Accept it already."

The last threads of Val's patience began to unravel. She'd spent the previous six hours visiting every gay bar and Chinese restaurant within walking distance of the spot Robby had been run down, and so far nobody would admit to knowing anyone who fit Chet's description. It was almost like they'd colluded and closed ranks.

"Look, I just want to talk to him. Chet's got a secret admirer—a very handsome millionaire—and I've been hired to track him down. Don't you want to help make a love connection?"

Mickey scoffed. "Bitch, please. It's not like all us queer people know each other, okay? And I don't give a shit about no love connection. You should've offered me money."

A spike of rage shot through Val and she slammed her fist on the countertop. Mickey flinched and jerked backward, his painted eyes widening with fear.

"No amount of money," she said through clenched teeth, "will make that lipstick look good on you."

Val stalked out of the bar while Mickey yelled about all the ways she was a terrible person, in his colorful fashion. She trudged back to her car, got in, and checked her cell phone. One text from Stacey: *Nothing yet. Going home to change. C U at the service.*

The service—Robby's funeral. She should give up and go home to change, too. Just give up. As if her back had turned to jelly, her head fell forward onto the steering wheel and she sobbed.

* * *

Val dumped a bowl of warm meatballs onto a serving platter and took her time spearing each one with a toothpick. She glanced through her kitchen doorway at the crowd that meandered around the living room in their black suits and dresses. They made small talk and smiled as proof that life went on. Val tried to play along but she wasn't selling it well, and the effort exhausted her. After the heart-wrenching spectacle that was Robby's funeral, the only thing that kept her from collapsing into a puddle of tears was the faint hope that she might get a lead on Chet from one of the gay bars or Chinese restaurants in Seattle that she hadn't visited yet—only fifty-plus more establishments to go. Val hung her head and sighed at the futility of it all.

"Can I help you with that?"

Val looked up to see Robby's sister, Josephine, standing in the doorway and pointing at the plate of meatballs.

"Oh, uh, sure, thank you."

Josephine walked over and put a hand on Val's shoulder. "You've done a great job today, with the funeral and wake, and gathering Robby's things for us. I know this must be hard for you, especially since you saw him…pass away. I can't thank you enough for everything you've done."

All Val could do was nod. She could barely look Robby's family in the eyes after her ridiculous, and ultimately pointless, tryst with Dirty John two days ago. Her ass still ached.

Not to mention whatever had happened with Max. Thinking back on it, the strange incident seemed like part of a dream where one minute she was drowning and the next she was flying. Dreams faded, though. The *want* she'd irrationally felt for him lingered in the back of her mind, shitting all over Robby's memory and reminding her what a terrible person she was.

Josephine took the plate and gave Val a reassuring smile, so graceful in her pain that she put Val to shame. She passed her and Robby's father, Dean, on her way out, and touched his shoulder before disappearing into the living room. Dean was more in line with Val's style of mourning, quiet and internal, silent as he poured himself a glass of water from the kitchen's tap.

"Dean, I wanted to ask you something, if you don't mind," she said.

He looked at her with sunken eyes, face thinner than it had been when she last saw him a couple weeks ago. "Go ahead."

She tried to proceed delicately, unsure what his reaction would be. "I've been thinking about what happened to Robby. It seems strange to me that he would be hit by a car right as he was about to talk to someone with information on the Max Carressa case. Since I was there, I can tell you that the car that hit him didn't even try to stop, and it had tinted windows so I couldn't see who was driving. Do you know if Max Carressa has enemies who might want to see him go to jail, or anyone who might have wanted to silence Robby before he could hear what the informant had to say? Or, I don't know, did Robby have any enemies at all that you know of?"

Dean's lips tightened and he turned even paler than he already was. "Robby died in an accidental hit-and-run, Valentine. The answer to all your questions is no. Why can't you let him rest in peace?" He slammed his cup on the countertop. "Not everything is a goddamn case to solve. I just buried my son today. I'm trying to figure out how I'll get on with my life. Maybe you should, too, and stop chasing shadows."

He stalked out of the kitchen, leaving Val breathless and sick to her stomach. She didn't think he'd get that defensive about it. Almost too defensive. Another shadow to chase.

Two hours later the mourners were gone, and only Stacey remained to help Val clean up. Her friend tossed paper plates into an open-topped trash can while Val sat at the kitchen table next to her own stack of used plates. She stared out the back window at the setting sun. Stacey picked up Val's trash and threw it away for her.

"I guess that's that," Stacey said. "Tomorrow we can hit a few of the Chinese places east of the highway, narrow down the list."

"Why bother?" Val said, still staring out the window. "Whoever murdered Robby is probably long gone by now—if Robby was actually murdered."

Stacey stopped cleaning and sat next to Val. "Do you think it might've been an accident after all?"

"I don't know!" Tears flooded Val's eyes. "I can't stand not knowing. If I could just talk to that bastard Chet and find out if what he had to tell Robby was worth Robby's life, then I could drop it and move on. But I can't let it go until I'm sure. And I might never be sure."

Stacey pulled Val into a hug, and she sobbed into her friend's chest for she didn't know how long. If she could've pushed her sorrow out through tears, by the time she took a breath and lifted her head, every mote of it would've been gone. But of course she couldn't, and when she finally met Stacey's eyes, her chest still overflowed with pain to a degree she hadn't endured since her sister died. Her friend's pretty almond-shaped eyes, familiar and safe, stared back at her, radiating a reservoir of comfort that trickled into Val, then streamed, until her starving soul began gulping it down in feverish desperation.

Seduced by their sudden intense connection, Stacey touched Val's face like she used to, and Val did what she used to do, what once made her feel good, and kissed Stacey. Her friend's lips, warm and inviting, tasted like she remembered, and responded like she remembered. Though a voice in the back of her mind begged her to stop and listed off all the ways she was making a terrible mistake and ruining a valuable friendship, the salve felt too good, and Val gave in to her most basic impulses.

In a frenzy of nostalgia, Val ripped off her ugly mourning dress while Stacey did the same. They fell into each other's arms, onto the floor, and back in time. Val found herself in a dream with Stacey's hand between her legs, their breasts pressed together, mouths fluttering like fairy's wings on each other's lips. She closed her eyes and enjoyed the fantasy, fetishizing the past, until for a few seconds the pleasure consumed her pain and her body melted—

Chet steps off a bus, checks his watch—half past eight in the evening. He walks two blocks, past a gas station and Magic Michael's Coffee Hut, then turns right onto Dowd Street. The song "Heart of Glass" cues up in his pocket as he enters a sliver of a building with white paint peeling off the walls, the words "Lakeview Apartments" stenciled on the side. He pulls out his cell phone.

"Hey, Dookie, wassup?" He climbs one flight of stairs. "Okay, so when are you coming over then?" He climbs another flight of stairs, passes an apartment with salsa music blaring and a baby crying. "Don't pull that shit on me. Just be here soon. You know I can't watch Making of a Diva *alone." He makes kissing noises into the phone and hangs up as he reaches the third floor. He unlocks apartment number 353 and walks inside.*

Val gasped as her ceiling replaced the vision of Chet entering his apartment. "I saw him!" She sat straight up, the image still so clear in her mind she thought she could stand and walk into his apartment right then. "I know where he lives!"

"Great," Stacey said as her fingers tickled Val's thigh. "We'll go there tomorrow and see what he has to say."

Val looked down at Stacey and blinked. What the hell were they doing naked on the floor of the kitchen? Then reality came flooding back.

Oh shit.

"Uh, no, I have to go now." Val sprang up from the floor and flew up the stairs to her bedroom. She threw on her clothes, then took her pistol and its holster out of the safe in her closet and strapped them on.

When Val came back down, Stacey wore her dress again and sat at the kitchen table, arms folded, her afterglow replaced by a scowl.

"*Excuse* me, I thought we were a team," Stacey said. "And we just had sex, in case you forgot that part."

"I didn't forget. Of course we're a team. I just... We just..."

What the hell had she been thinking? Why had she risked losing her best friend over a stupid, impulsive act? How could she fix this? Her chest tightened again, this time overflowing with panic.

"You just wish it hadn't happened," Stacey said.

"No, no, no, it's not like that," Val said, even though it was exactly like that.

"Then stay and talk to me!"

"I don't want to lose Chet again. I'll be back as soon as possible, I promise. Then we can talk." Val kissed Stacey on the forehead and forced a smile, then realized she'd made a serious tactical error when Stacey's frown somehow grew deeper.

"Listen, I—uh..." Val turned away and hurried out the door,

ran down the stairs, and jumped in her car, fleeing the scene of the shit storm she'd kicked up. "Goddammit," she muttered as she backed up.

Why did she sleep with her best friend and open up that long-sealed can of worms? She'd warned herself not to, and ignored the angel on her shoulder yet again. She should go back in there and talk to her. They were both adults. They'd had a post–junior high school fling before, though in that case Val had pretended to want to get back together to save Stacey's life. This time, she'd simply lost her mind for a few minutes in an irrational attempt to escape into the past so she could avoid the present. Stacey would think Val used her for a vision and then tossed her aside. It wasn't like that, though…was it?

No, it definitely wasn't. She should go back in the house and tell Stacey that. Endure her best friend's hurt and explain her feelings.

But shit, that could take hours.

She'd do it later. After she nailed Robby's killer.

Chapter Eight

The acrid smell of stale urine hit Val first when she walked into Chet's apartment building, followed by the echoes of salsa music from the second floor. Residents with shifty eyes loitered in the hallways and stared at her as she passed them on her way up the stairs. She was too white to be a local, too casual to be a cop. Whatever they thought she was, they were content to let her pass without a confrontation, for which Val breathed a sigh of relief.

She reached apartment 353 and rapped on the door. A moment later she heard footsteps, then saw the door shift as a body pressed against it to look through the peephole.

"Chet?" Val asked.

"Maybe," he said without opening the door. "Who're you?"

"My name's Valentine Shepherd. I'm a friend of Robby Price's, the guy you saw get hit by a car a few days ago. Can I come in and talk to you, please?"

Val heard the snap of a deadbolt sliding away and the rattle of a chain lock being disengaged before the door swung open. Chet waved her inside, then looked up and down his hallway before shutting the door and putting the locks back in place.

"That poor boy," Chet said, his wide, dark eyes and lanky brown limbs reminding Val of a frightened antelope. "I can't believe they ran him down like that. Did the cops get the killers yet?"

"They think it was an accident, so they're not really looking." Val glanced around his tiny living room, walls covered in colorful paintings he likely made himself given the easel in the corner. Teenagers sang from his TV. "Can we sit down?"

"Oh yeah, sure, sure." Chet showed Val through a beaded curtain to his cramped kitchen off the apartment's single bedroom. From Chet's kitchen window Val could see into the neighboring building's apartments, miniature theaters of people eating dinner, watching television, arguing.

"You want something to drink?" Chet asked as he closed the window blinds.

"No, thank you." Val took a seat at his kitchen table.

Chet cracked open a beer and sat across from her. "God, I can't get the image of him getting hit by that car out of my head. I didn't know he was Robby Price until I saw it on the news." He took a long swig from his beer, then looked at Val. "Hey, were you that chick with him?"

"Yeah, that was me. I can't get it out of my head, either."

"But I wasn't supposed to meet him until later, so I dunno what he was doing there. I've been telling myself it was just a weird coincidence. Do you think someone killed him because he was gonna meet with me?"

"That might be true."

Chet's gaze darted about the kitchen, an antelope scanning the tall grass for a lion. "Oh God."

"I'm trying to figure out why someone would want Robby dead. What were you going to tell him about the Max Carressa case?"

Chet took another swig, his hands shaking. "So, about six months ago I started volunteering for Norman Barrister's campaign for mayor. Handing out flyers in poor black and Latino communities, trying to get the vote out. I thought I was doing good, and earning community college credits. A month in, I met Norman at a rally and got a gay vibe from him."

Val's eyebrows rose. "Norman Barrister is gay?"

Chet shrugged. "He says he's not gay, but he sure seemed to like it when I stuck my dick in his ass in his hotel room after the rally."

Val's mouth fell open. Retired Colonel Norman Barrister, former battalion commander, decorated Army soldier, and noted opponent of the "Don't Ask Don't Tell" repeal was himself one of the queers he feared would ruin the military? She should have guessed. Then again, all she had was Chet's crude account of their alleged affair.

Chet went on, "We started seeing each other regularly after that. He'd have some kind of event, I'd meet him there, and we'd go at it afterwards, either in a car or a back room of wherever he was. He was good at losing his posse and picking spots where we wouldn't get caught—a military skill, I guess. At first he seemed like an okay guy, older and more uptight than my usual boys, but

I love me some manly man once in a while. When I started pressing him to come out, he turned into rough trade, all 'I'm not gay,' and 'If you tell anyone, I'll kill you.' He even slammed me into a wall once. Bastard."

"That's some, well, shocking information," Val said. "But why out Barrister to Robby? What does it have to do with Carressa?"

"I wasn't gonna out Norman—I mean, not specifically. It's not cool to force people out of the closet, even douchebags like him. Goes against gay code. The thing is, about six weeks ago, during one of our meet-ups before I quit his campaign, I heard Norman talking on the phone all secret-like about the death of Lester Carressa, like it had already happened. But this was *two weeks before Lester actually died*." Chet leaned toward Val like he was afraid to be overheard in his own apartment. "How could he know that Lester was gonna die before he died? Norman must have something to do with it. Which means that Max must *not* have anything to do with it, because why plot with other people to murder your father in the family mansion where you're bound to be the prime suspect?"

Val's mind went to a dozen places at once. Assuming Chet told the truth and heard what he thought he heard, why would Barrister want Max's father dead? Why try to frame Max for the murder? If they knew where Chet and Robby would meet, why not kill Chet, the source of the incriminating information, rather than Robby?

Val knew of one other way to know when someone was going to die before it happened. But that wasn't possible…was it? If other people could do what Val could do, it would be a well-known phenomenon, studied and documented. She'd found no trace of anyone else with her abilities, despite searching for over half of her life. It couldn't be.

"Why didn't you go to the police?" Val asked.

"Gay code, remember? If I went to the police, I'd have to out Norman. Lawyers have confidentiality privilege and stuff. And you can't trust the cops. Impossible to tell who's clean or dirty. But I couldn't let such a pretty boy go to jail for a crime he didn't commit."

As Val opened her mouth to ask another question, a heavy thump at the door announced another visitor.

"Oh, that's my friend Dookie," Chet said as he rose and exited the kitchen.

Val's head still reeled from Chet's information—what should her next move be? Should *she* go to the police?—when she heard someone bellow, "Seattle PD drug raid! Open up!"

"*Hijo de puta*," Chet said. "Again?"

She heard the locks release, the door open.

"Don't you guys have anything better to do than enforce racist stereotypes? No, I don't have any weed, just like I didn't have any two weeks ago."

BOOM BOOM. Two gunshots tore through the apartment, followed by the thud of a body hitting the floor. Down the hallway, a woman screamed. Val slapped a hand over her mouth to contain her own, then launched from her chair and backpedaled into the wall, as far away as possible from the beaded curtain that separated the kitchen from the living room. The image she'd seen two days ago of Chet lying in a pool of his own blood, pawing at his chest as his life slipped away, came back to her then. She knew the image was Chet at that moment, his future caught up to him.

Val heard a resident yelling at the cops, demanding to know what was going on. His voice was joined by another as one of the policemen, or men posing as police, told everyone to stay in their homes. She took the opportunity to sidle into Chet's bedroom and delicately shut the door, clicking the flimsy lock in place. She ran to the window and tried to pull it open quietly, but the damn thing stuck like it hadn't been opened in years.

"Come on," she whispered, strong-arming it open one inch at a time. It squeaked as she ratcheted it up. She had seconds before they noticed the noise. "Come on. *Come on.*"

Finally she forced the window open enough to squeeze through. With her heart pounding so hard her ribs hurt, Val pushed herself through the tiny opening as the bedroom's doorknob jiggled.

She stepped out onto a fire escape just as the bedroom door crashed open.

As fast as possible, she moved her arms and legs down the ladder, zigzagging the building's flank on rungs slick from the unending Seattle rain. On the final section she slipped and fell hard onto her back, knocking the wind out of her for a moment. She gasped for breath as she scrambled to her feet, then looked up in time to see a head poking out of Chet's window.

Sten. Fucking Sten. That son of a bitch. He *was* involved. And he was a murderer.

Val cried out when Sten stuck his gun out the window and fired at her. The fire escape prevented Sten from getting a clean shot, and the bullet clinked as it ricocheted. Val heard two more shots bank off the metal as she fled down the wet alleyway, then another that exploded the brick next to her head as she cut to the left, into another connecting alley.

Val sprinted down the narrow passage, crashing through mud puddles and leaping over bags of trash that littered her escape route. She followed the alley when it turned right, scanning her path for any opening into the street that might save her life. Before she found a way out, the alley dead-ended at a tarp-covered chain-link fence with barbed wire on top and a padlock trapping her inside.

"No!" Val yanked on the padlock. It didn't budge. She tried the only door in the alley, a metal behemoth flush with the brick—locked. "Goddammit, no!" She kicked the door, and it barely moved.

Val pulled out her pistol and pressed herself into the corner of the alley's dead end. She'd been in firefights before while in the military, though not against American citizens, and not alone. She didn't stand much of a chance against two armed cops when she had nowhere to hide and no cover for support. In all her visions she'd never seen her own death. There was no reason this couldn't be it.

But she'd be damned if she was going down without a fight.

Chapter Nine

Val planted her feet on the wet pavement, gun trained at the alleyway's bend, ready to shoot the first thing that entered her line of sight. The rain picked up, an icy October shower that matted her hair to her face and would have chilled her to the bone if not for the wild adrenaline racing through her veins. For what seemed like an eternity she listened to the approaching footsteps and stood her ground, waiting to die.

Then she heard it—a chain rattling. Val ripped her gaze away from where her killers were due to arrive any second to see a set of bolt cutters slip through the fence and snap the padlock off. The chain slinked to the ground, and someone pulled the gate open.

One of her pursuers had somehow doubled back, and now they surrounded her.

Val spun around to face her flanker, finger on the trigger to let loose a hail of bullets into Sten or his friend's smug face. She gasped and just barely stopped herself from firing as she registered Max Carressa standing in front of her, holding the bolt cutters and recoiling from her gun. She hardly recognized him in jeans and a black motorcycle jacket, a baseball cap deflecting the rain out of his startled face, though his gorgeous eyes were a dead giveaway.

"What the hell?" she said.

Max grabbed her arm. "Come on!" He glanced behind her, where Chet's murderers thundered up, just around the corner. "Do you wanna die here or not?"

No, she did not especially want to die there. With no time to consider any other option, she followed Max to his car, idling at the curb, and jumped into the passenger's seat. He flew into the driver's side and punched the gas. The car tore away as Val caught a glimpse of Sten and another man round the alleyway's corner and begin running toward her in a futile attempt to catch up or read the car's license plate number as it sped out of sight.

Val watched the world fly by through the back window as the car cut left and right down side streets, then merged onto the highway, until she was sure they'd lost her pursuers. She turned back and put her head between her legs for a minute, trying to catch her breath, then stole a glance around Max's car. It looked average, something a middle-class professional might drive, not a flashy status symbol of a rich playboy. He was trying to blend in, avoid notice from the cops. He'd planned this.

"How did you find me?" Val asked, still short of breath.

"The same way you found Chet."

For a moment Val didn't understand what he meant, because what she thought he meant couldn't be true. "No, I mean how did you know where I'd be at that moment?"

"*I mean*, I saw it in a vision of the future." He glanced at her. "Like you, right?"

Val stared at him, slack-jawed, and her heart began racing again. Was he telling the truth? How could he know otherwise? Could there be others like her, and how had she never encountered any of them until now? What did any of this craziness have to do with Robby's murder or Norman Barrister or Lester Carressa?

"You look like you're going to be sick," Max said. "Please don't throw up in this car. I'm borrowing it from a friend."

"I'll be fine," she snapped. "Just pull over somewhere. I need a drink."

He exited the highway and drove to a bar with peeling paint and a broken sign, careful to park out of view of the street in case someone was looking for their car. Blue-collar locals filled half the dimly lit tavern as country music crooned from an ancient jukebox in the corner. Max and Val sat at a booth in the corner, away from curious ears. An older waitress with too much eyeliner asked them what they wanted to drink.

"Bud Light," Max said, keeping his head down so the waitress wouldn't recognize him from news coverage of his father's death. Even a day's worth of stubble and a ball cap covering half his face couldn't hide the fact that he was an unusually handsome man with a mug that was hard to forget.

Val pushed her wet hair behind her ears and wiped away a smear of mud from her cheekbone. "Shot of tequila, please," she said. "Actually, make that two shots."

The waitress nodded and disappeared, leaving Max and Val

alone. They sat in silence for a while, studying each other. He looked calm, normal—a ridiculously attractive version of normal anyway. But she looked normal, too, and God what a lie that was. She'd often wondered if people could tell she was off, sensed the oddness in her somehow. Now that she'd met another like her—assuming he spoke the truth—she knew her secret was well hidden. She would never have guessed he was a freak, too.

And what a beautiful freak he was. His light brown eyes with starbursts of green around the pupils raked over her features and made her blush again. Why did he have to stare at her like that? He didn't make her uncomfortable as much as painfully aware of exactly how many inches apart their bodies were. Her heart still ached for Robby, but she wasn't blind.

He slipped off his coat, uncovering a Soundgarden T-shirt over exquisitely sculpted biceps, and handed it to her. Val looked at the coat for a moment, not sure what to do with it, until she realized that not only was the hand holding the coat shaking, but her entire body shook from the cold that saturated her wet clothes and chilled her to the core. She took off her own jacket and put on his, still infused with his body heat and masculine scent. His warmth soaked into her like a hot bath, and her tremors subsided.

"Thank you," she said, "for the coat, and for saving my life."

He nodded in response as the waitress returned with their drinks, eyed the unusual fractal tattoos on Max's forearms, then left again. Val threw back the first tequila shot and let it burn a path down her throat. She took a deep breath as her resolve fortified again and her thoughts untangled themselves.

"What the fuck is going on?" she said.

Max took a swig of his beer and shrugged. "Hell if I know."

"You can... You can really..."

"See the future when I come? Yes."

"Since when?"

"All my life. Since my first wet dream. As far back as I can re-member. You?"

She raised her eyebrows at him. "Why would you ask me that? Aren't you the expert?"

He laughed. "Hardly. You're only the second person I've ever met who can do it."

"There are *others*? Who? Where?"

"I only met the one guy. He was looking for something, like you. He implied there were others, but he came and went quickly—in more ways than one. I didn't get many answers out of him."

"If you knew there were others, why didn't you look for me—I mean, people *like* me? Like us?"

His eyes fell and he fidgeted with his beer bottle. "It's compli-cated."

She balled her hands into fists as a spike of anger surged through her. "I've felt alone my *entire life*. Even when I was with other people, I still felt alone. And you were just a few miles away the whole time? Did you even try to look?"

His face darkened, and when his eyes met hers again, she could practically count the bricks in the emotional wall he'd erected. "It's *complicated*."

Fine, he didn't want to talk about it. She knew how difficult it could be to discuss your deeply personal and weird ability with other people who'd probably dismiss you as a delusional sex addict. Whatever—his previous disinterest in finding others like himself wasn't important now.

"How did you know about me?" she asked.

"A hunch. I confirmed it right after you visited me at the Red Raven."

She smirked. "Did your little pussy cat help you with that?"

"Kitty's gotta work her way through nursing school somehow," he said with lazy sarcasm.

Val rolled her eyes, then asked, "What do you mean 'confirmed it'?"

"I saw a string of prime numbers. That's the same thing I saw with Ethan—the other guy with our condition."

"Condition?"

He sighed and took a long drink of his beer. "At first I saw images, and I couldn't figure out what they meant until I started interpreting them as numbers, because I'm decent at math. Now all I see is numbers. I've gotten pretty good at deciphering what they mean. But I still think of it as more of a sexual dysfunction than a gift."

"But it's how you got rich, right?"

Max's face hardened and his eyes turned cold. "Yeah, it is."

"At least you don't see dead people all the fucking time." The image of Chet in his death throes popped into her head—yet another person she'd failed to protect—and her hands began to shake again. She downed her second tequila shot, then slammed the glass on the table. "What's your connection to Norman Barrister?"

"The guy running for mayor?"

Val nodded.

"I don't have one."

"Bullshit." Gorgeous knight in shining armor or not, she was going to get some damn answers out of him. "Before Chet was gunned down in his own apartment by a couple of Seattle's finest, he told me that he heard Barrister talking about your dad's death two weeks before it happened. How would Barrister know that?"

Max furrowed his brows in deep thought. "I don't know. Maybe Chet was lying or misheard."

"Well, someone plugged him to shut him up, so I'm guessing there's at least a kernel of truth in what he told me." Val let a silence fall between them for a few seconds so Max could think about what she'd said. "Did you murder your father?"

He flinched, and his eyes turned cold again. "No."

"Then either someone else murdered him and is actively framing you—or at least letting you take the fall—or your dad really did accidentally trip and fall off his balcony, and someone like us predicted it. Which do you think is more likely?"

Fidgeting with the label on his beer bottle, after a pause, he said, "The latter."

"Why?"

"Because what are the odds that you and I are randomly involved, two people who just happen to be able to see the future?"

"True," Val said. She sighed, then stood.

"Where're you going?" Max asked.

"I'm going to call a friend to come pick me up and take me back to my car, and then I'm going home."

Max got up and blocked her exit. "You can't go home. The cops that chased you from Chet's place have probably run your license plate by now and know who you are and where you live."

Val frowned. He was right. In fact, they didn't need to run her plates. Sten knew who she was. It would take him a matter of minutes to track down her address. She imagined him parked across the street from her house right at that moment, just waiting for her to come home so he could choke her to death in her sleep, right after he raped her for shits and grins.

"Stay with me," Max said. "Whoever's after you doesn't know that we're together yet. We probably have a few days before they figure it out. Until then, we can have visions with each other, and compare what we see until we piece it together. That's why Ethan sought me out—two people with the condition have much stronger visions together than paired with normal people."

She cocked an eyebrow at what that information implied. "Was it true?" she asked. With an assistant like Kitty, there was no way he wasn't at least mostly heterosexual.

"Yes." He shrugged, reacting to the incredulous look in her face. "He needed help, so I helped him. If we ever meet again, he'll owe me a big favor. It's always good to have a healthy roster of people in your debt."

It was tempting to take him up on his offer, to see what sex was like with another of her...her *kind*, she guessed the correct term was. She'd slept with Dirty John just a few days ago, and then Stacey a few *hours* ago, but both encounters had been born of desperation. Something about Max gave her pause.

Despite how he'd helped her, she still didn't know much about him—or if she could trust him. She knew for sure, though, that he was dangerous. She still felt the fire in him that'd been there the first time they met, intense and tempting. He might kill her—in more ways than one. Maybe kill her softly with those goddamn eyes. Make her feel things she wasn't ready for. Not to mention how cavalierly he'd proposed the idea, like being ungodly handsome and rich meant she'd jump into his bed on command. Fuck that. She was nobody's submissive.

Val folded her arms. "I'll pass on being your crystal ball whore, thanks. I'll stay in a hotel."

"With what money? If you use your credit cards, they'll find you."

"I'll stay with a friend."

"Then you'll be putting that person in danger."

Val rubbed the bridge of her nose and squeezed her eyes shut, too tired to counter his argument.

"If you don't want to have sex, then we won't. It'll still be easier to work together if we're in the same location."

"Jesus Christ, we're two people who can see the goddamn future and somehow we don't know jack shit." Val shook her head and let out a long exhale. "We're doomed. Fine, I might as well stay at your place. Let's just get out of here."

Chapter Ten

The last time Val had been at the Carressa mansion, she hadn't made it past the gate. This time, Max punched a code into the keypad underneath the intercom and the wrought iron fence swung open with ease, welcoming its owner. The mansion itself was about a quarter mile from the gate, after a winding single-lane road that cut through a tiny patch of northwest wilderness with sky-high evergreens and ferns carpeting lush forest ground. Val gawked like the middle-class bumpkin she was when Max pulled up to a giant asymmetrical house made of vaulted glass walls framed by smooth pinewood beams, an integration of nature and the cosmopolitan that only a seasoned architect paid millions of dollars could have achieved.

Max unlocked the door and held it open for her, then punched another security code into the keypad adjacent to the entrance. It beeped, and the house lit up like the stage lights on an orchestra about to perform. The first floor was a sprawling open space that reminded Val of a *Northwest Living* magazine cover, with polished wood décor balanced against glass and steel fixtures.

Everything was in its place, immaculately clean. She followed him up a spiral staircase to a guest bedroom on the second floor, done up like a posh hotel room at the Seattle Westin with dark gray silk bedding, solid oak furniture, and framed pictures of pressed Northwest flowers. Nothing personal distracted from the room's elegance.

"Where's your room?" Val asked.

"I stay in the guest house," he said. "It's about a hundred feet away, on the west side of the property. There's a path that connects the two."

"You don't need to vacate your own home for me. I can stay in the guest house."

"Actually, the guest house *is* my home. I hate this place. It was my father's, not mine. I'm planning on selling it and moving to the city after the investigation into his death is over. I should have moved away a long time ago, but…" He trailed off, lost in a thought that darkened his eyes, before pulling himself back to the present. "Anyway, I've dismissed the help, so it's just you and me for now. Help yourself to whatever you want. I'll have Kitty bring by a change of clothes for you. Let me know if you need anything else."

Before she could thank him for his hospitality, Max said, "Good night," turned, and left, as if he couldn't get out of there fast enough.

Val would've loved to take a look around, but exhaustion from her long day dragged her brain into a stupor she was helpless to resist. She stripped off her moist clothes, slipped her gun underneath her pillow, and passed out on the guest bed.

* * *

Val woke with a start, not sure where she was for a moment until the previous day's events came flooding back in heart-pounding detail. She eased her hand off her gun, then checked her cell phone; four missed calls from Stacey. Val queued up Stacey's number, but stopped herself from dialing when she considered the massive amount of explanation she'd have to go through, as well as the inevitable talk about where their relationship stood. She texted Stacey instead: *I'm fine. 2 much 2 explain now. talk to u soon*, then turned off her phone.

She took a hot shower, washing away the grime from her mad dash down Chet's alley. Her clothes still felt damp, and she recoiled from the musty smell they'd acquired after sitting in a wet pile all night. Wrapped in a towel, she padded to an adjacent room, also impeccably decorated with no personal touches, and rooted through a dresser drawer until she found a men's dress shirt and boxer shorts for temporary coverage. She descended the stairs to the first floor, now awash in the early morning sun that filtered in through glass walls overlooking the crystal waters of Lake Washington. Her stomach growled, and she opened the stainless steel fridge to find it bare save for bottles of ketchup and mustard and other assorted condiments that would keep well into the next decade. She shut it and grumbled, shivering and hungry for a moment, then noticed the outline of the guest house through the window, behind a crop of trees. Val took a deep breath, steeling herself for the biting chill of the morning air, then opened the side door and ran across the cobblestone path to Max's house.

Strains of rock music reached her about halfway down the path, and she was grateful she wouldn't have to wake him up as she pounded on his cherrywood door. A few seconds later the door opened, and Max's eyes widened when he saw her outfit. She couldn't help gawking at him, too, shirtless in a pair of drawstring shorts and light boxing gloves, rippled muscles glistening with sweat. Her hands itched with the urge to touch him, and by the look on his face, he was thinking the same thing about her. Then she remembered how the last two times she jumped into bed with someone on a whim had ended in disaster, and she kicked the attraction away as she shoved past him.

"I need to talk to Barrister today," she said, rubbing the cold out of her arms. Stepping inside the doorway, she froze for a moment as Max's essence overwhelmed her. The scent of his workout infused the studio-style house, musk and male with overtones of sweat. She took in the worn punching bag still swinging from a chain in the corner, as well as his bed shoved against the wall, a tiny kitchen, and a bathtub shower all in the same space. It had the same aesthetic feel and open floor plan as the main house, except someone obviously lived here. Clothes lay piled in a corner, one of his expensive suits crumpled on top. Another suit was sheathed in plastic and draped across a love seat. A couple dirty dishes sat in the sink. Shelving with a hundred or more books took up the spot where a television would have been, next to more books stacked on the ground and a whiteboard with equations scrawled across its face.

Val felt as if she'd walked into a physical version of his mind, intimate and fascinating. Though she felt a little guilty for invading his personal space, she immediately liked it, and knew that was bad if she hoped to keep her distance.

"Funny," he said as he closed the door behind her, "you don't strike me as the suicidal type, but I've been wrong about people before." He pushed a button on his phone mounted atop a couple small speakers and the music turned off.

In his kitchen, she slathered peanut butter on a slice of bread she found paired together on his countertop. "We know he's somehow connected to Robby's and your father's deaths." She ate between sentences. "He's our only viable lead right now. If we move fast, he won't be expecting us. We can catch him off guard, rattle his cage."

"*If* he's involved—which we don't know for sure yet—then he's capable of murder, or at least fine with having other people do it for him. We don't know what he'll do if you confront him. It's not a good idea."

"Fine. You stay here. I'll go and let you know what happens."

He sighed and ripped the Velcro straps off his gloves, pulled them off. "When?"

"Now."

"May I suggest you put some real clothes on first?" He cocked his head to a stack of neatly folded women's garments on his bed.

Val finished her peanut butter bread, walked to the edge of the bed, and picked through the clothes. She was surprised to see them all in her correct size, including a pair of soft leather boots. "I'm impressed your girlfriend was able to guess my size after seeing me for only a few minutes."

"Who, Kitty?" He slipped off his shorts, and then his underwear, so he stood completely naked as he pulled his shower curtain back and turned on the water.

Val gasped and tried to avert her eyes away from his toned muscles and full endowment; she failed. A collection of deltoids, quadriceps, biceps, and abs filled her vision, all rippling beneath a sheen of sweat. A few long scars on his back and legs marred his smooth skin, and she wondered where he got them, what they felt like. For a fleeting moment she imagined licking all that salty water off him.

"Jesus, Max," she said after she came back to her senses. "Some people consider spontaneous nudity to be rude."

He shrugged. "I'm not prepared for company in the guest house. Anyway, I don't have anything you haven't seen before."

Of course not, but he still made her mouth water. Whether he was naturally fit or worked hard to look that way, his body matched his face for beauty in a way that confirmed how unfair the universe truly was. To give one man the build of a quarterback without the bulkiness, the face of a cologne model, the intelligence of a college professor, *and* millions of dollars seemed like a cosmic joke at everyone else's expense.

"And Kitty's not my girlfriend," he said as he stepped under the steaming showerhead, then whisked the curtain shut so only his head was visible. "I don't have a girlfriend. It's not practical with our condition. Women don't like it when you're always passing out during sex."

"I've had some decent relationships. You just have to work around it."

"That's easy for you to say. You can just lay back and enjoy the ride. I'm expected to *perform*."

Val hadn't thought about what her ability might be like for a man. He made a compelling case for how much worse it could be, especially for someone like Max whose looks, intelligence, and money allowed him access to almost any woman he wanted—women with high expectations. His perceived deficiency between the sheets could be crippling.

While he finished his shower, she picked out a leggings-skirt combo and a long-sleeved cashmere top; not her usual style, but she needed all the help she could get in the fashion arena. She looked around for somewhere to change and found none. There really was no opportunity for privacy in Max's home. Even the recessed bathroom was missing a door. It must've been quite a while since he'd had a visitor's comfort to consider.

She doffed her borrowed shirt and boxer shorts and changed, telling herself that *she* didn't have anything *he* hadn't seen, either, while pretending to ignore his half-second glances in her direction. So he liked the way she looked, too, made him squirm a little like he'd done to her. Val bit her lip to hide a smile. Turnabout was fair play, after all.

"Why do you own a sex club?" she asked as she pulled the boots on. "Are you just into freaky stuff?"

"There's some of that, I guess," Max said with a laugh. "I—" He stopped lathering his hair and looked away for a moment, as if considering how honest he should be. "I originally intended to use it to conduct randomized experiments on people."

Val cringed. "That's sick."

"I eventually came to that conclusion, yes. But by then I'd already bought it and done all the refurbishing, so it became an escape instead, and the observation room my office."

"Observation room?"

"Poor choice of words—"

"Were you *watching me*?"

"No," he said with a sliver of anxiousness, enough to convince her he was lying.

Val felt her cheeks heat up. Oh God, he'd seen her with Dirty John. She'd hoped to go through life pretending the unfortunate incident never happened, but now she had a damn witness. Of course Max had probably seen freakier people doing freakier things a million times before, but he'd still violated her privacy—like she'd violated his when she barged into his house. Maybe they were even—almost. She stood and marched to the shower.

"The existence of the observation room is in the contract people sign," he said. "Everyone consents. You would've known about it if you'd come in through normal channels—"

She whisked back the curtain with one strong yank. He gaped at the sudden intrusion just as she slapped him across the face. "Pervert," she said, and snapped the curtain shut again.

"Damn, you hit hard," he said, rubbing his cheek and eyeing her over the shower rod. "If I *had* seen you in one of the Red Raven's rooms, it wouldn't have been on purpose. Sometimes I'll do a general look around the club from the observation area to make sure everyone's safe and—"

"Yeah, whatever. Make it up to me by getting your ass out of the shower sometime today. And buy me a gyro for lunch."

She thought she heard him chuckle softly before the shower turned off. Val picked through his books and pretended not to notice his erection as he toweled down and got dressed.

"All right," he said after he'd changed into jeans and a black V-neck sweater that killed all the anger she had left. Did he *always* have to look so good? "I'm ready to go do something incredibly ill advised. You?"

"Just a sec." Val ran back into the main house and returned a minute later with her coat and handgun. She checked the magazine, slapped it into the hand grip and racked the slide back, then slid the gun into the shoulder holster under her jacket. "Okay. Let's go talk to Norman Barrister."

Chapter Eleven

The Barristers' white Colonial-style house in Arbor Heights reminded Val of something a Civil War general's wife might run out of to hug her husband returning from battle, but surrounded by evergreens instead of weeping willows. Val and Max drove past the house, not too slow to be suspicious, then parked a block away.

"How do you plan to catch the conscience of the king?" Max asked, baseball cap pulled down over his face again to avoid being recognized by passersby.

"What?"

"Catch the conscience of the king—convince him to incriminate himself. It's from *Hamlet.*"

Val snickered. "You are such a nerd. Don't worry, I'll think of something. A showboat like Barrister will want to talk."

"At what point should I charge in to save you?"

"Give me thirty minutes, or until you hear gunshots. Then call the fire department. I think they're less likely than the police to try to murder me."

Max's lips tightened like he might try one last time to talk her out of it, but instead he said, "Be careful."

"Being careful doesn't get shit done," she said as she got out of the car, "but thanks."

Val walked down the sidewalk, past white picket fences with immaculately manicured lawns of green grass turning brown with the season, up to Barrister's heavy white door with a wreath of red and gold polyester leaves propped on the front. She rang the doorbell, heard the *BONG-bong* on the inside. A few seconds later, a prim brunette in her early fifties answered. Val recognized her from Norman's campaign ads as his wife, Delilah.

"Good morning, I'm Val Shepherd. Is Colonel Barrister home?"

Delilah smiled a big toothy grin, exposing teeth as perfect as the milky white pearls strung around her neck. "No one's called him that in a while."

"I served under him while I was in the Army five years ago. Best commander I've ever had. I want to offer to help his campaign, testify to what a great leader he is. I'd like to say 'hi' and catch up first, before going to his campaign headquarters."

"That's sweet of you. Come on in, I'll take you to him. I think he's doing yard work out back."

Val followed Delilah through the house, an homage to French country living that was a spiritual twin to the Carressa mansion—beautiful and soulless. As they crossed through the kitchen, Val saw flyers for the Washington State Ladies for Family Values, a conservative action group based out of Olympia, stacked on the countertop. Delilah must be an active member. It made sense, given her husband's Republican leanings.

Past the kitchen and out the sliding glass door, the backyard extended for a quarter of an acre and included a rock garden with foot bridges over wildflower beds. Delilah asked Val to wait while she announced Val's presence to her husband. Norman Barrister, a six-foot-plus hulk of a man, stood at the edge of his yard, his back to the house and a shovel in his hand, watching something next to his iron fence posts. Tight piles of raked leaves were scattered about, waiting to be scooped into his meaty arms and dumped into the nearby compost heap. Val watched as Delilah walked to her husband, and at her words Norman smiled and waved Val over. Delilah met her halfway.

"Norman loves meeting people he used to serve with; so do I. It's the highlight of his campaign, really. Unfortunately I've got a meeting with the Washington State Ladies I need to go to." Delilah touched Val's shoulder like a doting mother. "It was great meeting you, Val. I hope I'll see you again."

Val forced out a warm smile in response.

After Delilah left, Val approached Norman where he stood at the edge of his lawn. A scraggly cat with a tail like a toilet brush dug its teeth into a dish of soft food at the base of the fence.

"We get a lot of stray cats around here," Norman said to her. "Poor things, half starved. No one will take them in."

"That's kind of you, sir."

Norman smiled at her, making his battle-weathered face somehow soft and approachable. He had a mug cut like granite, a thick jaw and flat nose, with piercing brown eyes tempered by laugh lines at their edges. It was a face a person could rally behind, friendly yet strong. Charismatic. Maybe she'd been wrong about him—though she remembered thinking the same thing the last time she'd laid eyes on the colonel, right before he sent his troops into an ambush.

"I'm Valentine Shepherd. Used to be Staff Sergeant Shepherd, part of the 510th Infantry Regiment. We met very briefly in Afghanistan when you went on a tour of the forward operating bases. It's okay if you don't remember me. You probably shook hands with thousands of people."

"Ah yes," Norman said. "I do remember you, actually. One of the first women assigned as a squad leader on the front lines, correct? How could I forget that red hair of yours?"

She smiled. "Your memory is impressive, sir. I hadn't realized that you grew up in the Seattle area until I saw your ads. I wanted to offer my help with your campaign, if you'll take it."

"Of course I'll take it." He laughed. "I'll take any help I can get, Sergeant. I'm behind in the polls right now, but not by much. This city needs some positive change, and fast. The crime rate has spiked under Mayor Brest, you know. This city runs through my veins like blood—yours, too, I'm assuming."

Val suppressed an eye roll. "You are one hundred percent right about that, sir."

He brushed some leaves off his flannel shirt and put his hands on his hips while he took a closer look at the woman in front of him. Val held the controlled demeanor and passive smile she'd perfected in the face of scrutiny by a superior officer.

He arched an eyebrow. "Are you packing?"

She glanced down at her coat, surprised he could tell. "For protection, just in case. The only way to stop a bad guy with a gun is a good guy with a gun, right?" She pointed her index finger at his chest, thumb pointed up, and pretended to shoot him. She chuckled like she'd made a joke.

He grinned, a little tighter than before. "So true. A lady can never be too careful. I didn't want to put you all on the front lines. I'm sorry you had to bear the consequences of the liberal faction's misguided attempts at 'equality.' The *things* they do to women in the war zone." He narrowed his eyes at her, the tempering laugh lines falling away to leave only piercing brown. "*Awful things.*"

He took a step toward her, his grip tightening on the shovel as he stared her down. Her breath caught in her throat. Jesus, he was *big*. His hands were nearly the size of her head. He could snap her in half if he wanted.

Don't let him intimidate you. She steeled her nerves and took a slow, deep breath, in and out through her nose. No way he'd try anything in his own home.

"So I've heard," she answered, forcing calm into her voice.

He switched his shovel for a rake and began corralling leaves. "What did you have in mind for this ad of yours?" he asked, chipper again.

"I wanted to get your opinion on that. I got the idea from a friend of mine who worked on your campaign. Chet's his name."

Norman stopped raking.

"I met him at this art class I was taking at a community college. He told me that he knew you well. He said I should do a TV commercial where I talk about what a great commander you were, and how you're the epitome of honesty and integrity. He was supposed to meet me here this morning to talk to you, but I guess something else came up."

Val tried not to hold her breath as she waited for his reaction. He stared at the leaves for a long moment, his face blank. When his gaze met hers again, his eyes were so cold she'd have sworn the dead of winter had rushed over them in the span of a few seconds.

"Chet, huh? I *do* know Chet, but not well. He was caught stealing from the headquarters building, so I fired him. You should think twice about who you associate with, Sergeant Shepherd."

"Are you sure you don't know him well? Because he sure seemed to know a lot about you. He said you guys were *tight*. He also told me how broken up you were when you heard about Lester Carressa's death. Was Mr. Carressa a friend of the family?"

Norman's lips peeled back from his teeth in a fanged smile. He tossed the rake to the side, then picked up the shovel again and gripped it to his chest with white knuckles. Adrenaline surged through Val as she stood motionless before him, doubting she could reach her gun before he could swing his shovel, but refusing to back down.

After a few tense seconds that felt like an eternity, he turned away from her and walked back to the mangy cat. She noticed now that it lay on its side, twitching as vomit trailed from its mouth.

"Wretched creatures," he said as he loomed over the poisoned animal. "They keep fucking breeding, and no one will do anything about it. No one cares."

He swung the shovel through the air and brought the flat aspect down on the cat's head. It made a sound like stomping on an orange. Val gasped and looked away as he slammed the shovel down two more times, until the cat's head was a pulverized mass of flesh and fur. Val cupped a hand over her mouth to suppress her gags.

Norman turned back to her, gore dripping from his shovel. His friendly mask had dropped away to reveal a man barely in control of himself, a knife hovering at the world's throat. "Get out of here, cunt."

Val stepped back, her resolve cracking under his primal glare. She turned and walked away, as fast as her legs could go without running.

* * *

Val jumped into the passenger's side of Max's car and heaved a sigh of relief.

A weary smile flickered across his lips, like he was thankful she'd come back in one piece. "Well? Did you get what you needed?"

"Oh yeah."

"So he incriminated himself?"

"No, but he's guilty as hell. He pulled a Dr. Jekyll and Mr. Hyde on me."

His hazel eyes widened, the green starbursts at their centers becoming visible. "Did he try to hurt you?"

"No." Val gave him a cockeyed smile. "Your concern is touching, though."

He looked at her thoughtfully, reading her as he'd done in his office the first time they met, until his gaze intensified and turned into something primal and hot. The car felt painfully warm, as if he'd jacked up the temperature, but the heat wasn't coming from the car's vents. It came from *him*, she realized, from the inferno that burned just underneath his outer façade, the hidden fire that drew her to him when she knew she should keep her distance.

He blinked, and his outer cool snapped back into place. "What now?" he asked in a calm, even tone.

Val cleared her throat and mentally slapped herself. *Of course he's not on fire. That's not even physically possible. Jesus, woman, pull it together.* How Max had learned to control his emotions so well, she could only guess. He put her lame poker face to shame.

She crossed her arms and looked off into the distance. "He didn't like when I talked about Chet, but he really lost his shit when I mentioned Lester." Her gaze cut back to Max. "You're sure that neither you nor your father has any connection to Barrister?"

"I know I don't. And I never heard my father mention Barrister, ever. He was totally uninterested in politics."

"Then we're missing something, because they're definitely connected somehow."

Max drummed his fingers on the steering wheel, then sighed through a grimace. "My father's home office is on the third floor of the main house. I haven't been in there since the day he died. It's packed full of papers and other junk I ignored. Could be useful information squirrelled away somewhere in there."

Val frowned. "Why didn't you mention this before?"

"Because you were dead-set on talking to Barrister as soon as possible, remember? And…I don't want to go in there unless I have to. I'm trying to keep it preserved for the police, in case they want to take another look around."

He looked away, and Val saw the darkness in his eyes again that made her wonder what his true reasons were for avoiding his father's office. Despite their unique connection, she knew next to nothing about him—he could have killed his father for all she knew, though the more time she spent with him, the more she doubted he was capable of murder.

"Then we need to go back to your house to poke around your father's office," she said, "right after we make one more stop."

He started the car. "Hera's House of Gyros?"

"After. First, the Washington State Ladies headquarters in Olympia."

Chapter Twelve

Norman scowled at Valentine Shepherd's back as she marched away, swinging her hips like she outranked him. It was all he could do to keep himself from chasing the bitch down and beating her face in. Why his Army contemporaries saw fit to give people like her leadership positions, he'd never understand. If the military insisted on clinging to the notion of diversity while ignoring the obvious differences between men and women's physical capabilities, they could at least put a premium on respect.

When he was sure she was gone, he tossed his shovel to the side and hurried back inside his house. In his den, he whipped out his cell phone and dialed as he paced across the Oriental rug.

"What do you want, Norm?" Dean Price answered. "I'm meeting with a client in five minutes."

"Do you know a woman named Valentine Shepherd?"

After a long pause, Dean said, "She was an acquaintance of my son's. Why?"

"Because she was just here asking questions about Lester Carressa. Why the fuck would she do that?"

"I don't know. She's aware that Robby was on the team of lawyers representing Maxwell Carressa—"

"How did she connect us? What did you tell her?"

"I didn't tell her anything." Dean's voice took on an edge of anger. "For some reason she thinks Robby's death is related to Carressa's case. Why would she think *that*?"

Norman cringed. Calling Dean had been a mistake. Just when Norm had finally managed to quell Dean's suspicions that his son's "accidental" death was nothing more than a coincidence, Norm had stoked the flames again. He rubbed the bridge of his nose with his thumb and forefinger, and nearly jumped out of his skin when he saw Gino behind him, lounging on the russet-colored leather sofa with his arms and legs crossed as he bounced a foot in the air, his thin lips twisted in a crooked smile. Goddamn Gino was like a fucking ninja—or a shadow, always there but only sometimes visible.

Norman turned away from Gino's distracting presence. "She didn't mention Robby," he said to Dean, "but she's connecting the dots somehow. You need to get her off the trail."

Dean scoffed. "She doesn't know anything. She *can't* know anything. Just ignore her. I need to go." He hung up.

Norman gripped his phone hard, then harder, until a crack appeared at its edge.

"Overreacting again, I see," Gino said in his obnoxious singsong voice.

"Shut up." Norman tossed his phone on his antique desk and took a couple of deep breaths. "How much so far?"

"Seven point six eight million."

"Goddammit. There's no way to move it faster?"

Gino laced his fingers behind his head and leaned back. "Not unless you want to catch the attention of the FBI. Oh, by the way—I saw Maxwell Carressa parked in a car a block from here, waiting for that woman who paid you a visit, I'm guessing."

Norman slammed his fist down on the desk. "Fuck!"

"Don't get mad at me. I did what you told me to. Killing the Price boy was supposed to clear our path to success, right? So you tell me why we've got Lester's kid and Little Red Riding Bitch on our case."

"I don't know why. It wasn't supposed to be like this…" He'd been told eliminating Robby was critical to the plan—exactly how, he still didn't know. He ran a hand through his salt-and-pepper hair. It was a little longer than he preferred, but his campaign advisers told him that voters wouldn't warm to the close-cropped military look. He glanced at Gino. "Criminal activity is your area of expertise. So how would you handle it?"

Norman watched Gino run his tongue across his lips as he considered their options—first his top lip, then the bottom. A heat clawed its way out of Norman's belly and down to his groin, pushing bile up his throat in its wake.

No, not here. Not again.

"Keep eliminating the weak links," Gino said. "Robby's gone—though that turned out to be pointless—and your boy toy's been removed from the picture—"

"Don't call him that," Norman growled. "He wasn't my 'boy toy.' We just…I just…That little faggot tricked me."

Gino laughed. "Sure he did, Norm."

Norman's fists tightened into leathery balls. *Goddamn* Gino, he knew how to push his buttons. He hadn't even known Gino for that long, met him through a friend-of-a-friend with connections to the criminal underground, but the skinny Italian man with shiny suits and a smart mouth had managed to work his way under Norman's skin in record time.

"Next in the chain would be Georgie Porgie," Gino said. "Get as much out of him as possible, then put him down. That piggy'll squeal eventually."

"Fine. Do it. The Carressa kid, too." War always involved casualties. The weak were the first ones to go.

"Uh-uh. We won't get away with killing a rich white boy, not so soon after Robby. Better to convince your pal Dean to pull the trigger on slipping the incriminating evidence he's got on Maxwell to the DA. That'll get the Carressa kid out of the picture. Maybe the redhead will disappear with him."

Norman nodded and cracked his knuckles. Dead people were easier to deal with, but Gino was the expert. Maybe after he became mayor and some time had passed, he could arrange for Maxwell and his whore to have an accident. Tie up those loose ends.

"You look stressed," Gino said. His eyes drifted down from Norman's face.

"Don't."

Gino chuckled. "It's hard running for office. Everyone needs to let off steam now and then." He stood and walked toward Norman.

Every muscle in Norman's body tensed, ready for a fight—a

fight within himself. "Stay away from me, you fucking fruit."

Like the ninja that he was, Gino's hand shot out lightning-quick and grabbed Norman's groin. Almost as fast, Norman grabbed the lapels of Gino's suit coat and yanked him close, staring murder into his eyes, ready to slam his skinny ass into the ground and end this game once and for all.

"How will you clean up this mess you've made without me, Norm?" Gino said as he ran his fingers across the outline of Norman's hard cock beneath the khakis.

Norman moved his lips to tell Gino to go to hell, to crawl back under the rock he'd come from, that he didn't need him for anything, that he had it all under control, but nothing came out. Gino popped the button off Norman's pants, the sound of unzipping as loud as a freight train, the feel of the air on his bare butt as sharp as a needle to the eye.

"No…" Norman said, but it came out as more of a moan when Gino knelt down and dug his fingers into Norman's ass cheeks, then flicked that sharp tongue against the tip of Norman's penis exactly four times before taking the whole thing in his mouth. Gino took his time sliding his lips up and down Norman's cock so Norman could feel every movement of Gino's tongue, every millimeter his wet lips slid down the shaft, every squeeze of his hand cupping the testicles. He was so excruciatingly slow that his legs began to shake and he whimpered like a baby for Gino to get it over with.

When Norman teetered at the precipice of his shame, Gino shoved him away like a child he'd gotten tired of playing with. They faced each other for a moment, the Italian's flushed mouth warped into an evil grin, snickering, as the colonel considered snapping his neck.

"Turn around," Gino said.

"Fuck you."

Gino grabbed Norman's arm and spun him, then bent him over his desk. Norman's bear-like body could have easily resisted, but his mind was weak. When the urge seized him, his military training and moral scruples dissolved in the sickening heat of the moment.

"I hate you," Norman murmured when Gino thrust himself into the colonel and painful ecstasy shot through every nerve of his body. "I fucking hate you."

"I know," Gino said, his voice slick with contempt. In and out he went, over and over, faster and faster, their thighs slapping into each other, grunting together in mutual desperation for release.

This is the last time, Norman swore as he came with a shudder on the rug under their feet. Every time he told himself it would be the last, but he meant it this time. Like last time. Norman cringed as Gino tensed with his own climax, pushing his life force where God and nature didn't intend it to go, just to spite Norman.

The last time.

Chapter Thirteen

And that's why we must take a stand against moral corruption and hypocrisy," Delilah Barrister finished her speech to the room full of Washington State Ladies for Family Values, "for the sake of our children, and the city!"

The audience erupted in applause. Val watched from the back of the room, keeping a low profile until the end of the meeting. It'd been a fight to get Max to wait in the car again, but he eventually relented after she convinced him talking to Delilah would be a walk in the park compared to her psycho husband. And with Sten and his assassination squad on her tail, it was important they weren't seen together. If Val could get Delilah alone and build a rapport with her, woman to woman, maybe she'd trust Val enough to spill whatever she knew about the connection between Norman and Lester, and how they were tied to Robby's murder.

As the ladies got up and began shaking hands and gathering their purses, Val did one last scan for cops or security who might ID her; still none, thank God.

When only a few women lingered, Val approached. "Hi again," she said with a friendly smile.

Delilah looked up from the papers she'd been gathering. "Oh, hello, Miss…Shepherd, was it?"

"You can call me Val. I'd like to talk to you about Colonel Barrister, if you don't mind. Do you have a moment?"

"Of course. Let's go to my office."

Val followed Delilah into a modest office with pictures of Washington State forest landscapes on the walls along with half a dozen certificates of appreciation. Atop the desk sat a fresh bouquet of flowers, next to a brass plaque that read "President." At Delilah's gesture, she sat down in one of the two seats in front of the desk.

Delilah took the other seat, crossed her legs, and leaned toward Val. "What can I do for you?"

Val laced her fingers on her lap and considered her words carefully. After thirty-something years of marriage, Delilah was in the best position to know what kind of man Norman was behind his carefully controlled public persona. True, many people chose to stay ignorant of their spouse's transgressions if facing reality could result in the loss of their cushy lifestyles. Val didn't know what went on between Delilah and Norman behind closed doors, but Norman definitely had a temper. If his wife feared him, she might be willing to turn on him and help Val in exchange for getting Norman out of her life.

"As I'm sure you know, sometimes people come back from war changed," Val said, "usually not for the better."

Delilah's mouth fell into a slight frown. "What do you mean?"

"When I visited Colonel Barrister today, he seemed…off. Not

the same man I used to know." That was a lie—Val always knew Barrister to be a two-faced bastard, but pretending to see it for the first time might bring Delilah around to her own realization. "He was more, I don't know"—Val cringed like it pained her to say it—"*violent.*"

Delilah sat back in her chair. She gripped the armrests and swallowed hard. After a long pause, she said, "He's had a hard time readjusting to civilian life. It takes a toll on you, all those years of fighting. You've been there. You know."

Yes, Val had been there. She'd been broken down and put back together again, to fight for Uncle Sam in one ultimately pointless skirmish after another. She might've had sympathy for Barrister if she thought he suffered from something like post-traumatic stress disorder, and wasn't naturally a cat-killing, woman-hating, homophobic hypocrite.

"He's changed, and…" Delilah's eyes filled with tears. "Sometimes he scares me."

Val leaned forward. "Has he hurt you?"

"Not yet, but…" Delilah shook her head.

"Has he hurt other people? Is he involved in anything…not right? Maybe illegal?"

Norman's wife narrowed her eyes at Val, suddenly suspicious. "Of course not. Why would I know that?"

She'd pushed too hard. Time to try a different tactic. "Listen, I'm going to be honest with you. I've been hired by Maxwell Carressa to look into his father's death and help exonerate him. The information I've discovered so far has led me to believe your husband is involved."

Delilah's eyes widened. "What information?"

"I can't divulge that right now. But the evidence is strong. I just don't know exactly *how* Norman is involved."

"Oh my God…"

"Delilah, I could help you. We could help each other. Your husband scares you, he's been unfaithful—"

"*What?*" Delilah sat up straight in her chair, anger overriding her shock.

"I'm sorry, it's true."

The prim woman said nothing for several seconds, clenching and unclenching her jaw as if she literally chewed on the information. Finally, she spat, "What do you want from me?"

"Give me evidence of Norman's involvement in Lester Carressa's death, or anything that might tie him to the death of Robert Price, Max Carressa's lawyer."

"I—I don't know anything about that."

"Come on, Delilah," Val said, her patience waning. "You're a smart woman. You must know something. You live with the man. If you help me, I'll make sure you're safe and help you leave him—"

"I can't leave my husband! I'd have nothing! I can't put my son through a messy divorce. I'd lose my position here. Everyone would *know*. I can't—" She launched from her seat, her back rigid. "Thank you for coming by, Miss Shepherd, but I really need to get back to my work. Though it was very nice talking to you, I have a lot of errands I must run today."

"Please let me help you," Val said as she stood. "No one should live in fear in their own home."

Eyes still awash in tears, Delilah shook her head.

Goddammit. She'd been so close to a possible breakthrough in her search to find Robby's killer. Why did Delilah have to be so goddamn stubborn? Sure, Val knew women in abusive relationships often went to great lengths to protect their abusers, but Delilah's main concern seemed to revolve around maintaining her perfect housewife image. Avoiding a painful divorce wasn't worth running the risk of being beaten to death.

Val swallowed a sigh. The sympathy gambit had failed. Delilah had made herself clear; now wasn't the right time. If Val pushed too hard, Delilah might never come around. "If you change your mind, please call my office—Valentine Investigations. Our contact info is on the website. I'm, um, in between phones right now, but my assistant can help you or put you through to me."

Delilah nodded and folded her arms, waiting for Val to leave.

With no choice, Val obliged her. At least there was still Lester Carressa's study to search. Maybe the day would conclude on something other than a depressing dead end.

Chapter Fourteen

Max stood at the threshold of his father's third-floor study and watched Val inspect Lester's bookshelves, end tables, glass desk, and glass display cases, until she finally stepped through the sliding glass door and onto the balcony. Lester loved glass. It gave the illusion that he had nothing to hide, which every magician knows is the perfect front for deception.

"Wow," Val said as she leaned over the railing and looked straight down to the rocky eaves that led to the waters of Lake Washington. "That's quite a drop."

"He liked to live dangerously," Max said. As he stepped into the room, a wave of irrational dread spread over him, like he expected the shadows to coalesce into the specter of his father and take over his life again.

He's dead, Max admonished himself, *Stop acting like a child.* He closed his eyes for a moment, focused himself on the task at hand, then reopened them with a new resolve strengthened by cold logic.

"Are you all right?" Val asked as she came back inside and slid the door closed behind her. "You look a little pale. If it makes you uncomfortable to be in here, I can dig through the room alone and let you know if I need help."

"There's nothing wrong with me," he said through clenched teeth. He took a breath and tempered the anger in his voice—anger at himself for letting his father get to him from beyond the grave. "You can tear this place apart all you want, but you'll never get through the computer files by yourself." He nodded at the sleek white laptop perched on the desk. "Most of them are probably password-protected."

She shrugged. "Okay, then."

He sat down in front of the computer and fired it up while Val pulled a folder from a neat row of them populating two bookshelves. He didn't expect her to find anything in his father's hardcopy files—old, miscellaneous papers Lester hadn't gotten around to shredding—but if it kept her occupied and out of immediate danger, then he'd play along.

Max still wasn't sure if this supposed conspiracy involving his father, Norman Barrister, and Robby Price's death was a real thing or just a series of coincidences. Meaningless concurrences were a lot more common than people believed, on account of the general public's poor understanding of probability. In fact, the chance that they weren't related hovered around seventy-three percent, by his back-of-the-envelope calculations. He could always try to check with a vision, but she wasn't up for it and it seemed inappropriate for him to do it himself with a houseguest in close proximity. In any case, whether or not they were related didn't change the fact that Val had witnessed Chet's murder, and his killers had an incentive to want her gone. She was safer with him than on her own.

And selfish as it was, he liked having her around. She was beautiful, smart, and tough, but above all she understood him, knew what it was like to bear a hidden curse that tore you apart from the inside. She'd experienced the long, locked-in-a-room-screaming torture that was a life of being completely alone in the world—well, not alone anymore. They had each other now, courtesy of Robby's death.

Max cringed. He shouldn't think like that. Max's junior lawyer had been a much better person than him. Robby deserved to be with Val, not Max. But…if Max and Val had discovered each other under different circumstances, been in healthier places in their lives and unattached, maybe they'd be more than…whatever they were. A woman obsessed with avenging her dead fiancé and a man accused of patricide, working together because they had no one else. The stuff fairy tales were made of.

He gave his head a small shake and turned his attention back to the computer. No sense dwelling on fantasies. She might understand him, but she didn't *know* him. He wanted to let her in, but if he did, she'd take off in a heartbeat, no matter their shared curse.

It took Max two guesses on a variation of his father's usual password to unlock the laptop. From there, he clicked through dozens of folders, each with dozens more files nested inside, and scanned the documents within. He spent the better part of two hours parsing through information he either already knew or was irrelevant to their search; no mention of Norman Barrister whatsoever. Val sat cross-legged on the floor, piles of paper strewn around her and growing larger as she read a document, found nothing, then tossed it to the side.

Rather than continue on this wild-goose chase, the best course of action for them was to just leave. They could go to Argentina, or Fiji, or Shanghai—anywhere in the world—until the mayoral election was over and the heat died down, then return. Or not. He could run Carressa Industries from afar or, better yet, sell the company and walk away from the past. Of course, there wasn't a chance in hell Val would go along with that plan, and he couldn't abandon her to her fate, even if it meant his own downfall. She was a good person—loyal, brave, and on the side of justice. The world would be worse without her; him, not so much.

"Who's Lydia?" Val asked, looking up from a clutch of college-ruled papers in one hand and a notebook in the other.

"My mother. She died in a car accident when I was twelve, shortly after I started having visions. Why?"

"This journal has your mother's name on it." She blew dust off the cover. "It's filled with random notes, like to-do and shopping lists."

"I remember my mom kept notebooks with her. Such was life in the era before smart phones. She was very organized."

Val held up the papers. "These fell out. They're love letters."

Max took them from her and flipped through almost a dozen short, handwritten declarations of love, none of them signed. Nausea gripped his stomach.

Val smiled. "Your dad was a real romantic."

"No, he wasn't. And this isn't his handwriting."

She raised an eyebrow. "Your mom was having an affair? Maybe with Barrister?"

"According to Chet, Barrister's a closeted gay man, so I doubt that."

"Maybe Barrister's bisexual."

Max threw down the letters. "No." He rubbed the bridge of his nose as the first throbs of a migraine coursed through his head. "Whatever these are, they're irrelevant, so let's move on."

Val studied him silently, her cool gray eyes searching his face for a reason why he'd so thoroughly shut down a potential lead. His reason was a stupid one: he didn't want to know. His mother had been the only person in his life who ever truly loved him. He couldn't lose her again.

He'd already resigned himself to accepting she'd died in a car accident, though the close timing of her death and the discovery of his ability always had him doubting. Lester had done lots of terrible things no one but Max knew about. Why not murder? It wouldn't even be the worst thing Lester had ever done. Not that Max could prove any of it. Maybe this possible affair was one step toward that—no. He wouldn't get his hopes up again. Hope only led to crushing disappointment, then despair, then drugs, then guns—

Stop. Think about something else. Max swiveled his chair back to the computer and resumed pounding away at it, his hands trembling but determined. This time, he pulled up his father's old e-mails. He had about an hour until the migraine took over his brain and he became useless. Best not to waste time agonizing over the past.

Thankfully, Val didn't press the issue. She stood and stepped out of her circle of papers, then started pulling books off the shelves and tossing them into the middle of the room.

When he raised an eyebrow at her book throwing, she said, "Families that keep secrets from each other are good at hiding things, often right under each other's noses. I'm guessing there are more gems in here."

Max wanted to tell her to stop, but he didn't want to explain why. Were his own secrets hidden in this room as well? He swallowed hard and let her turn the formerly pristine office inside out.

Orange light glinted off the office's many glass surfaces as the sun began to dip below the horizon. Like a spilled inkwell, the pain in Max's head spread from his temples and crept into the minute crevices of his brain until it was only with great effort that he could read an e-mail, recognize its irrelevance, and discard it. When he was about to give up for the day, he opened an e-mail that had been sent to his father about a month before he died, with no subject, no originating address, and only two lines:

Per our deal, we expect the grandchild upon delivery. Don't force us to directly intervene.

Max stared at the laptop screen as the pain in his head was overpowered for a moment by the fierce pounding of his heart, threatening to burst from his chest. Did this message mean what he thought it meant? Was this why his father had pushed him to find someone and settle down, even though he'd had a vasectomy years ago to make sure he could never have children and pass on his curse? Why Lester had gotten violent for the first time in over a decade? *Don't force us to* directly *intervene—*

"Bingo," Val said behind him. He turned and saw her kneeling beside a three-foot-by-two-foot safe that'd been hidden behind a false wooden panel in the wall, next to a display case she'd pushed aside. She looked at him and frowned. "Okay, now you really look like you're going to puke. Do you need to lie down or something?"

"I've got a headache." He closed the laptop. "I'll be fine." He'd tell her about the mysterious e-mail later. If he told her now, she'd start asking questions he didn't want to answer.

She furrowed her brows, unsatisfied with his response. The last rays of the setting sun caught the sheen of her strawberry-colored hair, and she tucked a lock of it behind her ear so it framed her delicate face, dominated by those steely eyes. He remembered the glimpses he'd caught of her disrobing in his house, how beautiful she was—slim and athletic—and his pain eased for a short moment. After a few seconds of staring at each other, she looked away, her cheeks flushed, and the pain rushed back as he kicked himself for reducing a woman he respected to a sex object.

"Do you know the code?" Val asked him, looking at the safe's electronic combination lock.

Max rubbed his temples and forced the cogs in his head to turn. "Try one-eight-six-zero-zero-three-five-nine-eight."

She punched in the numbers; the safe stayed locked. "Any other guesses?"

He glanced around his father's desk and opened the top drawer, where pens and paper clips rattled about. Inside, he found a sticky note with the word "ASCENSION" written on it. "Try two-seven-nine-five-four-two-four-four-two."

Val entered the numbers and the safe clicked open. "Nice. How'd you know?"

"The first try was my father's social security number, and the second was my father's social security number with the numeric place in the alphabet of each letter in the word 'ascension' added to each corresponding number, accounting for the rollover after the number nine back to zero."

"You *guessed that*?" Val gawked at him. "You told me you were 'decent' at math. My sister was decent at math. You sound better than decent."

He shrugged. She rolled her eyes at him, then started pulling things out of the safe. She handed him a large stack of twenty-dollar bills. Max flipped through it; fifteen thousand dollars in cash.

"I didn't know you had a sister," he said, putting the money on the desk.

"I did." She put a stack of receipts and accounting documents in his lap.

"Where is she now?"

"Dead."

"I'm sorry."

She looked at him with eyes tinged with sadness and gave him a weary smile. "Yeah, well, yet another example of how seeing the future can be totally useless when you only have minimal control over what you see, and most things can't be changed."

"*Most* things?" Maybe the vicious throbbing in his head had caused him to hear her wrong. "Nothing can be changed. I've tried. Ethan's tried."

She pulled a revolver out of the safe and turned it around in her hands. "Maybe you didn't try hard enough." She flipped the cylinder open. "Two bullets? Who only loads two bullets?" Val put the gun on top of the stack of papers in his lap, and continued digging.

Before Max could question her further about the impossibility of what she'd just said, a familiar notch on the gun's handgrip caught his eye. He picked it up and read the serial number—yes, this was the one, his father's old revolver that Max remembered from his teenage years. He thought Lester had gotten rid of the unassuming Smith & Wesson Model 60 after Max's "accident." He'd thought wrong. His eyes traced the barrel and the perfect circle at its terminus, and in a flash he remembered the coldness of the metal when he'd pressed it against his temple and pulled the trigger—

Max's vision blurred and his hearing dulled. His hands began to shake.

Son of a bitch, not now.

He shot up from his seat, knocking the papers and gun to the ground. He laid his palms flat on the desk, hung his head below his shoulders, and gasped for breath as he tried to control his panic attack.

Stop it, stop it, stop it—

He felt a hand on his back. "Max, sit down over here—"

"No!" He jerked away from Val's touch. His voice sounded muffled to his ears, like he spoke through a pillow. "It's my headache. My head hurts. I need my medicine."

He should've taken Val up on her offer to search the office

without him. It'd been months since he'd had a panic attack, and now he was regressing in front of an audience.

To hell with my father, and to hell with this fucking house and the fucking company and fucking everything.

He stumbled for the exit, desperate to get away from the ghosts of the past that haunted him.

Chapter Fifteen

After Max fled the office, Val dumped everything from the safe into a wire-rimmed wastebasket and carried it back to the guest house. She figured Max might be uncomfortable spending time in the same room where his father died, but she hadn't expected a full-on freak-out. Things must've been worse between Max and his father than he'd let on. She hadn't pressed him on exactly how he and his father had used Max's ability to get rich…Suffice it to say she couldn't think of any healthy scenarios.

At the guest house, she found Max bent over his kitchen sink, fumbling with a bottle of aspirin. He wrested the cap off and a cascade of white capsules clinked against the stainless steel basin. He scooped up a handful and shoved them in his mouth, then snatched a bottle of Scotch from the adjacent liquor cabinet to wash them down. She watched without moving as he stomped like the Tasmanian devil from the kitchen to a reading nook next to his mountain of books and dumped the contents of his brief-case onto the ground.

"Are you…" Val stammered. "Can I—"

"Did you get what you needed?" he said in a matter-of-fact voice that utterly failed to bring calm to the rest of his body. He picked up a lighter and a silver cigarette case from the pile his briefcase had thrown up. Val recognized the small box as the one she'd seen in Max's office at the Red Raven, the one that held his marijuana cigarettes.

"I don't know." Val nodded at the wastebasket in her arms. "I need to look through this stuff."

Max held the joint with the same hand that clutched the bottle of Scotch while he tried to guide the lighter with the other, but his hands shook too badly to mate the flame with the cigarette.

"Even if your dad's stash doesn't pan out, I promise you I'll get to the bottom of this—"

"*Fuck!*" Max threw the lighter and joint to the ground, having given up on trying to light it. He walked back to the kitchen, threw open a cabinet door above the kitchen sink, and pulled out a bottle of prescription something. Sleeping pills? Opioids?

Val's eyes widened. *He wouldn't…* She tensed, ready to wrestle the bottle away from him if he tried to down the whole thing, but he only swallowed two pills and tossed the rest back in the cabinet. Then he moved to his bed and lay down, back propped against the headboard, still clutching the liquor bottle. He squeezed his eyes shut, chest heaving while he tried to catch his breath.

So this was what happened when he lost control of his emotions. Jesus, no wonder he worked so hard to keep them in check. How could she help him? She might be able to offer him comfort if she understood where his extreme anxiety came from, but all she knew was some aspect of it included a deep loathing of his father. Val preferred to work through her pain alone, internally. In that, she guessed they were similar. She'd give him space, but she had nowhere to go. All she could do was stand uselessly in the doorway.

"I get migraines," he said after a minute of silence, eyes still closed. "I can't think when they happen."

Val walked to the bed and sat cross-legged next to him, putting the wastebasket down at the foot. She took the Scotch bottle from him and drank a mouthful, wincing at its potency. He didn't skimp on the good stuff.

"Do you want a back rub?" she asked him.

He let out a dry chuckle. "No, thanks. One thing might lead to another, God forbid."

They passed the bottle back and forth until dusk turned to night, and only the soft light from his bedside lamp kept the house from complete darkness. Val's body felt wrapped in a warm blanket, and she almost let her head drop onto Max's shoulder before an image of Robby popped into her mind's eye and caused her to catch herself. She retrieved the wastebasket from the floor and dumped the papers into her lap, leaving the money and gun in the basket. Combing through the pile, she held each one up to the light and scanned for anything that might be relevant.

"What happened to your sister?" Max asked, his body finally relaxed and slouched against the headboard.

Val didn't stop looking through the papers. "When we were in high school, she got drunk at a party and was raped. Someone took a video of it on their phone and sent it to a bunch of other people until the entire school had it. The cops did nothing, as usual—they said it was a 'community matter.' So she killed herself. And you already said you're sorry, so you don't have to say it again."

He turned his head toward her, eyes dark pools in the dim light. "Was the guy ever punished?"

"Sort of. Guys like that don't stay out of trouble for long. He eventually went to prison for dealing drugs, not sexual assault. I saw a lot of that when I was in the military, too. Unchecked predators left to their own devices because when sex is involved, everyone wants to pretend like there's this gray area where we can never really know what happened, so let's just look the other way until it blows over. Somebody had to do something, though, so I decided *I* would do something. That's why I started Valentine Investigations. I didn't want what happened to my sister to happen to anyone else." Val took a breath. "Anyway, that's probably more than you wanted to know."

Max's eyes closed again and his head fell sideways onto her shoulder. Electricity tingled down her arm. There was Robby again, but the aroma of the shampoo Max used in his morning shower dulled the image, and she couldn't convince herself to push the flesh-and-blood man away.

"It's not more than I wanted to know," he said. "Sometimes it feels like too much."

"Yeah." She rested her head against his. It fit nicely there. "Like the universe is against you."

"Yeah."

His dark hair tickled her cheek. An inch turn of her neck and she could kiss the top of his sweet-smelling scalp. If she hadn't felt Robby's eyes on her, maybe she would have.

"She was lucky to have a sister that cared. It's too bad she didn't realize it."

"What's too bad is that of all the future death I see, I didn't see hers—the one that mattered the most to me. I mean, what kind of sick God thrusts this weird ability on us and then…" Val trailed off, distracted by an accounting slip in her hand with a familiar name on it. "Does Dean Price have any involvement with the financial side of Carressa Industries?"

Max lifted his head and opened his eyes to slits. "No."

"His name is on this accounting slip." She held it up for him. "Why would that be?"

He gave it a cursory glance through heavy lids as the mystery pills he'd taken worked their magic. "I don't know."

She sighed at his unhelpfulness. "Why did you hire the Bombay and Price law firm to represent you?"

"My father had them on retainer. Has for decades."

"So why did your father originally hire Bombay and Price?"

"I think…my mother knew Dean Price from law school, and she introduced Dean to my father, before he got rich. That's the story I heard. When my father started raking in the money, Bombay and Price was there for all his personal legal needs. How fortunate for them." He deposited the bottle of Scotch in Val's lap, then shimmied onto his back. "Can we talk about this tomorrow? I need to go to work in the morning."

"But you'll look into this account with Dean's name on it, right?"

He waved a hand at her. "Sure."

In other words, he'd do it to humor her. What a great team they made. Val took a moment to assess what she knew so far. Dean had been Lester's business associate for decades. After Lester died, Chet came out of the woodwork with a claim of foul play involving Norman, at which point Robby was murdered to keep that information from getting out. She knew how Lester and Dean were connected, but how did Norman fit? Was the mayoral candidate connected to Lester through an affair with Lydia Carressa? Max seemed certain that wasn't the case, though Val couldn't rule it out. But why would Norman kill Lester *now*, when the affair ended decades ago? And why kill Robby instead of going straight to the source and killing Chet before he talked to Robby?

Goddammit, why did Robby have to die? She'd never stop until she got answers and justice for Robby. Never.

Val frowned at Max's chest, rising and falling in the steady rhythm of a man slipping quickly into sleep. He didn't care about the mayoral race, or Bombay and Price, or any other aspect of the conspiracy with his father possibly at its center. The only reason he was helping her was because he saw her in a vision. And maybe he felt a special connection with her because of their shared ability. She certainly felt a connection to him, however irrational it was for knowing him so short a time.

Val gathered the papers back into the wastebasket—setting aside the Dean Price accounting slip—and swung her legs off the side of the bed, ready to go back to the main house. She sat where she was for a moment, imagining the cold rooms and icy floor in contrast to the soothing warmth of Max's home, of his body. She turned off the bedside lamp, slid back into bed, and lay on her side next to him.

"Why didn't you look for me?" she whispered into the dark. "I stalked online message boards, went to weird fetish meetings, tolerated people thinking I was crazy, looking for you."

Though she'd thought he was asleep, she felt the bed bounce as he turned over, then his warm breath on her face only a few inches away. "I couldn't," he whispered back. "My father was always watching. He monitored everything I did, all the time. And everybody knew me. I couldn't blend in. I'm sorry."

Tears gathered at the edges of her eyes. They'd lived in the same goddamn city their entire lives, could have helped each other figure out what was wrong with them, why they were different, felt a little less alone, and *he was sorry* he didn't even try. Everything that could have been, all that lost time—

Something warm touched her face, and she realized it was his fingertips, skimming over her jaw like a feather, then across her lips, and her heart insisted *this* was their time, right here, right now, and if he'd kissed her, then she would've kissed him back and given him everything she was in a way she'd never done for anyone else. But in a heartbeat the moment passed and his hand fell away. Deep breaths against her face told her the pills and alcohol had finally forced him into sleep.

With the path of his fingers still warm on her skin, she rested her head against his chest, folded her body against his, and remembered what it was like to fall into another human being until, for that night anyway, the chaotic world retreated to a safe distance.

* * *

Val awoke to the swish of a razor blade, the tapping of the handle against porcelain, and running water trickling down the drain. For a moment she thought she'd had the most vivid dream of her life, and she'd open her eyes to find Robby getting ready for work, humming the theme song to whatever TV show he'd watched the night before. But the sheets felt thicker, smelled muskier, and the morning light warmed her from an unfamiliar angle. When she realized she was in Max's house, listening to him shave, she wasn't entirely unhappy about it.

She lifted her head and rubbed sleep out of her eyes. In the bathroom, Max splashed water on his freshly shaven face, a towel wrapped around his waist. He pulled the towel off and used it to pat his face dry. Val eyed the contours of his glutes, how they sloped into his smooth back like rolling sand dunes. For a moment she imagined running her fingers along those soft hills, then swallowed back a knot made of shame. It wasn't right she was so attracted to him. Robby had barely been gone a week, and she was already imagining what it might be like to touch another man. Seemed almost unnatural. Then again, both she and Max had some very unnatural qualities about them.

Val lay back down again and pretended to sleep as Max exited the bathroom and went about his morning routine, unaware that she watched him. Not that he'd care. She'd never met a guy so comfortable with his body. Though she supposed most people who looked like Max wouldn't be shy about showing it off, either—or maybe it was only her he wasn't bashful around.

He slipped on his underwear and socks, brushed his hair, and unwrapped a dry-cleaned suit from its plastic sheath. The cadence of his quiet movements lulled her into sleep again, until she felt the bed bow under his weight as he sat at the edge next to her, looping a blue-checkered silk tie into a knot around his neck.

He looked at her, saw her eyes were open, and smiled. "There's a board of directors meeting today that I can't miss. I need to make an appearance—instill confidence and all that. I'm afraid they'll try to vote me out because of the suspicion around my father's death, even though I'm the majority shareholder." He tucked the tie into the breast of his charcoal vest and buttoned the cufflinks on his white dress shirt, then leaned toward her, an arm propping him up. A slight bouquet of mountain spring shower gel and bay rum aftershave wafted off him, a smell that matched the green and brown in his eyes. His lips were, oh, thirteen inches or so from hers, she guessed. Too far to reach while lying down, but if he came closer—

"Can you wait for me here until I get back?" he asked. Then added with a hint of desperation, "Please?"

"You expect me to twiddle my thumbs here all day? I could set up a meeting with Dean while you're doing your work thing, twist his arm into talking."

"The guys that killed Chet are still looking for you." He picked up the accounting slip from the nightstand. "Let me ask around about this first, then we'll regroup and decide our next move."

"What am I supposed to do while you're gone?"

"Go through my things, raid the fridge, pocket some valuables. Or read a book."

"Reading is for nerds."

"Watch porn on my computer, then. Fill it with viruses."

She snickered. "Fine, I'll wait here." She nudged his thigh with her foot. "When are you coming back?"

Without seeming to notice what he was doing, Max took her bare foot in his hand and slid his thumb along her instep, sending shivers up her spine. "I'll try to sneak out in the early afternoon. I need to meet with a couple of people, but it shouldn't take long."

He looked at her foot like he just noticed her flesh cupped in his hand, cleared his throat, and let it go. She almost grabbed his hand and begged him to stay, to touch her again like he'd just done while he told her everything there was to know about himself, that they'd worry about the accounting slip later, and—and what the hell was she thinking? Barrister and his cronies were killing innocent people for God knows what reason, and she was the only person standing between him and a powerful public office. Her goddamn libido could wait.

Max slipped on his suit jacket, followed by a black wool overcoat. On the back of a grocery receipt he scribbled something and handed it to her. "Here's my cell phone number. Call me if you need anything." He grabbed his briefcase as he walked out the door, its contents collected back inside sometime before she'd awoke.

Val heard him drive away in the high-rev engine of a rich-boy car, the kind she would've assumed he used to compensate for some deficiency if she didn't know better. She pushed herself up and resolved to explore the main house, as she'd originally desired on her first night there. After she attended to her basic hygiene with the help of a spare toothbrush she found in the bathroom, she made herself a piece of toast and ate it over the sink. Through the glass of his cabinet doors she spotted the bottle of pills he'd desperately consumed the night before. She recognized the label as a medication for chronic anxiety, the kind her sister had been prescribed after the attack. Behind that bottle were more bottles, different drugs to treat anxiety, insomnia, depression, migraines. God, poor Max. Robby was right—the Carressa heir had some serious skeletons in his closet that he struggled to control. She felt a pang of sadness for him, then anger.

At least he didn't get run down in the prime of his life.

Robby's murder—that was the only reason she squatted in Max's house, slept in his bed, put up with his erratic behavior. Max was undoubtedly an *interesting* guy, and they had something in common that maybe a handful of people in the entire world possessed, but in the end he was irrelevant to her ultimate goal—extracting justice for Robby. Even if she had to rip out her own heart and sacrifice it in the name of vengeance, she'd make those bastards pay. She'd failed to avenge her sister. She refused to fail Robby.

Val threw the rest of her toast away and marched back to the main house, ready to get to work. She spent more than three hours opening every drawer, ransacking every closet, opening every container, poking into every nook for other hidden stashes. As each room failed to yield any further clues and her frustration grew, she held out hope that the freezer, a popular hiding spot for crooks and alcoholics, would give her something, anything. Its innards hid nothing but a freezer-burned pint of ice cream.

"Shit!" Val screamed and smashed a tray of ice on the floor. Great, now what? She could wait for Max to return, like she said she would, but she wasn't confident that he'd come back with useful information, given his relative disinterest with the whole conspiracy. She could call Dean and ask him about the account, but a phone conversation was no substitute for a face-to-face conversation, where she could read his body language and he couldn't hang up on her.

Val bit her lip. She needed to meet with Dean, the sooner the better. Just like she and Robby had tried to do with Chet, her best bet was to track Dean down where no one expected him to be, ambush him before he had time to develop a plausible lie, if he knew something worth lying about. God, she hoped he didn't, for Robby's sake.

Val returned to the guest house—promising herself she'd pay Max's housekeepers to clean the massive mess she'd left behind—and took her clothes off. She paused at the edge of his bed, remembering his offer to "help" her have visions, that they were more powerful when experienced between two people who had the ability. She considered his offer again and dismissed it. She couldn't. No matter how much she liked looking at him, the thought of *tasting* him scared her. Dirty John had been convenient and anonymous; Stacey, safe and familiar. Max was something more. If she'd met him under different circumstances, and she hadn't been engaged to Robby... It was too soon.

She lay down on the bed, had a thought, and pulled open his nightstand drawer. Next to more books and a black zip-up bag sat a little bottle of personal lubrication.

"Thought so," she said. No self-respecting person with prophetic orgasms would be caught without lube close by.

Val squeezed a glob on her hand—the self-warming kind. Nice. Manual stimulation wasn't as efficient as her vibrator, but she'd perfected the technique through the years. She rubbed the lube between her legs, making slow circles across her clitoris as the wetness and artificial heat helped hone the sensation, like tuning a string that began at her privates and threaded through her belly and into her spine. She played that string and visualized her last moments with Robby, what he'd felt like inside her, his hands caressing her backside, her breasts.

"Robby," she muttered as the string grew taut and resonated through her body, "where is your father? Show me Dean." She exhaled, long and ragged, her insides liquid as every muscle in her body tensed at the cusp of climax. She writhed on Max's bed and gripped his sheets, down feather duvet crinkling against her naked skin, the twin smells of his bath soap and aftershave still in the air—

A light rain trickles onto the pavement of an empty parking lot abutting a high-rise. Max walks outside through a metal door with "Carressa Industries: Deliveries Only" written on it in plain block letters, a "Closed for construction—use front entrance" sign taped underneath. Rain stains his expensive charcoal-colored three-piece suit and blue-checkered tie, but he doesn't seem to care. His eyes are fixed straight ahead, on something across the parking lot. He takes a couple quick steps across the pavement.

"And where are you going?" Sten says.

Max freezes.

"Don't you know that when you fight the law, the law wins? You should trust the Clash."

Blur.

Max lies on the ground with his hands cuffed behind his back, blood streaked across his white dress shirt, face a pulpy mass of red. His eyes are open but glazed over.

"Temper, temper," Sten says, kneeling over Max. He raises a collapsible baton over Max's head and snaps it to its full length with the flick of his wrist. "How am I going to live with myself, knowing what I was forced to do in self-defense?" He swings the baton down.

Blur.

Max lies in a hospital bed, tubes protruding from his body. A machine beeps in the background. His face is waxen where it's not covered in black bruises, his body limp, his eyes closed. A gas bag pushes air into his lungs.

"There was a lot of cranial hemorrhaging," one doctor tells another at the foot of Max's bed. "I'm not sure if he'll wake up—"

The beep becomes a continuous, unbroken tone.

Val gasped and sat straight up after her vision cleared. Holy shit—she'd seen Max die.

She'd seen him die *today*.

She had to call him *now*. Val cast about his house for a landline phone; he didn't have one. She threw her clothes on, sprinted to the main house, and grabbed the first telephone she saw—a cordless one perched atop the kitchen counter. She dialed Max's cell number, and swore when she got his voice mail.

"Max, it's me. You're in danger. When you leave your building through the deliveries entrance—which I'm guessing is in the back—a police officer will catch you there and beat you to death. So you need to either stay in the building or use a different exit or…I don't know, just don't go out that way. Actually, I'm coming to you now, so *don't leave the building*."

She hung up and ran to where she'd left her powered-down cell phone, atop the dresser in the room she'd slept in her first night at the house. After she turned it on, Val ran back to the guest house, snatched the keys to Max's borrowed car from the kitchen table, along with the wastebasket that held Lester's secret stash, then jumped in the vehicle. She estimated with traffic and stoplights, it would take her about twenty-five minutes to reach Carressa Industries Headquarters. She dialed his phone again; still no answer.

"Goddammit, Max," she said as she peeled out of the driveway, "if you die today, I will fucking kill you. And then myself."

Chapter Sixteen

The early afternoon sun peeked through dark clouds gathering in the sky outside Max's corner office window, glinting off the crystal Better Buying Power awards lining an oak shelf against the far wall. He counted the angles that their refracted light projected across the ceiling like mirror shards, before the sun disappeared with the shifting of the wind. The counting helped him concentrate, refocus away from the grueling board meeting he'd squeaked through, withstanding a barrage of criticism through a delicate tap dance of vision statements and iron-clad confidence to barely keep his job. Michael Beauford, Carressa Industries' chief financial officer, leaned back in a leather chair across from him.

"Charlene's itching to divest of Quality Foods," Michael said, resting his leathery hands on a once-toned stomach now sagging with age. "They posted a twelve percent loss this quarter. She's concerned they won't rebound from their organic spinach E. coli scare in July. Thinks their earthy-crunchy base demographic is too fickle to forgive. I told her if that were true, my wife would've divorced me forty years ago." Through a gray beard he gave Max a warm smile that faded when Max failed to reciprocate. "When are you moving into your father's office?"

Michael never ceased to amaze Max with his ability to cut to the heart of the matter with uncanny precision. Ever since Michael rose to CFO nine years ago, Max had trusted and respected him, in no small part because Michael's keen observation skills quickly deduced where the real power behind the company lay.

Max shrugged. "I don't know. Whenever I get around to it."

Michael scoffed. "That means never."

"I'm considering turning it into a janitor's closet."

The CFO folded his arms, another disapproving father figure Max didn't need. "Ignoring the situation won't make it go away."

"That's an interesting hypothesis. I'll let you know how my trial run goes."

"Yuk it up, buddy boy, but the board isn't going to tolerate your antics for much longer. You put on a nice show in there, and they like you better than they did your father, but the leeway you've been given to grieve is over. If you don't get your head out of your ass and start leading this company, it won't be yours much longer."

Max frowned at the far wall, avoiding Michael's stern gaze. Since his father died and the pressure to pulse the future for business advice had lifted, he'd disengaged from the majority of his responsibilities, probably to an extreme degree, he now realized. He'd stopped attending meetings, canceled appointments, holed up in his office, came to work high—when he bothered to come to work at all. At least most of the board mistook grief as the cause of his maladjustment.

"And for God's sake, get rid of the Red Raven in Moonlight." Michael said the name of Max's club like the words left a film of oil on his tongue. "It's bad enough that the police are *still* investigating you over Lester's death. If the press finds out about the place, it'll be a PR disaster. The board will turn on you for sure."

How the hell did Michael know about the Red Raven? The club was his sanctuary, one of the very few places he felt safe. He couldn't give it up, but Michael was right; only luck had kept the Red Raven out of the public eye for this long. He had to choose: the Red Raven or control of Carressa Industries.

"Do you recognize this account number?" Max handed Michael the accounting slip Val had found with Dean Price's name on it.

Michael rolled his eyes at Max's abrupt change of subject, but took the paper. "No." He read the slip, raised an eyebrow. "Dean Price is your defense lawyer, right?"

Max nodded.

"Huh. Odd." He turned the paper in his hand, looking for signs of fakery. "Where'd you get this?"

"From a stack of old papers in my father's study."

"I'll run it down in accounting," Michael said.

"Don't bother." Max took back the paper. "I'll do it. I'm overdue for a walkabout anyway."

Michael shrugged. "You're the boss." He drummed his fingers on the seat's armrests and ballooned his craggy cheeks out in a puff of air. "Listen, it's natural to have trouble reconciling conflicted feelings about the death of a family member when the relationship was…contentious. If you need someone to talk to, I can recommend a therapist who's discreet."

Max laughed at that. "Contentious" was putting it mildly. A therapist could write an entire book about his issues, right before she threw him into the insane asylum.

"I already have someone to talk to." He had Val—sort of. He could tell her more than most people, though not everything. Maybe one day. Or never.

Her sense of right and wrong seemed…not absolute, though well developed. Better than his. She knew one of his most closely kept secrets—but only one of them. To expect her to understand, and then forgive him, was unrealistic. She'd eventually find her fiancé's killer—of that he had no doubt—then leave him to go back to her normal life, find another normal man like Robby to love. Or she'd stay, and he'd have to tell her the truth someday, then she'd leave him. Either way, she'd never be his. He wouldn't beg her to stay. He'd already tried that with Ethan; he wouldn't embarrass himself again.

Max pushed away the black hole that threatened to swallow his thoughts, stood, and forced out a smile. "Thanks for the talk, Michael. I'll tag up with Charlene about Quality Foods later."

Michael nodded, an extended exhale betraying his skepticism. He paused on his way out the door. "Just promise me you're not off to throw on tights and start fighting crime."

* * *

Max stepped off the elevator onto the fourteenth floor. He walked through the cubicle farm that made up the accounting department, past number crunchers hunched over their computers who did double takes when he walked by. On his path to Dewey Dryer's office, the head of Accounting, he greeted employees. "Hi, Linda, how're you doing?" "John, how are the kids?" "Ben, finally housetrained that puppy of yours?" He liked talking to people about their normal lives, vicariously experiencing what it might be like to be a regular person. One man's banal story about taking his elderly mother to the dentist was Max's impossible dream.

Eventually he found Dewey Dryer's office with the door propped open. He poked his head in and saw the middle-aged man at his desk, deep into an earnings report packed with spreadsheets. Max cleared his throat, and Dewey's head snapped up.

"Mr. Carressa!" Dewey stumbled out of his seat.

Max shook his hand.

"Nobody told me you were coming down here. Um…How are things? Oh geez, that's a stupid question. Dead dad and all. I mean—what can I do you for?"

Ignoring Dewey's awkwardness, Max showed him the accounting slip. "I need to know more about this account. Do you recognize it?"

Dewey scrutinized the paper for a moment. "Hmm"—he rubbed his chin—"looks like an old one. Before my time, even." He poked his finger in the air. "I bet Georgie would know about this. He's been here since the company's beginning, I think. Have you met him?"

"No," Max said as he followed Dewey to Georgie's cube, tucked away in the corner. "I'm surprised we've never been introduced, if he's been here all this time."

"His name's George McOwen, but everybody calls him Georgie. Not sure if it's by choice, but he doesn't complain. He's a quiet guy, prefers to stay out of the spotlight. Real hard worker, though." Dewey stopped beside Georgie's cube wall and whispered to Max, "I mean, I assume he's not secretly a gun-toting psycho, but it's always the quiet ones, right?" He winked and chuckled.

Max tried to smile politely; it came out as more of a cringe.

Dewey rapped on the thin partition wall. "Hi, Georgie!" he said to the pudgy man in a wrinkled white dress shirt and too-short tie, plinking away at his keyboard.

Georgie jerked so hard at Dewey's voice that he knocked over a travel mug, spilling coffee onto the papers scattered across his desk top. "Dang it!" He struggled to his feet and grabbed fistfuls of other papers off his desk to mop up the mess.

"This is Mr. Carressa—Maxwell Carressa, I mean. The one that's alive."

Max righted the travel mug, stanching the flow of coffee, and smiled at Georgie. Georgie adjusted his Coke bottle glasses and swallowed hard.

"Oh, um, hi, Mr. Carressa," he said in a voice barely audible.

"I'd appreciate your help on something, Georgie," Max said. "Is it all right if I call you Georgie?"

Georgie shrugged. "Your father did."

Lester was on a first-name basis with this guy? Max made an

effort to be friendly and cordial with his employees; his father had not. Lester would never bother getting to know someone he considered a grunt unless that person had something he wanted. Why had Max never met Georgie before?

Max held out the paper. "What is this account?"

Georgie eyed the document. His face grew pale. "I don't know."

"Are you sure?" Max asked, ignoring his cell phone vibrating against his chest. "I found this in a stack of my father's records. Dewey says it looks like an old account. Will you take another look, please?"

"I...I don't know the account," he mumbled.

Max's cell phone vibrated again. As he reached into his pocket to check it, he froze when a plaque on Georgie's cluttered desk caught his eye. Worn oak the size of a half-sheet of paper surrounded a copper plate that read: "George McOwen, Employee of the Month, August 1995." Etched in the wood above the plate: "Bombay and Price Law Offices, LLC."

"You used to work for Dean Price," Max said. He looked at Georgie as the man's face scrunched with the effort of holding in secrets he didn't have the intestinal fortitude to keep. "You're *sure* you don't know this account?"

"I've never seen it. Never seen it before." Beads of sweat popped onto Georgie's brow. "I have to go to the bathroom."

"Why don't you check your archives?" Dewey said, oblivious to Georgie's growing anguish. "You've got all sorts of gems in there that've helped us out of a pickle. Like when we got court-ordered to hand over every record we had on Red Bell Ice Cream, and you dug up nuggets going back to its acquisition in like nineteen ninety-eight—"

A mother of a fart ripped from Georgie. His face turned red and he grimaced. "Oh, God!" he sputtered, "I have to go!" He barreled past Max and Dewey, leaving the rancid smell of his digested breakfast in his wake. His coworkers gawked and slapped hands over their mouths as he shuffled for the exit as quickly as his legs would go, a brown stain blooming on the rear of his pants.

"Sweet Jesus," Dewey said, holding his nose. "That stomach bug is really making the rounds." He pulled a tube of sanitizer from his pocket and rubbed a glob of it on his hands. "Sorry about that, Mr. Carressa. I guess we'll have to wait until he comes back from his emergency sick day. Maybe tomorrow?"

"Yeah." Max stared at the spot where Georgie had disappeared. "I'll come back tomorrow. Thanks for your help."

The fact that Georgie literally crapped his pants when Max asked about the account was a good sign he was on to something. And Georgie's previous employment at Bombay and Price couldn't be a coincidence, either. What in the world it had to do with Barrister, Max still had no idea. But Georgie might.

He could go straight to the source and ask Dean why his name was on this old account, but he should touch base with Val first—assuming she hadn't already contacted Dean despite his objections. Actually, that seemed like something she would definitely do. Might as well head home and compare notes. His phone vibrated yet again; he finally checked it, and saw four missed calls from Val, though it was Kitty on the line this time.

"Have you talked to your lawyers yet?" Kitty's silky voice had an edge of panic to it that immediately put Max on alert.

"Not today. Why?"

"Because a judge just issued a warrant for your arrest. The police are coming for you now."

"What? *Fuck.*" Max rubbed his forehead and tried to shield his crestfallen face from onlookers. For a second he considered asking Kitty how the hell she'd come by this information so quickly, but Kitty worked in mysterious and very effective ways that he preferred not to question.

"What are you going to do?" she asked.

"I don't know yet." He walked back toward the elevator, trying to appear calm as his thoughts raced. "Call my lawyers. Make sure they know what's going on. And keep them away from the Red Raven, if you can. I'll…be in touch."

He hung up and dialed his secretary. "Nadine, please have the valet bring my car around front." He pushed the "up" button for the elevator. "I'm going to swing by the office to grab my things, then I'm going home for the day."

"I'll do that now, Mr. Carressa," Nadine said.

After he hung up, he cut right, away from the elevator and into the building's stairwell. Hopefully the appearance that he was leaving out the front with no clue he was about to be arrested would throw off the police for a few precious minutes while he made his escape through the back, an area that'd been closed off due to construction in the parking lot. He didn't have a plan other than getting the hell out of there. He couldn't trust the cops, not after they'd tried to kill Val—

Shit, Val.

If they had a warrant for his arrest, they'd soon have a warrant to search his house, where they'd find her. The crooked cops who'd tried to end her life once might finish the job. He needed to escape, at least temporarily, to warn Val. Maybe ask her to meet him somewhere, if he could evade capture for that long.

As he bounced down the stairs, he tried to dial Val, then again, and again. Each time the call dropped. No reception in the stairwell. Damn—he'd have to wait until he got outside to call her.

After descending thirty flights of stairs, he reached the basement and jogged through a corridor used for equipment and supply deliveries, dark and deserted at the moment. No sign of police. When he reached the solid metal door that offered him egress, he pushed it open a crack and listened for sirens, car doors, or voices—nothing. He peered through the slit at what he could see of the back parking lot, a light rain beginning to darken the pavement—empty. Across the lot was a patch of woods with a short nature trail employees liked to hike through during their lunch breaks. On the other side he knew there was a gas station. He could make it. Play it cool, walk away like he had nothing to fear. Max took a deep breath and said a silent prayer for a clean getaway, then pushed the door open and walked outside.

"And where are you going?"

Max nearly jumped at a voice to his far left, an area he hadn't been able to see through the door crack. A plainclothes policeman in a gray hoodie and jeans, a badge around his neck, leaned against a backhoe with his arms folded across his chest. His mouth twisted into a shit-eating grin below a bush of a mustache.

"Don't you know that when you fight the law, the law wins?" the cop said as he walked toward Max, his gait casual despite a hand on his holstered gun. "You should trust the Clash."

Max gritted his teeth. There went his slapdash escape plan. He scanned his surroundings and noticed that he and the cop were the only people in the parking lot. How did this asshole know Max would come out this way, at this moment, and why didn't he have backup with him?

Goddammit. Val was right—there *was* a conspiracy. Only someone with their abilities could maneuver against them with this kind of clockwork precision. And this guy was part of it.

Max tensed up, ready to run. The cop noticed and pulled his gun.

"I'm no scientist, but I'm gonna guess you can't outrun a bullet," the cop said. "I think I learned that in high school physics class. Or maybe chemistry, I forget."

Max balled his hands into fists but didn't move. This bastard was itching for any excuse to shoot him in the back.

The cop got close enough for Max to read the name on his badge—Sten Ander. Sten pulled a pair of handcuffs from his back pocket. "Turn around and put your hands behind your back, pretty boy."

Max eyed Sten's gun. Though he seethed with the desire to bash the dirty cop's face in, it came down to fists versus guns, and the odds weren't in his favor. Clenching his jaw so tight his teeth nearly cracked, Max did as he was told. He felt the metal snap across his wrists and winced at his helplessness. Sten dragged Max back to the backhoe, then spun him around and shoved his back against the cab door. He grunted as his hands were crushed between wet metal and the small of his back. The cop paired a friendly smile with a sadistic glint in his eye that made Max shudder.

"Where's your new best friend?" Sten asked.

Son of a bitch, Sten knew about her, too. He wished he'd thought to call Val and warn her when he'd had the chance, before he'd lost reception in the stairwell. "I have lots of best friends," Max said, keeping his voice measured in an attempt to hide his growing panic. "You need to be more specific."

"The hot redhead. You know who I'm talking about." Sten winked. "You guys fucking yet?"

The rain picked up, matting Max's hair to his forehead. Water dribbled down his face and into his eyes. He blinked it back as best he could and considered spitting some in Sten's face. "Kitty has blond hair, not red. And yes, we've been fucking for about a year now."

Sten laughed. "You're clever. I like you. What's it like being smart and rich?"

Max stared at him for a moment while Sten waited for a response. And waited. He really wanted an answer. What the hell was this guy up to? At least if he was busy messing around with Max, then he wasn't hunting for Val.

Max thought of a smart-ass answer and said, "It's like—"

Sten punched him hard in the stomach before he could finish. He doubled over and fell to his knees, gasping for breath as pain seared through his torso.

"I'm just kidding," Sten chuckled. "I don't really care what it's like to be smart and rich." He pulled Max back to his feet again. "I do want to know, though, what it's like to have everything and nothing at the same time. What's that like?"

What the fuck? How did he know these things? Who told him? The mysterious people who'd e-mail his father, trying to pull the strings of his life?

"Lonely, right?"

Sten seized Max's jaw and dug his fingers into the sides of Max's cheeks. He writhed in Sten's grasp, struggling to breathe, old memories clawing their way to the forefront of his mind. This time he would *fight back*, goddammit.

"So lonely you wanna grab the closest thing you can find and fuck it rotten, just to feel a connection, like in a Hallmark movie?" His tone was jovial, like the two men were chatting at a sports bar. "Even fall in love with someone you just met?"

"Fuck you," Max managed to force out through Sten's vise grip on his face.

"You know, I think I'll do that when I see Shepherd again. I'll fuck her rotten, and we'll come together like two halves of the solstice moon, or whatever metaphor works here. She might say no at first, but if I've learned anything from reading romance novels, it's that every woman secretly wants to be dominated. They all have rape fantasies. I can do that."

Sten shoved Max away from him, a giant grin slapped on his face. The pain in Max's stomach and face dulled beside the rage that coursed through him, the desire to break every bone in Sten's body. To do everything in his power to keep this psycho away from Val.

"Aw, pwetty boy mad?" Sten opened his arms wide in front of Max, like a bird flapping its wings, or a toreador taunting a bull. "Now's your chance to prove you can take me with both hands behind your back. I know you're thinking it."

Max's world turned red. He struck out with his leg and nailed Sten in the chest. The cop stumbled backward and fell onto his side. His gun bounced out of his hand and slid ten feet away when he hit the ground. With a primal growl Max kicked him in the chest again, the urge to destroy him like a runaway train in Max's mind, barreling over all rational thought.

Max chambered his leg back to deliver another vicious kick, but before he could connect, Sten lunged forward and grabbed Max's front leg with both arms and yanked it toward him. Max slipped backward, unable to catch his fall with his hands cuffed behind him. He landed hard on his back, his head ricocheting off the pavement. Stars exploded in his eyes, and when they cleared, Sten stood over him, a joker smile back on his face.

"You just assaulted a police officer."

He kicked Max in the gut. More searing pain shot through Max's body as the air rushed out of his lungs.

"And you just resisted arrest."

Sten kicked him again. He wheezed out everything that was left in his chest, his insides turning to mush.

With the pain came a strange lucidity. He'd walked right into this trap. How much dumber could he have been? Sten *wanted* him to fight back, so the cop would have a plausible excuse for killing him. Sten's story might not hold up under scrutiny, but it didn't matter when the entire police force had his back. Like an idiot, Max had fallen for it. He'd let his anger get the best of him, just like with his father.

Sten kneeled down and punched Max in the face. Then he punched him again, and again, and again, and again, until the taste of blood and the dull thumping of flesh impacting flesh were the only sensations that reached him as the world spun away.

Sten's words floated to Max as if the cop spoke through a thick sheet of glass. "Temper, temper," Max thought he heard Sten say. "How am I going to live with myself, knowing what I was forced to do in self-defense?"

Chapter Seventeen

Val drove past the Thornton Building, home of Carressa Industries Headquarters, as slowly as she could without drawing attention to herself. Three police cruisers were parked out front, boxing in a Porsche that Val guessed belonged to Max, though Max was nowhere in sight. Two men in the cheap suits of police detectives talked to a valet driver, who pointed at the car and shook his head. By the way they blocked the entrance, she assumed they were there to arrest Max—which meant that Sten was close by, riding the wave of the arrest to waylay Max somewhere toward the back of the building.

"Shit," she said, scanning the outskirts of the building for a discreet way past the cops to the back.

She drove around the block and made two left turns until she could see the back of the glass skyscraper, then parked at a nearby gas station. After she checked her gun, she exited the car, glanced around to confirm that she'd still gone unnoticed, and cut through a patch of woods that separated the gas station from the headquarters building. Rain slipped through the evergreen canopy as she trotted along the soft earthen floor, cold darts of water spearing the top of her head, worry a vise on her chest. Dear Lord, please say she got here in time. As she crossed the well-worn trail, the outline of the Thornton Building began to emerge through the trees, along with the dark plane of pavement and the silhouette of a backhoe. She saw movement—two figures on the ground.

Oh no.

Val sprinted forward, bursting through the wood's edge and into a parking lot behind the building. Fifty feet in front of her Max was sprawled on the ground, unmoving, as Sten knelt on one knee and loomed over him, the retractable baton raised in the air, ready to strike.

"*No!*" Val pulled out her gun as she ran toward them.

Sten swiveled his head toward Val. "Oh, there you are." He lowered his baton when he saw her Glock.

She slowed to a quick walk to steady her aim at Sten's chest. Her eyes cut to Max. "Jesus Christ," she breathed.

He was just as she'd seen him in her vision, but the severity of his beating still shocked her. Blood soaked the front of his white dress shirt, his gray suit wet and streaked with dirt. His face looked like he'd been hit by a dump truck while his arms crooked painfully behind his back. Unlike her vision, though, his eyes were closed. She couldn't tell if Sten had already delivered the blow that would ultimately put him in a coma and end his life.

"Get those cuffs off him right now," she ordered Sten, her voice sharp with adrenaline and rage, "or I swear to God I'll blow your fucking kneecaps off. I am not bluffing."

"I know." Sten sighed, more disappointed than anything. He fished a key out of his pant pocket, unlocked, and removed the cuffs. Max's arms relaxed, but he still showed no signs of consciousness.

She nodded toward the backhoe. "Walk over there."

"We're playing 'Shepherd Says' now?" Sten said as he walked, Val following two strides behind so he couldn't wheel around and get the jump on her. "It's fun having a gun, isn't it? Such a versatile toy."

"Handcuff yourself to the boom."

He shook his head. "You drive a hard bargain." He snapped one handcuff onto his wrist and the other to a boom piston the size of Val's forearm.

"Tighten it."

"Ooh," he said as he pushed the metal bands closer together. "I'm starting to like this."

With all her strength, she kicked him in the groin. He collapsed into a writhing ball on the ground, and she pistol-whipped him as he lay prone, his handcuffed arm flailing awkwardly against the boom.

"*You murdering*"—she whipped him—"*son of a*"—she whipped him again—"*bitch!*"

He spit out a mouthful of blood and looked at her through more blood oozing from a gash above his eye. "Stacey's looking everywhere for you, just so you know."

She kicked him in the chest; he made a satisfying *oof* sound as the wind was knocked out of him. "I'll mail her all your goddamn teeth!" She raised the butt of her gun to continue pounding his face in—

"Val."

She froze, then spun around to see Max sitting upright, shoulders slumped and legs splayed like he could barely keep himself from falling over again.

"They're coming to arrest me," he said, his voice a disturbing monotone. "You should run. I tried to call you. I was stupid."

Thank God. Ignoring Sten, she ran to Max and knelt beside him, put a tender hand on his cheek, and looked into his eyes. With effort he met her gaze, though his eyes had a glassy sheen that made her stomach lurch at the possibility of a brain injury.

"Can you walk?" she asked him.

"I don't know."

"I'm sorry, but you're going to have to try. We can't stay here."

"Leave me," he said, and his face went slack like he might pass out again. "You should run."

"That's not happening." She threw his arm around her shoulders and struggled to pull him to his feet. "Come on," she said, grunting under his dead weight. "Get your ass up. Do you wanna stay here and die?"

"Yes."

Damn him—why did he hold such little value for his own life? "Then I'm going to stay here and die, too. Is that what you want? Because I'm not leaving you."

He looked at her again, and she saw the normally quicksilver wheels in his head turning like molasses. After a moment that felt like an eternity, he gripped her shoulder and pulled his legs in. Then, leaning on her heavily, he stood up. They stumbled forward together, almost falling over as Val scrambled to support most of his weight. When they were steady, they began to shuffle back the way she'd come.

"You guys are too cute together," she heard Sten say as they walked away.

She thought about sitting Max back down to get one more good punch into Sten, but grudgingly decided against it.

"Enjoy it while it lasts," Sten added. "They'll find you. They always find you." He laughed, a deep-throated wheeze on the cusp of a sob.

She could still hear him laughing as they fled into the woods. She dragged Max over the nature trail, the soothing smell of wet pine a sharp contrast to the urgency with which she pulled him along, as fast as his barely conscious body could go. Val was breathing hard with effort by the time they reached the opposite end of the wood patch at the edge of the gas station. After confirming there was no one around to see them, she hurried the final few feet to the car, threw open the passenger's side door, and dumped Max inside. She jumped into the driver's side and started the engine with shaking hands. As she reversed out of the parking spot, tires squealing in her haste to leave, she spotted the baseball cap Max used to hide his identity lying behind his seat. Val grabbed it and set it gently on his head, cocking the bill over his closed eyes. He looked unconscious again.

She turned left out of the gas station, away from the Thornton Building and the chaos that would erupt there when someone stumbled onto Sten. A police cruiser flew past with its lights blaring just as Val merged onto Interstate 5 going south.

She took a deep breath and tried to calm herself as they barreled down the freeway, checking the rearview mirror every few seconds to confirm they weren't being followed. They'd escaped by the skin of their teeth. For now.

They'll find you. They always find you.

Sten knew the score, but she didn't even know what game they were playing. Too bad she hadn't had more time to beat some answers out of him. She should have frisked him and taken his phone, or searched his car. Or kicked him a few more times for good measure. Or not dated his sleazy ass when they'd served in the Army together.

She gripped the steering wheel and tried to concentrate on the present rather than second-guess the past. Her eyes cut to Max, passed out with his head slumped to the side, his face red all over. Maybe the baseball cap wasn't necessary; she doubted anyone would recognize his pulverized face, though the clothes were a dead giveaway.

Val remembered getting kicked in the head with a soccer ball when she'd played varsity in high school, the confusion and stumbling around that had ensued afterward—a concussion, the doctors had diagnosed her with at the time. She guessed Max suffered from the same thing, albeit a much worse one. A concussion needed only time to heal, which they could do in hiding. But what if he had something worse? She had no medical training, other than the basic first aid she'd been taught in the military. If he had broken bones or brain swelling, she would need to take him to a hospital, where he'd be arrested on trumped-up murder charges, or murdered himself. Who knew how many accomplices Sten had? She prayed it didn't come to that.

After thirty minutes of driving, when the cityscape of Seattle had receded behind them and yielded to the suburbs, Val pulled off the highway and parked in front of a Walmart.

"What are you doing?"

Val jumped at the sudden sign of life from Max. He looked at her with groggy eyes.

"We need to load up on supplies before our faces appear on every news broadcast in the state," she said. "I figure we have about a sixty-minute window, which started forty minutes ago."

Voice flat, he said, "Let's go to Fiji."

"We can't clear your name from Fiji. We need to stay nearby."

"Then let's go to Fiji."

She couldn't tell if he was being facetious or brain damaged. "Dammit, Max! When I first met you, you told me that no one was more interested in proving your innocence than you were. Now you're telling me you suddenly don't care anymore?"

"I never really cared. I just want to be left alone." He closed his eyes again. "You should run."

"I don't run from my problems," she snapped. She reached into the backseat and retrieved Lester's cash and gun from the wastebasket. She pulled three hundred-dollar bills from the stack and shoved the rest into the glove box. "Stay here and act unassuming. I'll be back in a few minutes."

Max didn't respond; he'd passed out again.

Val left the car, locked the doors behind her, and entered the giant store. She glanced at the cameras perched in each corner, recording footage the police would probably show the public to aid in their manhunt for the rich murderer and his accomplice, the cop beater, depending on what version of events Sten told. She grabbed a cart and made a beeline for the medicine aisle, loading up on pain relievers, disinfectants, swabs, and bandages.

In the makeup aisle she grabbed fistfuls of lipsticks, eye shadows, and mascaras in the most garish colors she could find, the better to distract people from her actual facial features. She threw in a bottle of black hair dye. In the clothing section she snatched up clothes for herself and Max with no regard to color or style, ballparking Max's size. Finally she swung by the electronics section and grabbed a prepaid burner phone, then the first few games and books within arm's reach on her way to the cash register. The entire whirlwind trip through the store took her just short of ten minutes.

Val dumped her merchandise on the conveyor belt and kept her head down as the cashier spent about a hundred years scanning each item. Two shirts required a price check to confirm if they were twenty or twenty-five percent off.

"I'll just pay full price, I love them so much." Val slapped her cash down before the cashier could get on the intercom and spend more precious minutes haggling over how many cents she could save.

"Thanks," Val said after the cashier dropped change into her hand. She grabbed her bags and hurried for the exit. Her stomach dropped when she glanced up at a television screen on her way out the sliding glass door.

Breaking News: Multimillionaire Maxwell Carressa Charged with Murder, On Run with Girlfriend . . .

Chapter Eighteen

The black lipstick had an unappealing waxy taste that made Val cringe as she lathered it on her lips. When she was done, she checked her face in the car's vanity mirror—thick black eyeliner and shadow, no blush, the black lips, and the top of a fake barbed wire tattoo she'd drawn on her neck with the eyeliner pencil. She twisted her hair into a bun, then pulled the hood of her black sweatshirt over her head. Her red locks were her most recognizable feature, and she needed to keep them hidden until she could apply the black hair dye.

Val looked at Max, still asleep as he'd been the entire three-hour trip. She'd driven south along Interstate 5, then east on Route 12 until they'd come to a fleabag motel deep in the Cascade Mountains, a place that probably saw decent business from cash-strapped college students during ski season. In October, the off-season, the motel stood maybe a quarter full, occupied by truckers and malcontents passing through. A good place to lie low, she figured, while Max healed and they figured out what to do next. The police were unlikely to cast their net this far outside

Seattle, but close enough for Max and Val to return within a day when the time came.

Taking a deep breath and praying her disguise would hold, Val left the car and walked across the dark parking lot, past the neon "Stardust Motel" sign with the "o" burned out, and into the lobby that stank of stale coffee and cigarette smoke. The area was deserted save for an old woman behind the check-in counter. She clutched a cigarette between two prunes for fingers topped with long red fingernails, leathered face blank as she watched the local news on a cathode ray tube television perched on the counter.

Trying to commit to her Goth Girl look, Val put on a bitch face. "Need a room," she said to the old woman, doing her best "I'm acting tough to hide my inner pain" impression.

The woman threw Val a side-eye so full of loathing, Val knew she'd nailed it.

"How many nights?" the woman asked.

"A week. Probably."

"That equals *seven*, honey."

Val scoffed and pretended to be insulted. "Whatever," she muttered.

"It's forty-eight thirty-six per night for a queen bed room, including tax and fees. You have to times that by seven."

Val dropped a handful of crumpled bills onto the counter.

"I need your ID, too."

She bit her lip, letting her "inner pain" show. "My dad took it," Val said.

The old woman cocked one of her drawn-on eyebrows. "In that case it's seventy per night."

Val pouted and dropped two more hundred-dollar bills on the counter.

The woman snatched up the money in her knobby claws. She programmed a plastic room keycard while a banner that read, "Police Seeking Any Information on Whereabouts of Millionaire Murderer and Accomplice" scrolled across the bottom of her TV screen. Val turned her face to stone as photographs of her and Max popped up side by side. They used an official photo from her Army days, one with Val posing in her dress uniform in front of the American flag.

"You're in room one twenty-two, on the west end." The woman pointed past Val's head. "West is *that way,* where the sun sets." She handed Val the keycard. "Enjoy your stay, honey," she smirked.

"What-*ever.*" Val grabbed the keycard and rushed out the door.

Back in the car, she heaved a sigh of relief that the ruse had worked. Max stirred when the car door slammed. He turned his head in slow arcs to take in his surroundings.

"Where are we?" he asked, blinking back sleep as Val started the car.

"Packwood, according to the sign."

"Packwood, Fiji?"

She rolled her eyes. "Yes, Packwood, Fiji. The part that looks just like Washington State."

She drove the few hundred feet to their room. When she was confident no one saw them, she jumped out and opened the passenger's side door to help Max out. His broken face cracked into a painful-looking smile when he got a good look at her in the car's dome light.

"Is it Halloween already?" he said. "I can't believe I've been asleep that long."

"This getup saved our asses, so keep your snarky comments to yourself." She reached under his shoulder. "Let's get inside the room before someone sees you."

He groaned as she pulled him out of the car, less dazed but stiffer than he'd been during their escape from the Thornton Building. Leaning against her shoulder with one arm while clutching his chest with the other, he shuffled forward on unsteady legs to their room door. Val swiped the keycard and ushered them inside. The room smelled the same as the lobby, stale and smoky. A brown comforter enveloped the queen-sized bed below a generic picture of a pine forest panorama. Stains from nicotine tar spotted the white walls. A sink dripped in the bathroom. Better than a jail cell—or a shallow grave.

She led Max to the bed and helped him sit down. He inhaled sharply, eyes and teeth clenched shut, hunched forward as if protecting a ball of pain in his chest. If he could walk around and hold on to her, then his arms and legs weren't broken, but she wasn't sure about his ribs, or other possible damage to his internal organs. Val brought in the Walmart shopping bags and pulled out the medical supplies.

"Take this," she said, holding out a handful of aspirin and a glass of water for him.

He took the pills with hands still coated in pavement grime mixed with his own blood. Water dribbled down his chin as he worked to swallow them. Carefully she started to undress him, stripping all the pieces of his expensive, ruined suit from his battered body.

"I asked around about the mystery account," Max said as she pulled his coat off. "One of the accountants seemed to know something about it. He pretended he didn't, but then he shit his pants."

Val laughed. "Are you sure a night of greasy take-out didn't catch up with him?"

"No, it was definitely a guilty shit." He winced as she unbuttoned his dress shirt, rust-colored splotches dried down its front. "His name was…It was…Damn, I can't remember. I can't think straight right now."

"I'm just glad you can think at all—" Val gasped before she could stop herself. Thick bruises covered his entire torso, some already ringed with black. How could Sten have done this much damage in so short a time? She pushed back tears with images of doing the same to Sten.

"I think we should go to the hospital," she said in a quiet voice.

"Nah," he said, "then we'll both die, instead of just me. I'll be okay. I've been through this before. Help me lie down."

She pushed the sheets down and stuffed a pillow under his head as he inched onto his side. He pulled his legs up into the fetal position and closed his eyes.

"Are you hungry?" she asked him.

He mumbled, "No."

"Well, I saw some vending machines on the side of the building. I'm going to get something if you want it later. I'll be right back."

Val flipped up the hood of her sweatshirt and stepped back into the cold wet night, following the neon glow to the vending machines around the corner. She loaded up on chips and chocolate bars, and anything that looked like it might have nutritional value like peanuts or fruit snacks. When she was done, she moved the car to a parking spot where it couldn't be seen from the main road. Then she walked to a secluded spot away from the building, pulled the burner phone from her pocket, and dialed Stacey's number.

"Hello?"

"Stacey, it's me."

Val heard the muffled sounds of movement, then a door shutting.

"*What the fuck*, Val?" Stacey hissed in a semiwhisper.

"Yeah, I know—"

"Where the hell have you been? I thought you were kidnapped or dead until your face showed up all over the news. Are you really helping Maxwell Carressa? Are you with him now?"

Val sighed, the white tendrils of her breath disappearing into the black sky. "It's kind of a long story."

"I've got all night. You know I actually asked *Sten* of all people where you were? That's how desperate I was for answers. So tell me what the hell is going on."

Val gave Stacey a quick summary of everything that had happened since she'd run off to Chet's apartment three days ago, sidestepping the parts that involved Max's ability. She figured he wouldn't want her telling people without his permission, not even her best friend.

"We can't trust the police, and we're running out of options," Val said. "Chet is dead, Delilah won't talk, and Dean's hiding something that could connect him to Robby's death. He's our only real lead right now."

"I seriously doubt Dean would have anything to do with the murder of his own son."

"I know, but he's connected somehow. He's all we've got, besides the accountant whose name Max can't remember. I need you to arrange a meeting between us."

"Dean and I aren't exactly close. How am I supposed to convince him to meet with a wanted fugitive and not tell anybody about it?"

"I don't know. Appeal to his memory of Robby. Get creative."

"Hmm…I guess I could tell him I'm organizing a fund-raiser in Robby's honor, or something like that. But I'll have to wait until it's convenient for Dean. If I push him to meet right away, he'll get suspicious."

"That's okay. Max is in bad shape. He needs a few days to heal. Just give us at least a three-hour heads-up."

"Can't you just look into the future with him? Find Dean or this accountant that way, like you found Chet?"

"It's not like that."

"But it was like that with me?"

Shit, here we go. "Stacey, come on. What happened between us was a…a mistake. Neither of us was thinking straight. Can't we go back to the way things were?"

Stacey scoffed. "I don't want to be your girlfriend. But it would've been nice if you had at least stuck around to talk about what happened. You just *left* me with my vag hanging in the breeze! Even *I* don't do that to my girlfriends!"

"Look, I'm sorry. I panicked, okay? I—" Val shook her head. She didn't have the time or energy for this conversation. She let out a long sigh. "I promise we can talk about what happened when this is all over."

After an icy pause, Stacey said, "I'll call you back at this number when I get a day and time to meet with Dean."

"Thank you, Stacey, I really mean it. I owe you."

"Yeah, you do." Stacey hung up.

Val walked back to the motel room and dumped the junk food on top of the tiny microwave. She sat down on the bed next to Max, his head by her hip. She leaned over and dropped her face close to his, listening for his breathing to ensure it was smooth and unhindered. His bruised chest moved up and down in a steady rhythm. She lifted her head and ran her hand through his black hair, fine waves that slipped between her fingers. Looking down at his battered face, she couldn't hold back her tears any longer; they flowed off her cheeks and landed in fat dollops in his hair.

He stirred, put an arm across her lap. "You should run," he muttered.

"Shut up," she said.

Chapter Nineteen

Kitty enjoyed the sound of her heels clicking on the pavement as she walked down one of Seattle's seedier commercial streets, a throughway tourists ignored and locals avoided unless a specific purpose brought them there. A less assured woman might have feared for her safety; Kitty's stiletto shoes pounding the ground into submission told the world she was not that kind of woman.

Wrapped in a thigh-length red coat with fur encircling the collar, she smiled as she approached the Green Door Nightclub. It was nice to have a job that involved something other than keeping tabs on Max. Aside from the sex, spending time with him could get downright boring, his nose always stuffed in a book—that is, when he wasn't doing hard drugs, killing people, or running from the law. It'd been especially boring since he'd disappeared four days ago. Max was gentler than she preferred, both in his manners and sexual tastes. Tonight, Kitty anticipated she'd get to indulge in her own preferences for once.

The bouncer at the club's door—painted green, how clever—sized her up in one long head-to-toe leer, then gave his approval for her to enter with a curt nod toward the entrance. Kitty winked a baby blue eye at him and swept past.

She took a moment to orient herself in the dark, unfamiliar setting that throbbed with energy. Silhouettes gyrated on the dance floor as employees performed above them in cages hung from the ceiling. A shirtless man in a blond afro wig, white thigh-high kinky boots, and a thong swung his hips to the music while a woman in the cage opposite him matched his hip swinging in a black version of the exact same outfit, including the shirtless part. Three additional pairs of cages followed the same theme—men and women in the same outfit, different colors. The music thumped like a good, strong fuck. She'd never been to this club before, but she made a mental note to return for pleasure when she was off duty.

She checked her coat and cut through the dancing throng to the bar nestled in the back corner. On the far end she spotted her target. He leaned against the bar's edge, dressed in a shiny European-style suit, dark hair slicked back and graying at the temples, bony fingers clutching a Scotch on the rocks. He eyed every nubile young thing—male or female—who wandered into his line of sight, quietly judged them, then cut his gaze to the next. His attention lingered on the women; he was in the mood for the opposite sex tonight. He liked the curvy, sensuous ones, the slow dancers. Didn't seem to have a preference for hair color. Perfect.

She moved to the music and stepped into his field of view, the beat flowing from her neck, down her spine, and to her knees in thick, slow waves that lingered at her hips. She closed her eyes and imagined herself as a python wrapping itself around a rabbit in tighter and tighter circles. Kitty felt his stare before she opened her eyes and confirmed it. She'd passed his test, gotten her foot in the proverbial door.

After a couple minutes of showcasing herself to him without breaking eye contact, Kitty danced closer until she stood next to him at the bar. She leaned forward onto the counter, her full breasts pressed up and almost out of her halter top, and regarded him through thick lashes before turning her head away and flagging down the bartender.

"What can I get you?" her target finally asked.

"Rum and Coke," she replied with a thick Russian accent. She was feeling Russian tonight.

He ordered the drink. When the bartender brought it over, her target watched her wrap her lips around the tiny straw that came in the glass and suck out the liquid.

"Do you follow politics?" he asked.

She half smiled. "No."

"You should. Race for mayor is hot right now. Neck and neck. Exciting if you care about that sort of thing."

"I don't. I cannot vote, so why would I care?"

"Then get naturalized, baby. Marry some rich sucker, get your green card, then dump his ass and take half his money. It's the American way."

She laughed. "You are funny. No, what is right word—*cynical*. Yes, you are very cynical."

"You gotta be in this town. Seattle's known for being so *nice*—on the surface. Means you can't trust anybody." He ordered her another drink. "Your mother give you a name?"

"Yes. But I go by Katya."

"Katya. Pretty. My mother gave me a name, too, but I go by Gino."

"Nice to meet you, Gino."

"So…whatcha doin' here?"

God, finally. Any more tedious chitchat and she'd be forced to shove her hand down his pants just to get him to shut up. "Looking for fun," she said. "You?"

"Ditto—that means *the same.* How much is a fun time with you worth?"

Kitty's lips twisted into a smile she knew he would incorrectly assume was playful, and not predatory. He thought she was a prostitute—a Russian prostitute, embroiled in the sex trade, probably in the country illegally. Someone he could pay for and own for the night. A disposable toy to be played with and tossed when he'd had his fill. A woman he could talk freely in front of because she wasn't a real person. Too perfect.

"Eight hundred, all night."

"Can do." Gino pulled a thick wad of cash from his coat pocket and dropped some bills on the bar, then put his arm around Kitty's waist. "Let's blow this pop stand—that means *let's get out of here.*"

* * *

A cab ride later, Kitty followed Gino into his penthouse apartment.

"Welcome to my humble abode," he said as he tossed his suit

coat on a white leather sofa. A panoramic window framing the glowing cityscape forty-seven floors below dominated the living room. "My abode for now anyway. How long it lasts depends on the results of this election. That's why I care, babe."

Kitty surveyed the layout of the room. Leather sectional in front of the window, wet bar to her left, open kitchen to her right, bedroom past the kitchen. The couch was the best place for sex, tactically speaking. She took off her coat and draped it carefully across a kitchen stool directly diagonal from the sofa.

Gino poured himself a glass of vodka at the wet bar. "Your national drink," he said.

Kitty resisted the urge to roll her eyes.

"Want one?"

She shook her head.

He stepped close to her, sipping his alcohol. "I hear Russia's nice this time of year."

"Yes," she said. She grabbed the end of his tie with one hand and slid her fingers up its length with the other. "Very wet."

He reached under her miniskirt. His thin lips twisted into a smirk when he felt her lack of panties, her Brazilian wax. He inserted two fingers into her.

"Mmm, *very* nice."

She backed away from him, toward the couch. "You will be gentle with me?" She bit her lip.

Gino laughed. "Fuck no."

She grinned.

He shoved her down on the couch and pulled her skirt off, then spread her legs apart and licked her clitoris. Kitty let out a throaty moan. He was the kind of guy that liked a show, and she'd give it to him.

Gino put his drink down on the end table, then got down to business. He dropped his pants to his knees and propped Kitty's ankles on his shoulders, yanked her halter top off so her stilettos remained her only item of clothing, then slammed into her. No condom—not that it surprised her. Gino didn't seem like the kind of guy who cared much about the consequences of fucking people. Ah well, the cream Christophe made for Northwalk would ensure she'd stay STD and pregnancy-free. She didn't like the feel of the rubber anyway.

She gasped at the force of him, an insatiable animal, probably a sex addict. He fucked her hard, thighs meeting hers in a succession of satisfying, quick slaps. Her breasts bounced with each thrust, matched by her screams of ecstasy. Before she knew it, she'd come, but of course he kept going and she kept screaming like it was the best sex of her life. In truth, it was decent.

Five minutes in, Kitty heard the suite's door open and close.

"Pizza!" a man called from the foyer.

Gino didn't stop thrusting.

The visitor stepped into the living room area, shaking out his beige nylon jacket, which was spotted with rainwater. His face was blotched with partially healed bruises and a thick mustache above his lip. He didn't have pizza.

"Oh, I'm sorry, you have company," he said, then walked past them to the kitchen. He rooted in the fridge for a moment, then reappeared with an apple. He leaned against the kitchen counter and took a bite out of the fruit. "Still no sign of Shepherd or Carressa. Thought you'd wanna know."

Gino glanced to the side where his visitor stood behind him. "You checked with friends and known acquaintances?" His grip on Kitty's thighs tightened, and he thrust faster. Sweat bloomed on his brow.

"This ain't my first rodeo," the visitor said through a mouth full of apple. "Shepherd's a PI. She knows how to hide. Probably in Mexico by now."

"It doesn't matter where they are as long as they stay gone until after the election. So keep it that way."

Gino stiffened and he groaned, finally climaxing. He let out a long exhale, then slipped out of Kitty and pulled up his pants, retrieved his drink from the end table, and took a long gulp. His tongue flicked out and licked vodka off his upper lip. "Where are my manners? Sten, Katya. Katya, Sten."

Kitty rolled onto her side to face Sten, arm propping her head up, not bothering to cover herself. "*Privyet,*" she said to him.

Sten cocked an eyebrow at her, then focused back on Gino. "And what about the accountant?"

"We need to get as much money as possible out of that account before turning off the spigot. Wait two weeks, until right before elections, then make it look like an accident. Or a suicide, whatever. God knows I'd off myself if I woke up one day as a lonely, fat-ass accountant."

Sten shrugged. "Sure." He set the apple core down on the kitchen counter. "Though if I can give you some advice that I read in *Cosmo,* don't push your luck." He eyed Kitty for half a second. "Sometimes the hare doesn't know that the warren it's dug is actually a lair for snakes." His mustache ticked upward; it took Kitty a moment to realize he was smiling.

She frowned at him, and his eye twitched into an almost imperceptible wink.

"Gee, thanks," Gino said, "I'll file that nugget of wisdom right next to my Confucius verses."

"Just trying to help you out, bro."

A knock on the door interrupted their conversation. Sten answered on his way out.

"Ah, a distinguished visitor," he said as Norman Barrister entered the suite.

Norman's granite face, already etched with disapproval, fell farther when he spotted Kitty on the couch. She sat up and leaned back, draped her arms across the back of the sofa, and waved at him.

Sten tipped an imaginary hat to the mayoral candidate. "Have fun, Colonel," he said, winked, then left.

Fun indeed. Let the games begin.

"You know what I had to go through to get here without being seen?" Norman barked at Gino as the letch refilled his drink. "Why can't you live a little more modestly?"

"Because if I wanted to live modestly, I wouldn't bother helping you, and you'd be floundering in the polls right now. It's a win-win for everybody."

Norman kept his eyes resolutely off Kitty as she sat with her legs crossed and made circles in the air with her foot. He marched to the kitchen counter and slapped down a wad of cash. Gino picked up the stack and flipped through the bills with his thumb.

"It's all there, twenty thousand," Norman said.

"I never doubted you. I just like the feel of it. I'll need another infusion next week in order to keep operations running smoothly."

"I seriously doubt that this suite, and whatever *she* is, are necessary for your operations."

"Every good fighting force needs some R and R."

"Maybe take care of that *after* you do your job. Valentine Shepherd and Maxwell Carressa are *still* at large. They could know everything by now. What if they resurface and go public? I'll be sunk. All of this will have been for nothing!"

Gino slammed his glass down on the marble countertop. "They know nothing and they're long gone," he said with an intensity that finally matched Norman's. "Stop panicking. If you can't handle the risk of having your deep, dark secrets exposed, then you should've stayed out of politics. You're all in now. There's no going back."

Norman turned away, his face taut with anger before it collapsed into a defeated frown.

"Might as well enjoy yourself while you can," Gino said, his voice light again. "Have you met my friend Katya?"

"I'll see you next week," Norman said and took a step toward the exit.

"She's really something else," Gino went on, "enough to make a gay man go straight, even. Would you like a taste?"

Norman stopped and looked at her. Kitty uncrossed her legs

and let them fall wide open. She ran a hand up her thigh and smiled at him.

"No," Norman said, but he stayed where he was.

Kitty wondered if he felt anything when he looked at her—every straight man and gay woman's wet dream—or did he react out of conditioning, willing himself to feel something, *anything* rather than his desire for men?

"Are you sure?" Gino said, sensing weakness and moving in for the kill. "I've got her all night." He walked to Kitty and pulled her to her feet, then turned her to face Norman. He stood behind her and ran his hands up her torso, squeezing her breasts and putting a hand between her legs. "Any real man would want this."

Gino stripped all his clothes off and sucked on Kitty's lips while she stroked his penis into a steel rod. He pushed her head down, and she fell to her knees and took him into her mouth.

"Mmm, yeah," he moaned, thrusting himself down her throat.

From the corner of her eye, Kitty saw Norman look back and forth between Gino and the door. *Come on, Norman. Take the bait.*

"This is what men do, Norm," Gino said.

Successfully browbeaten, Norman slipped off his trench coat and sharp suit tailored to make his massive figure seem distinguished until he stood naked and wild-eyed, desperate. He approached Kitty from behind, and she had the surreal sensation that she was about to be mauled by a bear. Her lips still around Gino's cock, Norman hitched up her hips and entered her. He pumped, more determined than enthusiastic.

Gino pulled away from Kitty and moved to Norman's rear,

then slid himself into Norman. Norman grunted, and she felt him enlarge in her with each thrust from Gino until his bear-sized cock filled her up nicely. His thick fingers dug into her hips as the three of them moved together in one continuous piece of hot, sweaty flesh.

This *was* fun. Max should run from the law more often. Kitty chanced a glance at her coat and winked for the camera hidden inside it. She could only hope Mayor Brest turned out to be this good of a time, too, when she paid him a visit.

Chapter Twenty

Val bit her lip as she stared down at her white knight, a cheap piece of horse-shaped plastic half the size of her thumb. She surveyed the tiny chessboard where it sat in the middle of the bed, sandwiched between her and Max.

"So I could move the knight here, or here, right?" she asked Max, pointing at different squares on the board. She'd only played chess a handful of times in her life, but their limited options for entertainment forced her to revisit the game.

"Yes." He drummed his fingers against his cheek, his head propped on one arm while he sat cross-legged, eyes half open.

"But I could move the queen here, too?"

"You could."

"Or the bishop here?"

He sighed. "Yes."

Val could tell he worked hard not to roll his eyes. He'd sworn he wasn't a chess fan, either, but of course he knew all the rules and could even rattle off popular strategies involving openings and gambits. It seemed his mental faculties had returned in full despite his beat-down, though he still couldn't remember chunks of the day shortly before and after the attack, nor could he recall the damn name of the accountant who was somehow involved.

She hesitated for a few more seconds, then lifted the knight and moved it to a new square. "There!" She beamed at her cleverness.

For a moment Max chewed on his thumb, something she'd learned he did a lot when he was thinking hard. She almost grabbed his thumb to stop his fidgeting, but instead laced her own fingers together. If she took his hand, she wasn't sure she would let go. The last thing she needed was another spontaneous roll in the hay she'd probably regret the moment her vision cleared.

It'd been hard not to give in to desire when they spent every waking moment together, as well as slept in the same bed at night. Each day it got harder. But she had to resist. She couldn't get distracted from her goal—find Robby's killer and bring that person to justice. Whatever she felt for Max had to wait.

After a few seconds of intense concentration, he relaxed, slid off the bed, and sat down at the pockmarked table covered with their food supply—mostly bags of chips and beef jerky. He grabbed a bottle of water and aspirin and threw some pills in his mouth. The old chair groaned when he leaned back and sipped water as he stared out the window through a break in the curtains.

"What are you doing?" Val asked. "It's your turn."

He shrugged. "I'll win in seven moves."

"Seriously?" Val shook her head. "This is why I wanted to play Go Fish."

"I *would* play Go Fish if you didn't cheat all the time."

"It's called strategic thinking." She dumped the pieces back into the Cracker-Jack-size box they'd come in and folded the chessboard in half. She'd need to look up a way to cheat at chess next time she got a chance.

Watching him gaze out the window—slouching in oversized jeans and a gray T-shirt, a ray of early afternoon sun playing through his shiny black hair—he reminded her of an indoor cat that mewled each time a car drove by. For six days they'd been holed up in the hotel room, waiting for Stacey to call Val with a meet-up time for Dean. Max got a little bit better each day, until the swelling in his face was gone and only the bruises remained, black rings around his eyes and jawbone and streaks across his chest. He was almost recognizable, which could be a problem for them when they finally got the go from Stacey. No media outlet had mentioned that Max was injured, so no one would be looking for a black-and-blue version of the Carressa heir. Seemed Sten left out of his police report the part where he almost beat Max to death.

Val stretched out on the bed and clicked on the TV. She watched a local news anchor prattle on about the five-day weather forecast through a permanent line of static that cut across the ancient screen.

She glanced at Max. "Your favorite movie about weather...*Go*."

"*The Core*."

"Isn't that about astronauts who tunnel through the earth's crust to restart the core spinning?"

"Yeah, but space weather is critical to the plot."

"Goddammit, Max, can you *not* be a total nerd for even five seconds?"

He chuckled, then winced and touched his cheek.

"Tooth hurt again?"

"Yeah. I think it's cracked." His cheek bulged where he felt it with his tongue. "I hope they have decent dentists in prison."

Val sat up. "Don't you dare start with that again," she said in a voice sharp enough to kill their light conversation. She didn't know where his fatalist attitude came from, but he had no motivation to fight for his life as it had been before. When he wasn't talking about giving himself up to the murderous police, he badgered her to run away with him to Mexico or Fiji. Maybe he didn't want his old life back, but she did. "If I have to hear you whine one more time about how you should turn yourself in, then I just might let you do it. Your 'woe-is-me' rich boy act was old from day one. I'm sorry a life with infinite money was so tragically hard for you, but do you really want to be raped in prison? Because look at you—that's what would happen."

Max glared at her, and for a moment she thought her tirade had crossed a line. Then his gorgeous hazel eyes warmed and he gave her a half smile. "You're a hard woman."

She couldn't tell if he was being sincere. Max excelled at masking his feelings—until they exploded to the surface.

She crossed her arms and looked away. "I know. I'm sorry."

"You don't have many rich friends, do you?"

"I don't have *any* rich friends. Except you now, I guess."

Were they friends? They hadn't done anything romantic together, but he felt like something…more. She was grateful he hadn't brought up using their abilities to track down Dean themselves. Despite her concern for his injuries and her love for Robby, she wasn't confident she could say no again.

"Almost all my friends are rich, by necessity. We run in the same circles. When all your friends are wealthy, you don't have to worry if someone is only with you because of your money."

"So, say, in an alternate universe, if you had held some glitzy charity gala for war orphans and invited Robby and me, and we'd have met there and hit it off, you'd never ask me to hang with you, even as just a friend?"

"Probably not, if I only knew you casually. It wouldn't be anything personal."

"Well, now you know what you would've been missing—constant insults and bad chess games."

"Yep, now I know."

Their eyes locked for what seemed like an eternity as the television droned in the background. God, she wanted to kiss him so badly. Even with his current injuries and ill-fitting clothes, he was still the handsomest man she'd ever met, as well as the smartest. The fact that she'd never have known him if she hadn't barged into his weird sex club one night seemed like a narrowly avoided tragedy.

Not for Robby.

Val looked away from Max, her cheeks flushed. The urges to

jump into his arms and run away from him both seized her at the same time.

"Do you think your girlfriend's worried about you?" Val asked, her tone a hair too forced to sound natural.

"Kitty's still not my girlfriend. She never was. I haven't had a girlfriend in a long time…a really long time."

"Does she know what you can do?"

"Yeah. I've told her anyway. I'm not sure she believes me. She might just think I'm crazy, like almost everyone else I've told."

Val understood firsthand. She could count the number of people she'd told about her ability on one hand. Even fewer had believed her. "So you look into the future with her—for business?"

"Sometimes with Kitty. But"—he looked down at his feet—"mostly with just myself. No love life necessary. I don't need deep visions to get useful financial information. I always see the major stock exchanges, represented by certain strings of numbers. Then, based on the numbers clustered around those numbers, I can tell if they're going to be up or down, and by how much. It's pretty easy, actually. I don't even have to concentrate anymore."

"I wish mine were more useful. I usually see a bunch of junk, and dead people. Robby helped, though."

She played with a strand of her dull black hair. An ad for a nonpartisan science outreach event taking place at the Pacific Science Center tomorrow played through the silence that fell between them. Smiling children held up lab beakers while cartoon donkeys and elephants frolicked together against the backdrop of the Center's white arches. A political ad for Mayor Brest followed the spot. With the election less than two weeks away, every commercial break featured at least three of the damn things.

Max drank from his water bottle, making loud gulps as if his throat had gone dry. "When was your wedding date scheduled?" he asked, wiping his mouth.

She frowned and pulled her knees to her chest. "We didn't have one."

"How long were you engaged for?"

"About a year."

"That's a long engagement with no date."

"The timing was never right." *For me.* "I don't think I'm the marrying type," she mumbled.

I didn't really want to marry him. The thought hit her like a stake to the heart. She loved Robby, she had no doubt about that. But he wasn't the one.

So who *was* the one, then? Some guy she'd known for two weeks who had more skeletons in his closet than a Halloween party store? She willed herself not to look at Max, still slouching in his chair next to the window, picking the label off the water bottle, oblivious to his central role in the struggle she waged with herself. They'd spent too much time alone together. It clouded her judgment, made her feel something that wasn't there.

Val scowled when Barrister's face floated onto the TV. She stayed her hand from throwing something at the screen. She still didn't know how the bastard was connected to Lester. Max continued to claim he had no idea when she quizzed him on it, and he refused to entertain the possibility that Norman might have had an affair with his mother. Just talking about Lydia made him shut down, as if it caused him physical pain to unearth those memories. So she avoided the topic for his sake, though the question still gnawed at her.

Old hometown photos of Norman faded in and out of the television: a plump-cheeked boy in front of his childhood home, a smooth-faced kid in his junior Army ROTC uniform, a lanky teenager in short-shorts posing with his basketball team in the high school gym. *Norman Barrister: Hometown Hero. Change you can believe in!*

"Seattle Lutheran High School," Val muttered as a voice in the back of her head screamed something important but indistinct. "Robby went to Seattle Lutheran, too…"

And then she understood the voice.

…just like his father!

Val sprang to her feet. "Dean and Norman went to the same high school!" she yelled into Max's stunned face. "That's how they know each other. They were schoolmates!"

"Um, okay. What does that mean in the grand scheme of things?"

"It means Dean has to be involved somehow. There's no way it's a coincidence they went to the same school."

"Actually, there's a very good chance it could be—"

"We are two people who can honest-to-God *see the fucking future*. What are the chances that *anything* in our lives is a coincidence?"

Max raised an eyebrow. "So he killed his own son to keep him quiet?"

"Probably not. It must've been an unintended consequence. Or maybe Norman double-crossed him, and now he can't go to the police because he's in too deep. Or…or I don't know. But he's a goddamn liar. And he probably sicced the police on you because we were getting too close to the truth."

"You sound paranoid."

"Hell yes I'm paranoid! Haven't you been paying attention to all the insane shit that's happened to us? Your brain can't be *that* damaged." She paced around the hotel room for a minute while Max watched her with cool eyes, though he said nothing. Val grabbed the burner phone off the nightstand. "*Come on*, Stacey."

She nearly dropped the phone when it rang in her hand.

"Norman and Dean were high school classmates!" Val said to Stacey when she answered the phone.

"Okay," Stacey said. "So what?"

"So Dean is definitely hiding something. And what the hell took you so long to call me back?"

"You told me you needed time for your slam piece to heal."

Val glanced at Max and rolled her eyes. "Well?"

"I finally got in touch with Dean. It wasn't easy because he's been skipping work and disappearing for days at a time. I had to call Robby's sister to get a line on him. Josephine is worried about her dad, says he's not handling Robby's death well, that he's unraveling. Jo gave me Dean's phone number. When I talked to him, I told him that I wanted to meet to talk about setting up a scholarship for poor law students in Robby's name. He took the bait. Though he wants to meet at Robby's gravesite, for some reason. Today at six o'clock."

"Okay, we can do that. We can make it." Val started snatching clothes off the ground and throwing them into a pile. She nodded to Max; he stood and started to clean for their imminent departure.

"Val, you gotta be careful," Stacey said. "Dean didn't sound well. He might give you up to the police, or do something crazy. And your faces are still all over the news. Someone could easily spot you when you come back to the city."

"We'll take precautions."

Stacey whispered, "And you don't know the truth about Max. He could have killed his father. He could turn on you."

Val frowned. "He's not a murderer." She looked at Max. His eyes stayed glued to the trash he gathered into the wastebasket.

"Did you come to that conclusion with your noodle or your taco?"

"That's disgusting. And if you must know, his hot dog truck has not parked itself inside my taco stand. Happy now?"

Max snickered.

"Fine," Stacey said. "One more thing—Delilah Barrister called for you."

Delilah? Sweet, Norman's wife was finally taking the lifeline Val offered…Unless it was a setup, though Delilah obsessed over maintaining appearances, so it seemed unlikely she'd tell the police about their one-on-one chat.

"Why didn't you tell me this earlier?" Val asked.

"Because she wouldn't say what she wanted. She sounded fine anyway, all chipper. I thought she was trying to sell us cookies."

"Did you get her number?"

"Um, yeah…" Val heard rustling as Stacey moved papers around. "Got something to write with?"

Stacey read off the phone number while Val used a pen to write it down on the palm of her hand.

"Just be careful," Stacey said. "I don't want to lose my best friend."

"Thanks, Stacey. For everything. I'll be as careful as I can be." Val hung up, then dialed Norman's wife. If it *was* a setup, the cops wouldn't be able to track her burner phone. She'd have to be careful not to drop any hints as to where she was, though, just in case.

"This is Delilah Barrister," said a proper voice full of confidence and privilege.

"It's Val Shepherd. You wanted to talk?"

A shuddering exhale came through the other end of the line. "I didn't know who else to call," Delilah said, the confidence gone from her voice. "You were right. I—I think he's cheating on me. I can't live like this anymore."

"If you think he might hurt you, you need to leave immediately. You must have friends, family—"

"No, no, they wouldn't understand. I'd be breaking my vows. And he won't let me just walk away. He has friends in the police department. He'd find me. I need…I don't know. I need you to help me. Please."

Val held her breath and looked at Max. He met her gaze, matching her apprehension with his own.

"I'm wanted by the police. If I come out of hiding to help you, then I can't clear Max Carressa of his father's murder. Don't tell me you have no idea if your husband was involved."

A sound between a sigh and a whimper answered Val. She wanted to help Delilah, but she wouldn't risk getting caught and damning Max to a life of false imprisonment without a major payoff. The silent standoff lasted almost a minute.

"I'm sorry, Delilah—"

"I have e-mails," she finally said in a frantic whisper. "That's how I know he's cheating on me. And he's been corresponding with someone about money, and they mentioned Carressa. I don't know what it all means, but I can get them for you, if that's what it takes."

"That'll work." It was better than nothing, and if it *did* turn out to be something, it'd be worth the risk. In the best-case scenario, she'd help Delilah, clear Max's name, and nail Robby's killer. Three birds with one stone. "Will you be at that Science Center thing tomorrow?"

"Yes."

"Okay then. When you have the opportunity, slip out of there and meet me at—"

"Oh God, he's coming. I have to go." The phone went dead.

"Delilah? Delilah!" Val dialed the number three more times—no answer. "Shit!" She dropped the phone on the table, folded her arms, and drummed her fingers on her biceps. Why couldn't anything ever be easy?

"Well?" Max asked.

"We've got a date with Dean at the Lakeview Cemetery at six o'clock, which means we need to clean up and hit the road in twenty minutes. And Delilah says she'll give us possible evidence of Norman's connection to your father if we help her leave her husband, but she hung up before we could nail down a place and time other than tomorrow at the Pacific Science Center." She threw up her arms. "We'll figure it out later. If you gather stuff up, I'll carry it to the car. Then we'll wipe down all the hard surfaces to remove our prints." She grabbed the keys off the dresser, then stopped at the door. "Did you ever learn how to hotwire a car during your rebelling-against-rich-daddy days?"

"No. They didn't teach you that at PI school?"

"No. Damn. What are the chances that the friend who loaned you this car has told the police about it?"

"Low."

"How do you know?"

"Because he wouldn't talk to the police. He's my dealer."

Val raised an eyebrow. "Your *car* dealer?"

Max's lips tightened and he looked off to the side.

"You know marijuana is legal now."

"Sometimes I need something stronger than marijuana."

"Like what?"

He cringed like he kicked himself for bringing it up. After a long pause, he said, "Heroin."

"You're a *heroin addict*? Are you fucking kidding me?"

"I'm not an addict." Max dropped the wastebasket and crossed his arms over his chest. "I haven't done it seriously in ten years. But sometimes I just need my brain to stop."

They stared each other down. What other critical pieces of his past did he keep from her? He didn't *look* like an addict; she hadn't seen any track marks on his arms or signs of withdrawal, so he was probably being truthful. Probably.

After a tense few seconds where every bird chirp and car engine was a thousand decibels, Val sighed. "Holy shit, you're a hot mess," she said. "Some women are really into that. Not me, for the record, but some."

He unfolded his arms, and a hint of a smile touched his lips.

She flipped up the hood of her sweatshirt and opened the front door. "Tell your dealer thanks for his car."

Chapter Twenty-one

A light rain misted the car where Val and Max waited at the base of the rolling hillside that composed Lakeview Cemetery, five minutes late for their meeting with Dean at Robby's gravesite. She wanted to be sure they'd arrive after Dean, in case he saw them and bolted.

"Come on, Max, just put it on." Val held the tube of black lipstick out for him. "When someone looks at you, all they'll see is a beat-up, overgrown Goth kid."

He pushed it away. "I'd rather be raped in prison."

A line of cars with their headlights on filed past, then began to park around Max's car. Mourners in black exited their vehicles and loitered for a moment, popping umbrellas open, then shuffled up the hill. Max and Val sank into their seats and lowered their heads together.

"Do you know you're *still* on Seattle's Twenty Most Eligible Bachelors list? That baseball cap and hoodie combo is not going to cut it if someone gets a good look at you. Put on the damn lipstick."

"I'll do it if you beat me at rock-paper-scissors."

"No. You always win."

"Then it's settled."

Val sighed. "Okay, fine."

They put their fists together and shook them one, two, three times—Val had paper, Max had scissors.

"Dammit!" she said. "You're jerking off so you can look into the future and know what I'm going to throw, aren't you?"

He snickered. "Actually, you have a really obvious tell."

"That's still cheating."

"Interesting observation, coming from the world's biggest Go Fish cheater. I'm not wearing the lipstick."

Val scowled at him, then gave up and slathered the lipstick on herself to complete her Goth Girl disguise before letting it drop into the cup holder. She checked her watch, adjusted her gun in its chest holster underneath her hoodie, drummed her fingers on the steering wheel, and glanced at Max. He watched the rain streak down the windshield as he chewed his thumb, lost in thought. The patchwork of bruises on his face made his already sharp jawline even sharper. The shadow of facial hair left by the cheap hotel razor contrasted with his pale skin to give him a gaunt, heroin chic look, though he probably wouldn't appreciate the observation.

"Are you sure you're up for this?" she asked him. "You still don't look one hundred percent, no offense. It's okay if you want to stay here. I won't think of you as any less of a man."

"I feel fine," he said, like she knew he would.

"Suit yourself." She tried to squelch her worry that he was

pushing himself too hard, though they didn't have much of a choice at this point. With every cop in the city looking for them, they wouldn't get far if his strength failed and she had to drag him away from trouble again.

She rechecked her watch. "Dean should be here by now. You ready?"

He nodded. They flipped their hoods up over their faces and got out of the car.

The last of the day's sun cut through a wisp of clouds on the horizon as they hiked up the hill together, side by side, heads down. Despite Max's previous assurance that he felt fine, he walked up the incline with effort and steadily slowed as they ascended. At the crest he stopped, put his hands on his knees, and leaned forward, breathing hard. Val put a tender hand on his back while she waited for him to recover. She looked around and spotted Dean, alone at Robby's gravesite on the far side of the funeral party. He stood with his back to them, facing the gravestone, shoulders slumped in a black trench coat. Max touched her arm and straightened, recovered enough to continue. They walked around the group of mourners, all quiet as a priest recited a eulogy for the dead, and approached Robby's father from behind.

"Dean," she said when they reached him.

He turned his head toward them, but otherwise didn't move. "I figured as much," he said. "You just don't give up, do you?"

"Your son was murdered," Val said, struggling to keep her voice low, "and you know it. You've known all along, haven't you?"

Dean turned to face them, and Val stifled a gasp. He'd lost at least fifteen pounds, his skin pulled taut over a skeletal face, dark circles under his eyes. The smell of alcohol wafted off him. His gaze cut from Val to Max and stayed there for a long while, studying the Carressa heir with an intensity that made Max squirm.

"Yes, I know," he said, still staring at Max. "I guess I've always known."

"Was your friendship with Barrister worth more than Robby's life?"

The corners of his mouth twitched into a mirthless smile that quickly fell away. "No. But it was never about friendship."

Val stepped closer. "Then what?"

"Revenge."

She grabbed the collar of his trench coat in her fist. "I hope it was worth it, you son of a bitch," she hissed. "You managed to kill your own son, ruin my life, and ruin Max's life. Do you feel better, now, huh? Do you—"

"Val." Max gently pulled on her arm from behind. He made a subtle nod to the funeral party only thirty feet away.

She forced herself to let Dean go, her hand still clenched in a fist. "Revenge against who? For what?"

Unaffected by Val's simmering rage, Dean's eyes wandered to Max again as the crowd of mourners launched into a group prayer. "You have her eyes," Dean said to Max. "And my nose, I think."

Max froze. "*What?*"

"I loved her, but we were young and stupid then. I had Robby to think of, and you didn't want for anything. Who was I to take you away from that?"

Val's eyes widened. "You're talking about Lydia Carressa, aren't you? Holy shit, *you* were the one having an affair with Max's mother! Did you kill Lester over her?"

"I didn't kill that bastard," Dean said, "but I let it happen. For what he did to Lydia."

"So Barrister killed Lester?"

"Yes." Dean wiped tears from his bleary eyes with the palms of his hands. "He told me he could make it happen if I made a donation to his campaign using the money Lester stole from Carressa Industries over the last couple decades. It was easy, since the offshore account was already in my name, because what's a little embezzlement between *friends*?"

So *that's* how the three men were connected—Norman wanted Lester's money that only Dean had access to, and Dean wanted Lester dead. Then another connection clicked into place.

"The accountant at Carressa Industries—he helped you embezzle that money, didn't he?"

Dean answered by rubbing his face and mumbling something incoherent into his hands.

"What's his name?"

"Doesn't matter. He's probably dead by now."

"*Goddammit*, Dean—" She was close to yelling again, or punching him. Forcing herself to calm down, she concentrated on optimizing the little time they had left before Dean took off or someone recognized them. "Lydia's been gone for twenty years. Why wait until now to get revenge?"

He scoffed. "What was I gonna do, hire a hit man? Smother him while he slept? I'm a lawyer, I know how this shit works. The more you plan, the more likely you are to get caught. And I had Robby, Josephine, and my firm to think about." He nodded toward Max. "And keeping an eye on you, making sure he didn't hurt you, too."

"Don't forget your cushy business deal with Carressa Industries," she said. "Wouldn't want to give that up, right?"

His unsteady gaze met hers again, and his mouth twisted into a snarl. "All these years I've wanted to punish him, thought about how I might do it, waited for the right time. Norm finally gave me the opportunity without putting my own family at risk. But Robby"—his face fell—"God, Robby…"

Dean put his head in his hands and sobbed. A softer person might have felt pity for the man who'd only wanted to avenge his lost love and ended up losing everything he had left. But Val wasn't a sucker for tragic irony, nor was she soft.

"Why did Robby have to die?" Val asked, her voice like a knife.

"I don't know!" he cried. "I don't know."

"Well, I know one thing at least," Val said, "He died because of you."

Val folded her arms and turned away from him in disgust. This whole mess revolved around a two-decades-old revenge fantasy? It was almost too pathetic to accept. She considered laying into Dean some more, until she saw Max. He'd been silent through Dean's confession; now she saw why. His already pale face looked completely drained of blood and he swayed half an inch from side to side, like he'd done in Lester's study right before his freak-out. He stared at Dean with a roiling mix of emotions.

Crap—Max was about to have another panic attack. That was their cue to leave, fast.

She turned back to Dean one last time. "I hope Robby's life was worth it."

"It wasn't," Dean said.

Then he pulled a gun from the pocket of his trench coat, put it in his mouth, and pulled the trigger.

Chapter Twenty-two

The gunshot cracked through the cemetery, drowning out every other sound so all Val could hear was its echo ringing in her ears. Dean's head jerked back with the blast and his body slumped to the ground, six feet above his dead son. She watched blood leak out of the back of his head and pool in the grass, the gun still in his limp right hand.

Did she just goad Dean into killing himself? Or had he planned to commit suicide before he'd even shown up? Maybe he'd been on the edge, and Val had pushed him over. God knows he looked like hell, was drunk and probably not thinking straight. Racked with grief as his murder-for-campaign-donations scheme had spiraled out of his control, culminating in his son's death for reasons even he didn't understand. Dean made a terrible mistake entering into a deal with the devil in the form of Barrister, but Robby wouldn't have wanted this. She'd pushed Dean too hard.

I killed him, she thought as she stared at his body, the gunshot still ringing in her ears. *I killed Robby, and then I killed his father.*

Dean's figure began to recede from her vision as if her mind left her body and floated away from the cemetery. After a moment Val realized that her mind was still in fact attached to her body—it was her body that moved, dragged away from the gravesite by Max. He held her arm tight and pulled her across the grass, dodging headstones and members of the funeral party that had suddenly appeared all around them.

"Oh my God!" "Was that a gunshot?" "There's a man on the ground over there!" "Is that a pistol in his hand?" "I think they shot him." "Is that Maxwell Carressa?" "It *is* Maxwell Carressa, and his girlfriend!" "Someone call the police!"

Their voices drifted past her, faces blurs as Max pulled harder on her arm, forcing her to move faster. She tried to yank herself away and tell him she could walk on her own, but her body wouldn't respond to her commands.

"Somebody stop them!"

They stumbled downhill, her legs struggling to keep her body upright out of reflex. Max stopped her in front of the car, threw open the door, and shoved her inside.

"Get the license plate number!"

Max jumped into the driver's side, started the car, and punched the gas. He threaded around the vehicles that surrounded them and swerved to avoid a would-be vigilante who jumped in front of their path. The single lane of pavement that wound through the cemetery turned into a side street, and the side street turned into a main street. Grocery stores and coffee shops zipped by.

With a shudder, Val's mind snapped back into her body and she regained control of herself. She opened her mouth to ask Max where they were going, but a sob burst forth instead. It seized her whole body and surged in a tidal wave of grief she was helpless to stop. She pulled her knees to her chest as the pain flowed out in heaving sobs while Max drove. What had she done? How many people would die because of her? He'd put the gun in his mouth and pulled the trigger, no hesitation. She'd pushed him. *It was my fault. My fault…*

My fault echoed in her mind until darkness enveloped them and the car stopped.

Val sat with her head buried in her arms until the flow of anguish ebbed and her thoughts began to clear. She looked up. "Where are we?" she asked between hiccups.

"A parking garage in Eastlake," Max said, his face still a sickly shade of white. "Parents of an ex-girlfriend of mine have a boathouse here that's in foreclosure. She asked me for a loan a couple months ago. It's probably still empty." He leaned back into the headrest and squeezed his eyes shut. "We need to ditch this car. I couldn't think of anywhere else to go that was close to the cemetery."

She wiped the tears from her face with her sweater sleeve. Streaks of black stained the gray cotton, runoff from her Goth Girl eyeliner. She almost laughed; now they both looked like strung-out junkies.

Max lifted his head upright and let out a long exhale. "We have to walk four blocks." He opened his eyes and stared at the concrete wall on the other side of the windshield for a few seconds, like he steeled himself with what little strength he had left, then looked at her.

Val took a deep breath, pushing away the image of Dean eating a bullet. "Okay." She took Lester's gun and the burner phone out of the glove box and shoved them into the deep pockets of her hoodie, and handed Max the stack of Lester's cash to carry. Then they left the car and everything in it, a bunch of stuff they wouldn't need anymore and couldn't carry down the street without attracting attention anyway.

Outside the parking garage, cars ambled past as streetlamps popped on in the twilight. They were in what looked like a quaint tourist area, with restaurants and antique shops lining both sides of the narrow road. Val listened for police sirens and heard none. Max began walking down the street, his head down and hood up over his baseball cap. She hurried to catch up with him, then grabbed his arm and swung it over her shoulders as she hooked her arm around his waist. He didn't ask what she was doing, so he must've understood—a young couple arm-in-arm who looked like hell might just be trust fund kids coming back from a rough party, while two shady characters stalking down a well-to-do street would garner more suspicion from curious onlookers. Max walked at a good clip but she felt his chest heaving with the strain, and his hand was like ice in hers. Every second they strolled in the open felt like dodging a prison spotlight.

He cut across the street and down a hill into a posh residential area nestled against the waters of Lake Union. Many of the houses stood dark—either second homes that were empty for the season or homes that were for sale. Max turned right and stopped at a small two-story house with lush wood siding, a burnished blue front door, and a sign that said "Foreclosure" next to the mailbox. After confirming that no one in the sleepy neighborhood was obviously around, they walked to the back along a porch that floated over the water. Max punched a code into a keypad at the back door—of course he would know the code, probably guessed it based on the Julian date of his ex-girlfriend's sister's birthday or something—and the door clicked open. Val followed him inside.

The house was dark and cool, permeated with the musty smell of a place that hadn't been occupied in some time. Val squinted to make out the kitchen they stood in, counters bare save for a decorative bowl with plastic apples in it, the hallmark of a home staged for open houses. She followed Max through the kitchen, into a living room, then up a set of stairs. A master bedroom occupied the entire second floor, with a sliding glass door that led out to a deck overlooking the lake. Max closed the blinds while Val fumbled in the dark of an adjoining bathroom for a hand towel. She yanked one off its hook and draped it over the nightstand lamp before turning it on, giving them a dim halo of light to see with.

Val went back to the bathroom and used one of the two sinks to wash the black crap off her face. Max appeared next to her and used the other sink to splash water on his face. Then he lunged for the toilet and threw up.

She was surprised he'd gone this long without losing it. He was already weak with a lingering concussion when they'd arrived at the cemetery. Then he had to watch a man who confessed to being his real father blow his brains out, *and then* drag his partner to safety after she froze up. God—all the ways she'd fucked up, and forced him along for the ride. Maybe it would've been better if she'd stayed out of his life.

When his retches stopped, she handed him water in a fish-shaped glass she found next to the sink. Without looking at her, he took the cup from where he slumped over the toilet and rinsed out his mouth, then drank the rest in desperate gulps. He pushed himself up, stumbled to the bed, and collapsed into a sitting position on the floor, his back against the mattress.

Val took off her laden hoodie and gun holster and let them fall to the floor. She sat on the ground across from Max. "Is it true?"

"How the fuck should I know?" He took off his baseball cap and ran a trembling hand through his dark hair. "Dean was a friend of the family—my parents' friend, not mine. I saw him maybe twice a year at most before my father—Lester—died."

"Robby was your half brother—"

"If Dean was telling the truth. He wasn't thinking clearly, obviously. Who knows what the truth is."

"I don't think he'd lie and then kill himself."

"Then why'd he leave me there?" Max's hands balled into fists. "If I was his son, why'd he leave me with a piece of shit like Lester? Because Lester had money? Because money makes people good parents? Because a guy who murdered his wife would make a wonderful father?"

"Are you sure Lester murdered your mother?"

"I don't know! I don't know anything!"

Max took a deep breath and raked another hand through his hair as he struggled to calm himself. They needed to keep the noise down. If the neighbors noticed activity from a house that was supposed to be empty, they'd surely call the police.

"I'd always suspected," Max said, his voice quieter. "I was told she died in a car accident. I hoped it was true."

"Okay, well, the past is the past." Val stood and paced across the shag throw rug as Max eyed her with heavy lids. "Now that Dean is gone, all we have is the accountant who helped embezzle the money to corroborate the murder-for-political-donations scheme. And maybe Delilah, if whatever evidence she has is worth anything. But it could be nothing, so you need to remember the accountant's name."

Max sighed. "I can't."

"Try again."

"I already have."

"Try harder!" She rounded on him. "If you can't remember, then we have nothing! Dean and Chet and Robby will never be avenged. You'll go to prison for a crime you didn't commit, and Barrister will get away with multiple murders."

"So what if I go to prison? I don't have any family left, and my 'friends' are acquaintances at best. No one would care."

"*I* would care!" She scoffed. "You know what? Fuck you, Max. *Fuck you* for making me care when you can't even be bothered to give a shit that you're being framed for murder."

"I'm not being framed."

"The hell you're not." Val wanted to yank him off the floor by his shirt collar and shake the apathy out of him. "Dean told us Norman killed your father. It must've been either Dean or someone else working for Norman that leaked fake evidence to the police that you killed Lester. That's a pretty classic frame job to me."

Max looked at the floor. "Norman Barrister didn't kill my father."

"He probably hired someone else to do it, but if he ordered it, then he might as well have done the killing himself—"

"I know Norman didn't do it because I did it," Max said. He looked at Val. "I killed my father."

Chapter Twenty-three

Val thought she'd heard him wrong. She stared at him, waiting for him to explain how she'd misunderstood what he said.

"You know how Lester made his millions?" Max said, his eyes filling with fire. "By molesting me. For years. As soon as he realized what I could do. He was already a wealthy stock broker, but it wasn't enough. He needed *more*. So he used his stupid little boy to get it, a kid who had no idea what sex was or what the weird images I kept seeing were, who thought his dad could teach him something about becoming a man. I don't even think he was really a pedophile. I was just a means to an end, a golden goose. Probably killed my mother so she wouldn't find out what was going on and stop the gravy train. And like an idiot, I went along with it out of a pathetic sense of loyalty. Eventually he let me handle it myself, and I thought we were some kind of fucked-up money-making team, equal partners."

He laughed, a cackle so mirthless it felt like sandpaper to Val's ears.

"Until a couple months ago, out of nowhere, he orders me

to have a baby. With anybody, he didn't care. Said it was my duty to carry on the 'special' Carressa line. I told him I couldn't because I'd had a vasectomy years ago, as soon as I could give legal consent. I'll be damned if I'm going to bring a child into the world that could end up like me. He freaked and attacked me, punched me in the face because I ruined his plans to become richer than God by destroying some other kid's life. He hadn't hit me since I was a kid, and I realized that nothing had really changed. We weren't equals. I was still his slave. So I snapped. I hit him back, so hard I broke his jaw. Then I threw him off the balcony. I hated him. *Hated him.* He was a sick fucking bastard. His death was merciful compared to what he deserved."

Max breathed hard as if he'd run a sprint. Val stared at him, slack-jawed. After a few seconds, the anger leaked out of him like a popped balloon and his body began to shake.

"You know what the worst part was?" he said, sadness quieting his voice. "Up until that moment, I thought even though he'd let his greed get the better of him, deep down he loved me like a father's supposed to love his son. But he never did." His shoulders slumped, and he squeezed his eyes shut as tears leaked down his cheeks. He wrapped his arms around his chest as his face warped into a mask of concentration, like he was trying very, very hard to regain control of his emotions.

All of her life, Val had considered her visions to be a burden with limited utility. She'd even given up sex for a while during her enlistment in the Army, when she'd tired of witnessing her platoonmates' deaths before they happened. She'd cursed the fact that her visions weren't more useful, been jealous of the normal lives others seemed to have. How petty she'd been. It could have been so much worse.

"So that's it, that's everything," he said, his voice choked up. "I'm a murderer. I make excuses, but that's the truth. I should've confessed and turned myself in to the police from the beginning. If you want to part ways now, I understand."

She studied his despondent face, his dark eyes wet with tears. A face she thought she knew. She'd warned herself not to trust him.

Close to a whisper, Val said, "You lied to me."

"I did," he said. "I didn't know you then."

She didn't know him then, either. Who was she to judge? She might have done the same under similar circumstances. Not to mention how she'd unwittingly led Robby to his death, and pushed Dean to his. She was a killer herself.

Val slid down the wall into a sitting position across from Max. She touched her foot to his, connecting them. "This means our initial guess was correct. Only someone like us could have known you would kill Lester in a spontaneous fit of rage. They must have told Norman about it, and then Norman told Dean it was a planned hit, to dupe Dean into giving him access to the money Lester embezzled from the company."

Max didn't agree or disagree. He looked at her like the Barrister conspiracy was the farthest thing from his mind.

"I'm tired of running," she said. "I want my life back. Norman's a monster in sheep's clothing, just like your father was. Someone needs to stop him like you stopped Lester."

A slight smirk cracked his somber face. "You wanna throw him off his balcony?"

"I would if I could, but I'd rather expose him for the piece of shit that he is."

"How?"

"Get Delilah to back us up. If she turned on him, she could ruin his career and send him to jail. She might also have evidence that exonerates you. When I talked to him at his house, he almost attacked me just for mentioning Chet and a possible connection to your father. He's ashamed of his sexuality and also has no impulse control. He's a loose cannon. It only takes a little push to set him off."

"When?"

"At the Pacific Science Center outreach thing tomorrow. We'll go in there, find her, and bust her out."

"So your plan is to pop in, look around for her, and hope no one notices us?"

"It's our only option, okay? Either that, or find the accountant whose name you can't remember and get him to spill his guts to the media before Norman uses his stable of dirty cops to murder him, if he's not dead already. Or better yet, do both. If we split up, we can find the accountant *and* grab Delilah. Divide and conquer." She folded her arms at the incredulous look on his face. "I'm open to any better ideas—and turning yourself in is not an option, so don't even start with that again."

Max threaded his hands behind his neck and closed his eyes in contemplation. He'd stopped shaking, and some color had returned to his cheeks. "Okay, but first: we no longer have a car.

Second: the rally will be swarming with security. Third: I'm not lying when I say I can't remember the accountant's name. Those are fairly sizable obstacles."

"I can beg Stacey to borrow her car. She's still pissed at me, but she'll come through. And you ask Kitty for her car, if you think she can be trusted. You go get the accountant, I'll get Delilah, then we'll meet at the back of the Pacific Science Center either right before or right after the event starts. As for how we get to them...we'll have to look."

His eyes snapped open. "I thought you didn't want to do that."

"We don't have a choice now. We're up against someone like us who's always one step ahead. It's time to start fighting fire with fire. You said the visions are stronger together than apart, right?"

He nodded slowly.

"We need all the help we can get."

"Are you sure?"

Val took a deep breath. "Yes."

"I don't have my books. I won't be able to completely interpret what I see."

She rolled her eyes. "God, Max, just do the best you can, all right? We have these tools, we need to use them. So let's just do it and get it over with."

He deadpanned, "You make it sound so romantic."

"Romance and desperation don't go together well."

With no fanfare or foreplay, she kicked off her boots, stood up, and pulled off her skirt, leggings, shirt, bra, and panties while Max stayed seated and watched her with a mix of curiosity and awe. It might have been the least sexy strip tease ever. When Val stood naked before him, it occurred to her how bad they both looked—exhausted, disheveled, strung out from yet another day that ranked among the worst of their lives. She realized he'd never actually seen her looking good, in makeup or a flattering dress or something else a normal girl might wear. Now that she'd presented herself to him, she felt embarrassed, then stupid for feeling embarrassed.

But hey, she finally had an excuse to fuck the hottest guy she'd ever met, even if he was more than a little beat up, had serious psychological problems, was the secret half brother of her murdered fiancé, and a part-time heroin addict…Oh yeah, and he also killed his child-molesting father. Robby would be so happy for her.

Scowling at her selfishness, Val walked past Max to the other side of the bed, where the sliding glass door looked out over the black waters of Lake Union. Through slits in the closed blinds she saw the surface glitter with lights from the shore and ships passing in the night. She heard Max stand up behind her, his sneakers drop to the floor.

"Robby wanted to live by the water," she said. She hugged herself against the chill in the room. "He didn't even like water sports. He just wanted to buy a house where he could get on a dingy and paddle around. 'Our kids will like it someday,' he told me." Her eyes filled with tears, and the lake became a blur. "I thought it would be dangerous for kids to live next to water—someone else's kids."

Val felt Max approach her from behind. He stepped close, the heat from his body warming her through the thin fabric of his clothes and the sliver of space that separated them. He touched her arms and slid his fingers along her skin, up to her forearms. His lips brushed against her shoulder.

"We don't have to do this if you don't want to," he said, his voice husky.

A tiny groan escaped her throat in response. She closed her eyes and leaned back against him as a fire ignited in her belly and overwhelmed all her other senses. God, she wanted him, all of him, despite what a mess he was. She wished it wasn't so, for Robby's sake, but it was. She couldn't recall wanting anything so badly in her life.

He kissed every inch along the soft arc up to the nape of her neck. "Tell me when to stop."

His breath against her skin was so hot, it nearly burned. Val lifted her arms above her and wove her hands around the back of his head, curling her fingers through his hair, pulling him closer. His lips traveled up her neck, to her ear, where his tongue caressed her earlobe. His hands slowly slid across her flesh, drifted to her front, and cupped her breasts, his fingertips tracing arcs across her nipples.

His left hand moved down her torso, and a jolt of lightning shot up her spine when his fingers slipped between her legs, then inside her. She moaned as he caressed her in slow, deep strokes, her head nestled into the crook of his neck, his flesh against her lips made moist by her breath. Her hips moved to his tune as he played the string that threaded its way through her gut and into her spine, until she danced at the precipice of climax.

No—it was too soon.

"Stop," she said, breathless, and he did. She turned to face him. His face had gone slack like a drunk man's, though his gaze gripped her with an animal intensity. Her fingers traced the contours of his rough mouth, the cut healing at the edge, wetness gathering where she skimmed the soft inner flesh of his bottom lip with the tip of her thumb.

Don't kiss him, she ordered herself. *I owe Robby at least that much. I'm only doing this because I have to. Stay focused on the real goal. Get the vision and be done with it.*

Before he could pull her flush to him, she grabbed the bottom of his sweatshirt and yanked it up to his chest. She helped him work the hoodie and T-shirt underneath over his head, slipping the clothes off his skin with the same satisfaction she felt when peeling the lid off a pudding cup to get to the sweet insides. She pressed her bare chest to his and slid down his torso, gentle over his patchwork of bruises. Falling to her knees, she unbuttoned his jeans and pushed his pants and underwear to his ankles. Her eyes followed the thin trail of black hair that led from the faint fist-sized diamond on his chest, through the hard folds of ab muscles, to his erect penis.

He inhaled sharply when she wrapped her lips around him. A steel rod in a velvet sheath, he tasted like she imagined he would—sweet and salty, musky and hot. Her hands traced the soft slopes of his backside, leaving goose bumps in their wake. She played him like he'd played her, sliding her tongue up and down his shaft in long, luxurious strokes. The essence that leaked out was delicious because it was his, and she lost herself drinking it up.

She nearly fell forward when, without warning, he stepped out of the clothes bunched at his ankles and away from her. He backed up and sat at the edge of the bed.

"What are you doing?" she asked, still catching her breath.

"It has to be like this."

Oral wasn't enough? "But...you're hurt."

"So be gentle."

"We don't have protection."

"I can't have kids. And I don't have any STDs. Do you?"

"No."

"I guess we'll have to take each other at our word then."

He might have been lying, but she didn't have the mental strength to argue. Even if she did, she trusted him completely. It was herself she didn't trust. She needed to stay focused, make this act more than a lust-fueled romp. If he was inside her...well, she'd have to concentrate harder. She stood and walked to him while he watched her, motionless except for his heaving chest. For a moment all she could hear was his breathing.

"Think about the accountant," she said. She gripped his muscular shoulders and swung her leg over his lap so she straddled him.

"Okay."

Max grasped her hips, slid his hands along the small of her waist and up her back. He pressed his face to her chest and she felt his mouth engulf her nipple. A wave of dizziness hit her. She cradled his head in her arms and clutched his hair as she struggled to stay upright and concentrate on anything that wasn't him.

"Think about...the Pacific Science Center event tomorrow,"

she said, her voice strained as his lips worked their way up her neck, tugging at her skin with such force it almost hurt.

"Mm-hmm," he mumbled into her flesh. He cupped her backside in his hands.

"Think about—"

Her words caught when he pulled her onto him and thrust deep.

"*Oh, God*," she muttered as every nerve in her body seemed to fire at once.

He rocked his hips into hers and she matched him, deeper each time, clutching his chest to hers until she thought she might melt into him like a stick of butter left on a hot stove. The furnace of his mouth breathed a cadence into her ear, his stubble branding her cheek, and before she could stop herself, she'd let him take her mouth with his. He kissed her deeply and she kissed him back, long and hard and desperately, as if they were lovers who'd been apart for years and not strangers who'd met only two weeks ago. The wisp of self-control Val had left slipped away, and he dominated all her senses. In the brown of his eyes she watched flecks of glittering amber, like embers from a fire, pop in and out of existence as he moved through her, gazing into the depths of her being as she gazed into his, looking for something that'd been missing in their souls and finding it in each other. He'd finally released the inferno she'd sensed in him, the fire he struggled to keep hidden. It was hers now. And in that moment, she was completely his.

His thrusts became stronger, faster, deeper, until he moaned and his eyes closed. His hips stopped; he was climaxing, and in the midst of a vision. Though her body screamed for him to continue, at the very edge of her own orgasm, she took a few seconds to observe his slack face—this was what she must look like when she climaxed, like she'd slipped into a trance. Now she knew.

Val kissed his unresponsive lips, wrapped her arms around his neck, and rolled against him. Still hard and throbbing inside her, his taste still ripe on her tongue, she buried her head in his neck and fell over the edge into orgasm—and saw fire.

Chapter Twenty-four

I'm in a park. Wet, brown leaves litter the ground. I feel the heat of a vicious fire behind me. People are screaming. I run from the flames, following a paved path that winds around a big white building underneath wide arches. The Space Needle looms straight above me. I round a corner—right into a clutch of terrified bystanders.

"It's her!" one of them yells. "She set it off!"

Someone else yells, "She's got a gun! Help!"

"Put your hands up!" a man orders me from behind. I turn to face a plump-cheeked police officer, his baby face twisted in fear as he aims a pistol at me. His gun shakes. I raise my arms. The gun goes off. My chest explodes as a bullet rips through my heart—

Blur.

I'm running away from the fire. I cut to the left, off the paved path and away from the group of people I know are around the corner, one of whom will flag down a police officer

*who kills me. I skate along the back of the building until I find
an unlocked door. I go through it and enter a dimly lit storage
area, metal shelves with tagged boxes and knickknacks divid-
ing the room into slender hallways. I cut down the middle at a
quick trot, panting from the adrenaline coursing through my
veins. Suddenly I stumble and fall to the ground; a searing
pain tells me I've been hit in the head from behind. I try to get
up but I'm struck from behind again. I collapse flat on my face.
Bony hands flip me over, and an older man with a gaunt face,
thin smirking lips, and a shiny suit looms over me.*

"Miss Shepherd, I presume?" he says.

*My head is swimming and my body stays limp despite my
desperate pleas for it to move.*

*He checks his watch. "I've got a few minutes. Let's see if the
carpet matches the drapes, shall we?" He pulls down my leggings and starts to unzip his slacks.*

"No," I moan as sheer panic grips me. "No!"

*He frowns and puts a hand over my mouth. "We can't
have that." He lifts a crowbar above my head—the same one
he likely hit me with from behind—and brings it down with
crushing force—*

Blur.

*I hug the wall of the storage room, gun drawn, scanning
for the man I know is lying in wait to rape and murder me. I
see movement to my right. I spin around just in time to catch
him lunging at me with the crowbar. I shoot him three times
in the chest. He crumples to the ground, dead. Resisting the
urge to spit in his face, I continue through the room until I get*

to the other side, where a door leads out to a service hallway. I run through the hallway, past stacks of pallets stocked with merchandise for the gift shop. At a fork I make a left, and go through another door into a space exhibit that's been closed off for renovations. I search frantically for the exit, trying to navigate the maze of displays in near total darkness.

As I'm making another lap around the Mars section, I run straight into Norman Barrister. Before I can raise my gun, he clocks me in the face so hard I fly backward and crash into the wall. My gun falls out of my hand and disappears somewhere on the ground. He grabs my sweatshirt in both hands and throws me against the wall again. I pound his chest with my fists and kick him in the shins, but his massive frame absorbs the blows with more irritation than pain. He lifts me in the air and slams me into the ground, knocking the wind out of me. Then he wraps his giant hands around my neck and squeezes. I claw at his hands but they're like metal vises, and his grotesque face, warped in homicidal fury, fades from my vision as blackness closes in—

Blur.

"You know what you must do, and yet you keep dying."

I'm in a high-rise penthouse office. Walls of glass surround me. A city of neon glows in the night outside. Not Seattle—Shanghai or Tokyo maybe. The city provides the only light for the sparse office composed of a single desk and a couple of chairs. A woman with silky black hair and an all-white skirt suit stands in front of the glass wall, her back to me.

"Who are you?" I ask. "Do I know you?"

"We have always known each other," she says. She has a strong English accent, and speaks slowly with the high-pitched breathiness of a child but the deliberateness of a sage.

I address her blurred reflection in the glass. "I don't want to die."

"Nor do I. But some things cannot be avoided."

"I can't. I need to…I was…" I try to recall how I got here. What I'm doing here. I can't. "I was with Max—"

"Excellent."

A kernel of memory pops in my brain. "Barrister. Norman Barrister. I need to stop him, expose him. How?"

"By living."

"But how?"

"Pray at the base of the mountain that touches heaven."

"I don't understand."

"Consider what happens if you do not."

Blur.

I'm standing on the balcony of Max's house, the balcony where he threw his father to his death. The sky is overcast, the water is black. All of the glass is cracked, and trash is strewn everywhere. At my feet I see a weathered newspaper with a headline that reads:

President Barrister Declares War.

Before I can check the date or read the article, the brightest light I've ever seen bursts in the sky and mushrooms upward. I hear and feel a rumbling that grows louder, shattering the *glass around me, until a shockwave hits and I'm engulfed in flames—*

"Val."

I'm screaming as the fire chars the flesh off my body and roasts my bones—

"Val!"

Max's face came into focus, his brow knotted in worry. He grasped her wrist with one hand while the other covered her mouth. With a shudder of relief she realized she was still in the boathouse, naked on his lap, her flesh uncooked. He removed his hand so she could speak.

"You started screaming," he said.

"I died, over and over, and then I saw the whole world die…" She couldn't get out any more before a wave of tears overwhelmed her. She buried her head in his chest and sobbed.

Max hugged her to him and lay down on the bed. Arms wrapped around his chest, she cried into his bare skin while he stroked her shoulder. As his essence infused her senses again and she remembered the ecstasy of being with him right before her horrible vision, her tears began to wane. She focused on the beating of his heart underneath her ear, the warmth of his skin against hers. When she'd calmed down enough to be coherent, she told Max what she'd seen.

"Have you ever had a conversation with someone in a vision?" she asked him.

"No, but all I see is numbers, so I wouldn't know even if I did."

"She said we've always known each other, but I've never met her before. I wouldn't forget that voice. Then again, if she's from the future, then maybe we'll meet later? I don't know how all this *Back to the Future* shit works." She sighed. "What do you think 'Pray at the base of the mountain that touches heaven' means?"

"Mount Everest could be 'the mountain that touches heaven.' Or it could be another tall mountain. Or a metaphor for something else entirely."

She rolled her eyes. "That's helpful. It'd be nice if she'd just spoken like a normal person, but I guess that would be too easy."

"Maybe she has to interpret her visions, too, like I do. Ethan told me his were like flipping through the pages of a graphic novel—static images with captions and dialogue bubbles. He said sometimes they made no sense."

"What were your visions like with Ethan?"

"It was an unending string of nondifferentiable numbers. After some research I realized it was two different fractals."

Val took his hand from her shoulder, turned it over so his forearm faced up, exposing his tattoo. "Are these what you saw?" She ran her fingers across the intricate shape that repeated itself the closer she looked, like thousands of brilliant aquamarine snakes eating their own tails.

"Yeah, that's one of them—it's called the Julia set." He held up his other arm. "This is the other—the Davis-Knuth dragon, also called 'twin dragon.' Ethan said they were important and I shouldn't forget them, but it's been six years and I still don't know what their significance is."

"What else did you see with him?"

"That was it. Just the one vision."

She lifted her head and met his gaze. "Are you saying he didn't rock your world?"

Max shrugged. "I wasn't that into him honestly. It was an effort to work myself into just the one vision. And he insisted on being on top, and that I call him 'big brother,' which was fucking weird."

Val buried her head into the crux of his shoulder and laughed.

"I'm glad you think it's funny." He ran a finger up her spine; she yelped and arched her back at the tingling sensation. "Just be happy I didn't ask *you* to do anything bizarre." He let out a long exhale and stared at the ceiling. "Even though I wasn't attracted to him, I still begged him to stay. I was so tired of being alone."

She lifted her head. His eyes met hers when she touched his cheek. "You're not alone anymore."

He cupped her hand in his. "And neither are you."

"What did you see with me?"

He frowned. "The number *pi* until it terminated."

That didn't sound especially interesting, but Max's sudden haunted look made her think it had some significance in the world of numbers that she missed.

"Will you get that tattooed on your arm, too?"

"I don't have enough room for that unfortunately. *Pi* is a lot of ink."

She rested her head on his chest and traced the outline of his abs with her finger. "Well, this is great. I saw myself die horribly a bunch of times and met a woman who talked in riddles, and you saw the number *pi*. Real useful, all around."

Val adjusted herself against him. When her thigh rubbed against his manhood, she felt him harden. He must have the same accelerated libido she did, always craving something that remained eternally out of reach. She pushed herself up so she was face-to-face with him, his warm hazel eyes with their starbursts of green in the center studying her in that way that melted her from the inside.

"Do…you want to try again?" she asked him.

"Yes."

"You're not feeling sick or tired or anything?" She pushed a lock of hair from his brow and searched his bruised face for hidden signs of distress.

Max bear-hugged her, and with a whoosh, he'd rolled on top of her. "I feel great actually."

There was no way he felt great after everything that'd happened that day, but his full smile and the joy in his eyes convinced her, at that moment anyway, it was true.

"What about you?" he asked. "You sure you want to risk seeing something horrible again?"

"We need to keep trying until we have a plan. And as long as you're on the other side, I think I'll be all right."

His lips seized hers, and Val didn't consider stopping him this time. She hugged him close and relished his weight on top of her, her rock in the storm that raged around them. With her legs wrapped around his waist, he slipped into her and flowed in and out, slow and deliberate, prolonging the act. They both knew the journey to climax was the best part, the buildup, the falling into each other until she didn't know where he ended and she began. Her fingers traced a lazy path over every soft hill of his vertebrae, up to his thick hair and the fine coat of sweat that misted his scalp.

Like before, Val tried to think about the accountant or how to save Delilah without dying, and like before, she could think of nothing but Max. She breathed in his breath, tasted his tongue, smelled his sweat, felt his mass atop and inside her. When his thumb caressed her lips, she seized it with her mouth, clasping it with her teeth, running her tongue along the folds and grooves until he filled her completely. He moaned into her ear, and she couldn't hold out any longer. Every muscle in her body tensed and her chest arched into his. She dug her fingers into his flesh as a wave of ecstasy rolled over her. A desperate cry escaped her chest to stay with him and not slip away—

A Frisbee flies overhead, caught by a teenage girl, who throws it back to her partner. I'm surrounded by families in a public park, the Seattle skyline glinting in a clear, azure sky. A warm breeze tickles my skin. The grass around me is so green I think someone's littered the ground with emeralds. A little boy runs up to me with blond hair and gorgeous brown eyes with bursts of green at their centers.

"For you, Mommy," he says, and hands me a dandelion.

I reach for him as he runs away from me to gather more flowers. I feel kisses on the back of my neck, hands resting on my shoulders.

"Let him go," Max whispers into my ear. "He'll be back."

Blur.

A Frisbee flies overhead, caught by a teenage girl, who throws it back to her partner. I'm surrounded by families in a public park, the Seattle skyline glinting in a clear, azure sky. A warm breeze tickles my skin. The grass around me is so green I think someone's littered the ground with emeralds. A little girl runs up to me with silky black hair and gray eyes.

"For you, Mommy," she says, and hands me a buttercup.

I reach for her as she runs away from me to gather more flowers. I feel kisses on the back of my neck, hands resting on my shoulders.

"Let her go," Max whispers into my ear. "She'll be back."

Blur.

Max grabs fistfuls of clothes from a dresser drawer and shoves them into a duffle bag.

"Fine, just run away," I say, my voice shaking. I tremble with rage, and there are tears on my cheeks. I don't know why. "Run away like you always do."

"I can't do this anymore." His face is haggard and his eyes are red like he's been crying, too, though his anger has overwhelmed his sadness. "We're never going to find her. They will always be one step ahead, and I can't...I can't." His voice chokes up. "I'm sure that, wherever she is, they're treating her well." He zips up his bag.

"You fucking coward. Get out and don't come back!"

He brushes past me, wiping tears from his eyes.

"When I find her, I'll tell her that Daddy gave up!"

Blur.

I run along a path through a tropical forest. Max runs in front of me, barefoot, wearing only board shorts. I'm barefoot, too, in a bikini. I hear a roar through the trees. We burst from the forest, into a clearing at the edge of a cliff. Water cascades down the side into a crystal blue pool fifty feet below us. My stomach lurches as I consider the drop.

"You can't chicken out now," he says, panting from our run. He takes my hand, and I see he wears a wedding ring; I have one, too. "Come on. On three: one, two, THREE!"

We sprint off the side of the cliff, screaming as we fall, hand-in-hand, until the cool water envelops us.

Val breathed in as she broke the surface of the pool. When she opened her eyes, she was back in the boathouse, Max staring down at her, his weight on top of her. He cupped her head in his hands.

"Are you all right?" he asked, his gorgeous eyes with their emerald centers searching hers—the eyes their child would one day have.

Val had assumed the child she'd seen in her vision at the Red Raven was the son she and Robby might have had someday if he'd lived, but it wasn't—it was Max's son. Or daughter—apparently fate hadn't decided which one they would have yet. And they would fight—their daughter would go missing—but at some point they would marry.

They were meant to be together. She'd finally found the part of her she didn't even know was missing. Elation burst through her, and she almost laughed with delight.

"I'm all right," she said, beaming up at him.

"Do you want me to stop?"

Val pulled him down for a kiss. "Don't stop." She took him into her again, as deep as he could go, taking in his pain, his joy, everything he was, good and bad. "Don't ever stop."

Chapter Twenty-five

Stacey breathed hard from where she lay naked on her bed. She strained against the bindings around her wrists and ankles that fixed her to her bedposts, her legs spread wide.

"God, please don't," she begged.

Kat stood at the foot of the bed and sneered. "There's no getting out of this, cunt."

She flicked a light riding crop across Stacey's breasts. Stacey cried out as the sting resonated through her chest. When the crop came down across Stacey's thighs, she yelped.

"Hey, ow, that kind of hurts."

"It's supposed to hurt a little. The pain enhances the pleasure."

"When does the pleasure part begin?"

Kat folded her arms. "*You're* the one who said you wanted to know what the big deal was with rough sex. Should we stop now?"

"No. I'll get back into character." She'd hoped this little experiment would get her mind off the chaos Val had left behind in her freight-train approach to catching Robby's killer. If she didn't try harder, of course it wouldn't work. She closed her eyes and took a deep breath, channeling the method acting skills she'd learned from a free class a few years ago. Back in the zone, she opened her eyes. "Stop, no more. It hurts—*hurts so good.*"

The corners of Kat's lips ticked up, and Stacey could tell she worked to stifle a laugh. She straddled Stacey's waist, flipping her honey blond hair over her shoulder so it grazed the tops of her plump, exposed breasts. Through the opening at the bottom of Kat's leather bustier, she rubbed her completely shaven groin against Stacey's while Stacey lay trapped underneath. Kat's cold blue eyes leveled Stacey with a look of pure desire so hard that Stacey thought she might come from her stare alone. The woman was an exquisite piece of ass so perfect Stacey could hardly believe she was real, and hers. Then again, Stacey always thought that when they were together.

Kat drizzled lavender oil onto Stacey's skin and rubbed her torso down, kneading her breasts, digging thumbs into her nipples.

"Ah, that's—that's"—Stacey's chest heaved against Kat's hands—"that's kind of painful."

"Oh, we're just getting started, bitch."

"Do you have to be so mean about it?"

Kat's grip loosened. She chuckled and poked Stacey in the shoulder. "Oh my God, you are such a baby. I think we can officially declare that rough sex isn't your thing."

"Well, at least now I can say I tried it next time my sister asks." She yanked on the ropes around her wrists. "Untie me?"

Kat folded her arms across her fat breasts and tapped a finger against her lips. "Hmm…no."

Kat's hands shot down and she tickled Stacey's sides. Laughter exploded from Stacey's chest as she writhed underneath Kat's legs. "*Stop it!* Bad kitty!" The neighbors were going to complain about the noise again.

She kissed Stacey's collarbone, and her tickling fingers drifted down to her girlfriend's thighs.

Stacey breathed, "You are so naughty—"

Tchaikovsky's *1812 Overture* erupted from Kat's cell phone on the nightstand. Kat glanced at it. "Shit, I have to take this."

"*What?*" Stacey panted. "Jesus, Kat, let it go to voice mail!"

"I can't. We've got a big client we're supposed to be on standby for. If I don't answer, I could lose my job." Kat hopped off Stacey and snatched up her phone. "Sorry, baby."

Stacey rolled her eyes and sighed. "Can you at least untie me now?"

Kat loosened one of Stacey's wrist straps, then disappeared into the living room.

Stacey swore as she freed herself from the bed, threw on a terrycloth robe, and stepped out onto the deck off her apartment's bedroom for a smoke. The cold air helped clear her senses. She didn't totally understand what Kat's profession entailed—something about international trading—but the job required her to do their bidding at the drop of a hat. Kat had explained the situation to Stacey when they'd met three months ago, and Stacey had said that she understood and accepted it, but it was awkward times like these that made Stacey reconsider.

Of course, it wasn't like Stacey was in any position to criticize Kat's judgment. Stacey had admitted to Kat that she was in a relationship with Natasha when the two had first met at a coffee shop—now their *special* coffee shop—but she let Kat pursue her anyway. When their friendship inevitably turned romantic, Stacey beat around breaking up with Natasha for chicken-shit reasons Val would've rolled her eyes at. And when Stacey cheated on them *both* with Val, it was time to come clean. By that point, Natasha already had one foot out the door; Stacey just absolved her of any guilt.

But Kat stayed. Kat understood and forgave her. And thank God she had; otherwise, Stacey would be totally alone. She didn't know what the hell she'd been thinking, sleeping with Val. Stacey knew she'd never be more than Val's friend and business associate, but she'd seized the opportunity to relive old times anyway. It wouldn't amount to anything, but at that moment it had felt so right. And then Val literally *ran away*, like she'd broken a dish in a china shop and didn't want to pay for the damage. They'd both made a mistake. Fine. She could accept that.

What she couldn't deal with was constantly bearing the brunt of Val's bad decisions. In a few short weeks everything had changed—Robby and Dean were dead, Val was aiding and abetting a murderer, and the business was faltering. Almost all of the Valentine Investigations clients had jumped ship after the shit storm with Maxwell Carressa hit the fan.

Ah, Maxwell Carressa—*that guy* was right up Val's alley. Stacey wasn't too gay to recognize a man worth salivating over: rich, dangerous, unattached, ungodly handsome. Though if he barely scraped through Harvard Business School—as the Carressa exposés that played round the clock claimed—maybe he was none too bright. Val got wet for intelligent men, Stacey knew. Hell—that was wishful thinking. There was no way Val wasn't tapping that ass by now, idiot or not.

Stacey pushed thoughts of Val's love life away. She didn't care. She *did not care*. This who-was-sleeping-with-whom bullshit was trivial compared to the whole situation with Robby's murder, and now Dean. Poor Dean…

A shiver ran up Stacey's spine. She heard Kat at the bedroom doorway.

"Main and Third, okay," Kat said into her phone. "I'll be there." After a short pause, she laughed and said, "Twenty percent raise *at least*. See you then. Good luck."

Stacey heard the phone drop back onto the nightstand. She took a drag from her cigarette. "Gonna keep your job?" she asked over her shoulder.

"Things are looking good." Kat walked onto the deck despite wearing nothing but a cupless bustier. The woman had no shame. With a body like that, Stacey couldn't blame her, though more complaints from the neighbors were sure to follow. She rested her head on Stacey's shoulder. "All going according to plan so far."

"Fantastic."

Kat raised an eyebrow. "What's got you so sour?"

"Other than my blue bean, you mean?" Stacey exhaled a long column of smoke. "Valentine Investigations is going under unless Val can somehow fix this giant mess she got herself into. I'll have to go back to selling hemp bracelets at Pike's Place Market."

"I'll buy one of your bracelets, baby."

Stacey half smiled. "Gee, thanks. It's not really that, though.

I'm just having a hard time not thinking about Dean. I'd like to know what the fuck is going on—"

The trill of Stacey's cell phone interrupted her.

Kat shrugged. "Guess it's your turn." She went back inside and lay on the bed, flicking the riding crop across her thigh. "Let me know when you're ready for more punishment."

Stacey checked her phone on the kitchen counter, dreading another long talk with a client to explain the "misunderstanding" with Val and the Carressa situation until the inevitable "I'll take my business elsewhere" declaration. Her heart jumped when she saw the number for Val's burner phone in the caller ID. Stacey hesitated, knowing Val was going to ask her for something, then answered.

"I suppose you've got a totally logical excuse for why you killed Dean today," Stacey said.

"Is that what the news is saying?" Val asked. "We didn't kill Dean. He killed himself."

"That doesn't change the fact that I sent him to meet you." Stacey tried to keep her voice low so her nosy neighbors wouldn't get an earful. "I sent him to his death!"

"You didn't, Stacey. Dean was in bad shape already when we met him. Before he died, he admitted that he knew Barrister killed Robby."

Stacey let out an exasperated sigh. "Oh my God. Now they're both dead. This is crazy, fucking crazy."

"I know. I'm close to nailing Barrister, though. I've got Delilah on my side, but I need to meet her during the science outreach event at the Pacific Science Center tomorrow and help her escape. We had to ditch our car after everyone saw us at the cemetery. So…I need to ask you one last favor."

"No shit."

"I need to borrow your car."

Stacey scoffed. "I'm not going to be an accessory to another person's death."

"Stacey, please. I just need to get to the Science Center. We'll be recognized if we try to use public transportation, and neither of us knows anything about stealing cars. I'll park your car far away, and that's all we'll do with it."

"*We*, huh? You two some kind of crime fighting duo, now? Screwing for justice?"

Val sighed. "Stacey—"

"I don't suppose you ran away from him afterward, too?"

A long silence followed.

"I'm sorry I left. I know it was wrong. I panicked that I'd screwed up so badly I'd lost you as my best friend. I only need to get to Delilah, and then I won't ask anything else of you again."

Stacey's resolve weakened. Every friendship had their ups and downs, she figured. She and Val were having a *serious* down moment, but would she rather have Val as her friend than not?

Probably…yeah…yes, she would. They'd experienced too much together to throw in the towel now. Even after everything that'd happened, including Dean's death—

Oh God, poor Dean.

"This whole thing has gotten way out of control," Stacey said. "You need to deal with your own shit, Val. I can't help you anymore. I'm done." She hung up.

Stacey collapsed on her couch and pulled another cigarette from her pack with unsteady hands.

"That was Val, right?" Kat asked from the doorway. "I can tell because you look upset."

"She said Dean killed himself. And she wants to borrow my car. I told her to go to hell."

Kat sat down next to her. "That's kind of harsh."

"The bodies are piling up, Kat! I don't want to get sucked any deeper into this craziness."

"But I thought she was trying to avenge her murdered fiancé and stop Norman Barrister from taking over Seattle and being evil, or something along those lines."

"That's what *she* says."

"You don't trust her anymore?"

"She hooked up with a guy who killed his own father—"

"Allegedly."

"She may not be thinking straight, is all I'm saying. I'd help her if I didn't think she might get herself or someone else killed doing it. And since when did you become Val's defense lawyer?"

"I had a friend once who got himself into a bad spot. His deal was drugs, though. Owed the wrong people money. I had the opportunity to help him but I didn't, because I didn't want the hassle. Then the police found him floating in the Puyallup River. He was killed as an example to others, I guess, because you can't get your money back from a dead man. I thought he might get beat up a little, but…I often wish I had at least tried to help him. I don't want you to have the same regret. It eats at you."

Stacey laid her head on Kat's lap. "What if they catch her with my car and charge me with accessory to whatever the hell she's doing? I don't think I'd do well in prison."

Kat stroked Stacey's hair. "You could borrow my car instead of using your own. My company leases the vehicles we use. If someone recognizes her in the car and runs the plates, they'll probably assume she stole it. It would be hard for the police to connect the car from my company to me to you, I think."

Stacey sighed. "I guess that could work. I just…I really think she's making a mistake throwing her lot in with Maxwell Carressa. He seems all kinds of shady to me, a master manipulator."

"Maybe. But no one can control who they love." She leaned over and gave Stacey a tender kiss. "Oh, before I forget—have you ever been to a club called the Green Room?"

Stacey shook her head.

Kat smiled. "Then have I got a treat for you."

Chapter Twenty-six

From where he sat cross-legged and naked on the bed, Max held a couple pages of stationery up to the dim lamplight. He chewed his thumb as his eyes raked over the numbers scrawled across the paper, searching for meaning. After the third vision he'd finally realized he needed to filter out the big numbers—*pi*, a Fibonacci series, the fractals that popped up again for the first time since Ethan—and focus on the numbers in between for useful information.

He recorded the in-between numbers using paper and a pencil he'd found in a kitchen drawer. Then he wrote down what he thought they meant: the intersection of Main and Third Street, 2:33 p.m., white Ford Taurus. Silver SUV—stay to the right. The number 7 kept appearing; it was important for some reason. And of course, he also saw a bunch of financial information he'd been trained since puberty to pay special attention to, no matter how much he tried to ignore it.

He circled the numbers he thought might be related. It was hard to tell without his books for reference. He possessed an impressive memory, but even he couldn't remember every value in every table. It might've been a Fourier series, which usually implied a body of water, like Lake Union, Lake Washington, or the Sound.

"Goddammit," he muttered and slapped the papers on the bed.

"What's the problem?" Val asked from where she lay next to him underneath the covers.

He thought she'd finally fallen asleep after the half-dozen or more times they'd made love that night, but she looked at him now with clear gray eyes set in heavy lids.

"I'm horrible at this without my textbooks."

"What are you trying to find out?"

Max showed her the papers. "I think these numbers are connected, but I don't know how."

She pushed herself up onto one arm, the blue comforter falling away to reveal her naked torso. Despite the many times he'd already done it, he fought the urge to seize her and run his lips across every inch of her soft skin. He had a hard time controlling himself with her, and it bothered him. He feared he might have hurt her in his zeal to be inside her, though she hadn't complained yet.

She touched his bare shoulder. "Do you need help?"

He felt himself harden underneath the sheet across his lap. All it took was her touch. What was he, some kind of sex fiend now? He'd never been this *enthusiastic* about a woman before, and there had been plenty of others. But she knew things about him he'd never told anyone else, and she accepted them all.

Maybe that was the heart of his intense attraction to her—she'd seen his dark side and didn't run. No matter what he wanted, though, she looked tired. They'd been fucking pretty much all night.

"Don't worry about it," he said. "You need some sleep."

He needed sleep, too. His many bruises ached and his head throbbed. He smirked a little, wondering if his doctor would say he was healthy enough for sex.

Val asked, "What does this mean?" She pointed to the only letters on the paper: "RR."

"Oh, that's the red raven."

She raised an eyebrow. "Your sex club?"

"No, I named the club after this. It's the only thing I still see in my visions that's not a number—a red-colored raven. I've seen it sporadically my entire life. I never knew what it meant before I met you."

"What does it mean?"

"Well, I…I think it's you."

Val blinked at him, then laughed awkwardly. "I'm not that important."

"You said before that you've been able to change things that you saw. How?"

She shrugged. "I don't know. It's not special—I mean, apart from being able to see the future to begin with. Sometimes I'll see different versions of the same event—usually someone dying versus not dying—and I try to make the not-dying version happen. Most of the time it doesn't work. Sometimes, very rarely, it does. That's it."

"What have you changed?" Max asked, hanging on her words.

Val frowned, lost in thought for a moment. "Stacey was one. I saw her drown in a boating accident with some of her community college buddies. I made up a reason for her to stay with me and not go on the boat. She really wanted to go sailing since she'd never been before, so I had to think of something compelling. I told her I still had feelings for her, that maybe we could take our friendship to the next level. I knew she still had feelings for me, so I used that. It was really mean, what I did. Awful. I broke her heart. Our friendship barely survived when I told her I'd changed my mind." She hung her head and stared at the far wall. "But it worked. She didn't die. I've never told her the truth. I don't think she'd take it well."

She rested her head on his shoulder like she was suddenly out of energy. "I saw you die, too, and you lived," she said in almost a whisper. "I saw Robby live, and he died."

"I've never been able to change anything," Max said, "and I've tried many, many times. Sometimes I'd lie to my father about what I saw in a vision, like some company was about to declare bankruptcy, so he'd sell all his shares. That alone should have done *something* to change the market or hurt the company, since by that point he was a major player. But it didn't. Everything turned out just as I'd seen it in my vision, and the company was fine. After I tried that a few times, he caught on and made sure I didn't lie to him again." Max cringed, remembering those awful beatings.

Val hooked her arm around his as if she sensed his unease.

"Then I tried a bunch of non-finance-related experiments, like every day I would lay out a series of random numbers on flash cards and take two numbers out of the deck. Then I'd try to use a vision to see which one I would put back in the deck the next day, and purposely put the other number in to change what I saw. But each time I did it, either my vision would be unclear, or somehow the number I saw would get back in the deck, despite my intention to keep it out. I thought someone was messing with me for a long time, so I'd alter the experiment to eliminate variables, control for outside influence or tampering. The experiments still turned out the same. For years I tried different experiments—trying to outwit Schrodinger's cat, you could say. But nothing changed. Eventually I gave up. I was trapped, a slave to the future.

"After some"—*suicide attempts*—"soul-searching, I accepted it and learned to make the most of a bad situation, be as normal as possible. Kick my drug habit. Have relationships. Enjoy sex. Get some hobbies. I thought I had things under control, as much control as I'd ever have anyway. Until I threw my father off his balcony."

Val laced her fingers through his and hugged his arm tight. She kissed his shoulder, and he realized she was trying to comfort him. He was blubbering like a sad sack.

"Anyway…" Max cleared his throat, pulling himself together. "The point is, I've never been able to change anything. Ethan admitted the same when I quizzed him on it. That makes you unique, even amongst *our kind*, I think. So what I'm saying is…maybe this whole thing isn't about the mayoral race, or my father, or my money. Maybe it's about you."

Val scoffed. "Don't say that. It's not true. It doesn't make any sense, because... It just doesn't."

"Maybe not," he said, but he was pretty sure it *was* about her. The red raven, finally appearing in the flesh right as his life imploded and everything he thought he knew turned out to be false. His real father was Dean; his half brother was Robby, Val's fiancé. He could have a DNA test done as proof, but the more he thought about it, the more he felt like an idiot for not realizing it sooner. The way his mother would light up when Dean was around, how Dean often asked personal questions that Max mistook for social awkwardness. Lydia and Dean's enduring "friendship" from college until the day she died. All signs pointed to the obvious.

The truth about Max's real father, Lester's embezzlement, Dean's thirst for revenge, or Norman's manipulation of Dean to get at Lester's embezzled money wouldn't have come to light if Val hadn't shown up at his club one night, if her fiancé hadn't been run down. Robby's death was the fuse that had set her off, and brought her and Max together. Add to that someone or some group who had demanded that Lester give them Max's child—a child he wasn't capable of having, not without reversing his vasectomy.

But if he was to one day change his mind... he'd only do it for her. Like Val said earlier, it couldn't be a coincidence that he'd only be willing to have children with one specific person in the entire world, and that person just happened to show up on his club's doorstep. Why their theoretical future offspring were important, he didn't know. In any case, everything depended on her actions in some way. It made sense to him.

In fact, now that he thought about it, the Julia set—one of his fractal tattoos—was defined by its chaotic nature, in which small perturbations caused drastic changes in future functions. Sounded a lot like Val. Could he have had her "name" tattooed on his arm all this time?

"Think what you want," she said like she knew he placated her. "All I care about is wiping Barrister off the goddamn map and making him and whoever's helping him pay for all the lives they've ruined. Nothing else matters."

Max wondered if that included him. He frowned, then wiped it away before she could see.

Val picked up his papers. "What part are you having trouble with?"

He pointed to the circled numbers. "I think these are a Fourier series, but I can't tell without referencing a table of integrals. If it is, then I can confirm that it represents a body of water, and the base number will tell me which body of water."

Val smiled and buried her face in his neck. "You are so nerdy." Her lips tickled his skin when she talked. "I love it." She dropped the papers on the nightstand, slid her leg over his lap, and laced her fingers behind his neck.

"I can figure it out later," he said as heat rushed to his groin. "If you want to sleep, you can—"

Warm wetness enveloped his cock. The heat in his gut shot through the rest of his body, refueling the fire of lust that refused to go out, giving him energy he thought had been sapped.

"How many bases are there?" she asked as she slid up and

down him, slow and deep. They'd learned to talk during these sessions, though they often veered off onto random subjects. It helped to focus the visions, as Val had said she'd done with Robby.

"An infinite number." He cupped her soft breasts in his palms, perfect handfuls, and massaged the flesh. "But I only see the first ten or so. Those are the ones in the Seattle area, for obvious reasons."

His fingers traced a path over her rib cage and around to her back, running along the valleys of skin made by her shoulder blades. He pulled her chest to him and rolled her nipple with his tongue, savoring the smooth, hard flesh in his mouth. She gave a faint, throaty moan that gained in pitch as she breathed out—the sound she made when she particularly liked something he did to her. He loved that sound.

"Where did you learn all this stuff about numbers?" she asked, her voice strained now, breathy.

He moved his mouth off her breast and focused on rolling his hips in time with hers, thrusting hard in, lazy out. She made the sound he loved again.

He spoke with some difficulty himself. "I'm mostly self-taught, though I took some easy math classes in college." He breathed in her flesh, ran his lips across her collarbone, up the nape of her neck to her ear. "I hated college. Giant waste of time. Why learn market analysis when you can just look into the future to see what it's going to do? I only bothered to finish because I thought the receipt they hand out on graduation day might be useful."

She threaded her fingers through his, clasping both his hands with hers. "You know you're probably some kind of genius. Idiot savant, at least."

If I were a genius, I would've left my father long before I lost my mind and killed him.

"I don't want to talk about me anymore," Max said.

He pushed against her hands. She pushed back, and they fought in a playful shoving match before he forced her arms behind her back and held them there. Val threw her head back and laughed. He nipped her ear with his teeth, and she yelped in delight.

"Where's your family?" He pulled her arms down so she leaned back, arching her torso toward his. She braced her knees against his hips and closed her eyes as he took full control.

"Mom's in Canada somewhere," she murmured, her face flushed and lips the color of sweet wine. Her eyelids fluttering like she was dreaming. "She's a radical left-winger. Moved away when I was five to protest the Gulf War. Dad remarried and moved to Oregon. Cousins scattered around."

He nuzzled her neck. "Tell me why you joined the Army," he whispered.

"I wanted to shoot something. I was mad about my sister, didn't have money for college—"

She moaned and her fingers clasped harder with his as he picked up speed against his will, the frenzy right before the climax bearing down on him with a passion he couldn't resist. He wanted to be inside her as far as he could go, to taste her and smell her and feel her completely. He wanted her to experience the most intense pleasure she'd ever known. He wanted to know everything about her, to make her happy. He wanted her to feel the same way about him.

"It was either the Army or Walmart—" Val shook her head. "*I can't,*" she whimpered. Her face twisted into what looked like pain.

Oh no—did he hurt her again? With every ounce of self-control he possessed, at the cusp of orgasm, Max stopped, released her hands, and pulled out. He panted with the effort.

Val gasped. Her eyes popped open. "No! Don't stop!"

She threw her arms around his neck and kissed him, her sweet wine lips devouring him with a desperate need he matched with his own. He pushed as she pulled him back in, and they began their dance atop the sheets again, a faster, deeper rhythm than before, breathing in time with each other. She made her special sound, louder and louder as she threaded her fingers through his hair until he thought she might pull a clump of it out. The pain of the past left him when he gazed into her eyes, getting lost in them, wishing he could stay there and never come out. She was his new sanctuary, now and forever.

"I can't concentrate on anything but you," she breathed. "I—" She gasped as she came, and was silent.

Her grip on him slackened. Max caught her before she fell, and hugged her tight. He pushed her hair away from her beautiful, placid face, still hot to the touch.

"I love you," he whispered into her ear.

He didn't know why he said it, or even how true it was. He'd never told anyone he loved them, save for his mother in the way children do. Love was a weapon others could use against him, he'd learned at an early age. But it felt safe to tell her if she would never know, because it *was* true. He loved her.

The realization swept over Max, a tidal wave of emotion flowing from his heart and crashing through the rest of his body as Val clenched around him in the throes of her silent orgasm. The sensation was too much to resist, and though he didn't like to finish in her while she was in the midst of a vision, the world fell away and exploded with numbers—

31415926535897932384626433832795028841971693993751058209749445923078164062862089986280348253421170679821480865132823066470938446095505822317253594081284811174502841027019385211055596446229489549303819644288109756659334461284756482337867831652712019091456485669234603486104543266482133936072602491412737245870066063155881748815209209628292540917153643678925903600113305305488204665213841469519415116094330572703657595919530921861173819326117931051185480744623799627495673518857527248912279381830119491298336733624406566430860213949463952247371907021798609437027705392171762931767523846748184676694051320005681271452635608277857713427577896091736371787214684409012249534301465495853710507922796892589235420199561121290219608640344181598136297747713099—The red raven regards me with her clever black eyes, lustrous crimson feathers shimmering in the light of a moon I can't see. She soars atop

*the numbers like a loon on the surface of a lake, obliterating
some, clipping others, rearranging segments, leaving a trail of
chaos in her wake. She flies close to me, what I recognize as the
edge of my consciousness, so close I think I can reach out and
touch her—*

Max opened his eyes and blinked a few times to orient himself
in the darkness. He'd moved somehow; he lay on his back with
his shoulders propped up against the headboard slats. He reached
behind him and felt Val's hand providing a cushion between his
head and the backboard. She lay molded to his side, her eyes
closed, legs and arms intertwined with his.

"You were falling backward when I woke up," she said, sounding half asleep. "I didn't want you to hurt your head again."

"Um, thanks." He hated the awkwardness that always accompanied his temporary helplessness. At least Val understood, and he
didn't have to make up a lame excuse about low blood pressure.

Max inched down until his head rested on a pillow. He pulled
the covers over himself and Val, enveloping them in a cocoon
of warmth. The tendrils of exhaustion wrapped around his brain
and began to pull him under, unrelenting this time.

He picked at a piece of Val's dull black hair spread over her velvety shoulder as her chest rose and fell against his side.

I love you.

"How long is your hair going to stay like this?" he asked.

"Twenty washes, according to the package." The rhythm of her
chest skipped when she chuckled softly. "Did your raven turn
bottle black?"

"Nope. Still red. Good news for the future of your hair."

He desperately needed sleep, but he fumbled for any excuse to stay awake. Sleep meant the end of their night—maybe their *only* night together. He rolled toward her. "Do you think your friend will come through with her car tomorrow?"

"She'll come through. She's a good person, better than me. What about your girlfriend?"

"She's not my—" He sighed, knowing she was only teasing him. "Kitty will come through. She always does."

Max stared at the top of her head nestled in the crux of his shoulder, his mind going numb with exhaustion.

Val asked, "Do you need to write down what you saw?"

"No. It was…no new information. The Dow Jones will be up three hundred and twenty-eight points tomorrow, though."

After a long pause in which he nearly fell asleep, she said, "Puget Sound."

Max jerked awake. "What?"

"The water for your base, or whatever—it's Puget Sound. I saw it in my vision. I'm pretty sure it was meant for you."

"That's nice of your vision."

Her chest bounced against his as she laughed, then all he heard was her deep breathing. Max strained for the shrouded lamp on the nightstand and clicked it off. It was cruel to keep waking her for his own selfish desires. He held her in his arms and tried to sear the moment into his memory, wishing daybreak and the horrors it would likely bring wouldn't come.

Chapter Twenty-seven

Norman adjusted a deep red tie in his bathroom mirror, careful to line the knot up exactly with the buttons of his black suit coat. Attention to detail was the difference between someone who truly cared and someone going through the motions, those born to lead and those who only wished to lead. His troops—and voters—could tell the difference. He practiced a warm-but-authoritative smile and flexed his orating muscles.

"By targeting measured tax breaks at married couples struggling to provide for their children, my Family Values Initiative will promote strong family bonds and a platform for success…a *springboard* for success…*ensure* the success of committed married couples…of any gender." *Don't cringe.*

Today's outreach event at the Pacific Science Center was critical. He needed to nail all his talking points. He and Mayor Brest were neck and neck in the polls, despite Norman's right-leaning views in left-leaning Seattle. Brest hurt his lead by siding with the Puyallup Indian Tribe in a dispute over building a casino on contested wetlands, royally pissing off the environmental nuts.

Unfortunately for Brest, those nuts made up most of the Seattle population. Norman opposed the vice of gambling; pretending he cared about the environment led to the same result. His political action committee got his message across loud and clear thanks to ads and endorsements funded with Lester Carressa's secret stash. It wasn't like Lester needed the money, and the manhunt for Maxwell and his bitch Valentine Shepherd were exactly what they deserved. The Carressa kid was guilty of murder, after all.

It was too bad about Dean, though. At least his high school chum's suicide meant one less weak link to worry about.

He wished all the dirty dealings hadn't been necessary, but sometimes you had to play dirty for the greater good—a valuable lesson he'd learned on the battlefield. Regrets wouldn't bring his mood down. Everything was moving in his favor. He was a townie, an experienced leader, an honorably retired colonel with a firm but fair leadership style the civilians craved. Victory was so close, he could taste it.

And when he won—no more Gino. He'd be done with that shameful part of his life. He could disconnect himself from the hysteria of campaigning and get back to his conservative roots, take the city where he *really* wanted it to go.

Norman tightened his tie so it choked him a bit; the pressure kept him on his toes. He smiled in the mirror, checked his cosmetically whitened teeth, and moved the corners of his mouth up and down by fractions of an inch for the perfect smile.

"I can't stress enough my deep support for free-range farming—"

Movement at the bathroom's entrance caught his eye. His wife stood in the doorway in a red knee-length dress that matched his tie, delicate white pearls around her neck, and her dark hair in a sensible, loose bun. Mascara streaked down her cheeks as she cried.

"Honey, what's wrong?" he asked. Did their idiot son get himself suspended from his ROTC detachment again? Hopefully Norman could get whatever it was this time straightened out before the Science Center event in a couple hours.

Delilah held up her cell phone with a shaking hand. "What the hell is this?"

Norman walked to her and looked at the phone's screen where a video played. It took him a moment to recognize what it was. When he did, his stomach dropped and a cold sweat broke out over his entire body.

The world stopped as he watched himself, Gino, and that blond prostitute having sex together in Gino's penthouse suite. Their moans of passion through the tinny phone speakers made them sound like cartoon characters.

"What is this, Norman?"

He couldn't speak for several seconds. "It's not me," he finally stammered. "It's...it's some kind of trick." His consciousness seemed to float away from him, his mind desperate to escape the situation. "I would never do something like this," he said in a voice that sounded smaller and weaker than his own. "Please don't tell anyone."

Delilah slapped him hard across the face. He staggered back from the shock of it.

"You disgusting pig." She spit the words out. "After thirty-two years of marriage. After everything I've done for you." Delilah threw the phone at him. It bounced off his chest and landed on the ground at his feet. She turned on her heels and fled to their bedroom, slamming the door behind her, sobs echoing down the hallway.

Norman stood frozen for a moment as he reeled. Muffled moans still issued forth from the phone, lying facedown on the linoleum between his wingtips. This wasn't happening. No, no, no. He would wake up any moment now and it would've all been a nightmare, a cautionary tale…

He didn't wake up. Norman wasn't sure how long he stood staring into the empty doorway until his mind slinked back into his body and demanded he do something. He picked up the phone, a crack now splintered in the corner of the glass. How was this filmed? Who filmed it? The Russian whore? The man that'd left Gino's place right as he arrived? Gino himself? How did his wife get it?

Norman stopped the video and backed up through her phone's menu until he reached the text through which the video had been transmitted. *Norman sends his love* was all that was written in the body of the message. He looked at the phone number from where the text originated. It was Gino's.

Rage exploded through Norman, so hot it blurred his vision. Gino sent the video to Delilah because he was a psychopath, or maybe he wanted more money, or he wanted Norman to leave his wife. Who else would send the video to her and not directly to him with a demand for cash, or to his opponent, or reporters?

He could work things out with Delilah. She'd given up her own Army commission from West Point and stayed with him throughout his entire military career, through his year-long deployments and assignments to remote bases. She supported him when he told her he wanted to get into politics. They could weather this. He'd go to counseling, beg God for forgiveness, repent. As long as no one else saw the video, his political dreams weren't dead.

As the initial shock wore off, his tactical acumen kicked in. He knew what he had to do—eliminate the source. He didn't need Gino anymore. With less than two weeks until Election Day, he could ride his current momentum into office.

Norman pulled his own phone from his pocket and texted Gino: *Let's talk terms. Meet me at the Pacific Science Center today, 30 mins before showtime. I'll unlock a back door for you.*

It was a risky move. Norman and Gino had been careful never to be seen together, so no one could connect the known criminal to the political upstart. But it was a risk he had to take. The endgame had arrived. Time to start sacrificing pawns for the checkmate.

Chapter Twenty-eight

Val racked back the slide of her nine millimeter Glock handgun and peered down the barrel, confirming once again that it was free of debris or defects.

Max looked up from the half-dozen papers he'd laid out on the foot of the bed, pencil in his hand, a swath of light from the afternoon sun cutting across the mess of numbers. His eyebrow cocked. "Has your gun spontaneously stopped working yet?"

She snapped the slide back in place. "It never hurts to be sure."

"Unless you break it by checking too many times."

Val gave him the side-eye, set the gun down on the nightstand, and picked up Lester's revolver.

"If you're itching to kill time," he said, "there's something called a 'quickie'—"

"No," she said more harshly than she'd intended.

Max's face hardened, putting in place the mask he wore to hide his feelings. "I was kidding."

Val took a deep breath and forced herself to relax. "I mean *no* because we'll never get out of bed. You are not quick."

He eyed her as if judging her sincerity, then gave her a cock-eyed smile. "I'll take that as a compliment."

He should. Their long night together seemed like a strange, erotic dream completely separate from the chaos that raged around them. She'd felt things for him that, in the light of day, she wasn't sure were real. After they'd slept through the entire morning, she'd awoken convinced she had imagined the best sex of her life as a distraction from the horrible reality of Robby and Dean's deaths. But it *had* happened, and Val had leapt out of bed and busied herself with preparations so she wouldn't be trapped there with Max, lost in him, denying reality. She wouldn't trade justice for Robby for bliss with Max.

"*Mercy*," he said as he leaned over the stationery. He poked one of the pages. "This section is an alphabetic cipher that spells out the word 'mercy.' Why mercy?"

"Sure it's not *Mercer*, as in Mercer Island or Mercer Street?"

"No, the word is definitely 'mercy.'"

Val shrugged and checked her watch. "Better figure it out quick. We need to leave soon." She flicked open the revolver's cylinder and sighed at the two bullets loaded within. Buying more ammo was out of the question. One of them would have to make do with the bare minimum for self-defense.

"Do you know how to shoot a gun?" she asked him.

"Yeah."

She held out the revolver. "Have you shot this one?"

He looked at the gun and hesitated. "Not…really."

"What do you mean?"

"I tried to shoot it once, but it jammed."

"When?"

"A long time ago, when I was a teenager."

"Have you shot it since then?"

"No."

Val frowned and shifted her gaze between the revolver and the Glock. She needed to be ready to fight off Norman and his henchman so they didn't fulfill her vision and murder her, but Max was in danger as well. She had military training; he didn't. He was injured; she wasn't.

"You take my gun," she said.

Max shook his head. "You saw yourself die multiple times. I think you need it more than me."

"Two guys will try to kill me, and I have two bullets. It'll do."

He folded his arms. "I am not taking your gun."

Val scowled at his stubbornness. They didn't have time for this fight. "Okay, fine. You take your father's gun, then." She held the revolver out to him.

Max looked at the gun, and a hint of deep unease flickered in his eyes. "I'm not taking that one, either."

"Max, come on." She pushed the revolver at him. "You need a gun. It's nonnegotiable. People are trying to kill us—*both* of us. At least take it so you can wave it around if you have to."

He swallowed hard. "I can't."

"Why not?"

"Because *I tried to kill myself with it*, okay?"

Val pulled the gun back. "But it jammed," she said softly.

"Yes, the fucking thing jammed."

Was it the gun that set off his panic attack in Lester's study?

Seemed likely, considering his awful childhood and monster of a father. The revolver was the ultimate reminder of his status as a prisoner in his own life. Fate wouldn't even let him commit suicide.

She held her Glock out to him. "Take mine," she said, quiet but firm. "You need a gun."

His lips compressed to thin lines, and he reached for the revolver. As he held it, his hand began to shake. Max clenched his jaw and stared at the hand, willing the tremors to stop. He grabbed his wrist with his other hand and squeezed until his knuckles turned white.

Val cupped his hands in hers and eased the revolver out of his grip.

He scoffed and shook his head. "Goddammit," he muttered.

"Take—"

"I'm not taking your gun!"

She hugged him, absorbing the tiny earthquakes running through his body. The feel of his stubble pressed against her cheek brought back the most intimate memories of their night together, the parts that felt most like a wonderful dream. She had to force herself to let him go.

"If I have the revolver, then the future is already different than what I saw." Val looked into his eyes, the most gorgeous pair she'd ever seen. "Please take my gun, Max. Do it for me."

A tumult of emotions flashed across his face as the twin desires to honor her request and maximize her protection fought with each other. She ran a finger along the edge of his ear, and felt a pang of guilt for so shamelessly manipulating his emotions to get what she wanted. But it was stupid for him to go forth without any protection for her sake. She couldn't live with herself if he died, too, another lost love…

Max let out a long exhale and took the Glock. He wedged it into the back waistband of his jeans. "Please tell me you've won marksmanship awards."

"No, but I'm an expert pistol whipper." She looked at her watch. "We'd better go."

Max gathered up his papers and put them into his jean pockets, then pulled on his sweater and baseball cap. Val considered cleaning up, but there was no way they could hide evidence that they'd been there, so why bother? It didn't matter anyway; once they walked out the door, hiding ceased to be an option. They'd either grab Delilah, find the accountant, and expose Norman Barrister, or die trying.

Val left a couple hundred-dollar bills from Lester's wad of cash on the counter as compensation for the owners, then followed Max out the back door they'd come through the night before. He reset the security code as Val took in the crisp afternoon air, a rare sunny day that also happened to be unseasonably cold. She hugged her hoodie around herself and walked to the quiet street with Max.

They stopped at the sidewalk and looked at each other. Beneath the bill of his baseball cap, the light hit his face in such a way she could see a shadow of Robby in him. The eyes and lips were different, and Max's face was more angular, but if he'd lightened his hair and gained thirty-five pounds, the resemblance would've been uncanny. She couldn't believe she hadn't seen it before—or maybe she had unconsciously, and that explained why she was drawn to him.

Max pointed behind her. "Remember to take a left at the church to go the back way to the gas station."

"Okay."

"And wait for me to get there with the accountant, if at all possible. I mean it—*wait for me*."

"I'll try."

He opened his mouth like he wanted to say something else, but closed it again. Val took a breath and hardened her heart, narrowing her mind's eye for a fight. As she began to turn away, he touched her hand. She turned back, threw herself into his arms, and kissed him deeply, drinking him in like it might be the last time they would ever taste each other, until they ran out of breath.

"Come back to me," he breathed.

She caressed his cheek. "I will."

They turned from each other, their entwined fingers slipping apart as they walked in opposite directions.

Val pushed back tears. *He'll be fine. Focus on reaching Delilah. Don't look back.* When she reached the corner, she looked back. He'd already disappeared down another street. They were each on their own now. She felt weaker somehow.

After she'd made a left at the church and reached the local gas station, Val loitered at the corner and pretended to talk on her cell phone while she waited—and prayed—for Stacey to arrive.

"Come on, Stacey," she muttered into her dead phone while her eyes scanned the street. "Please, please, *please* show."

As the seeds of panic began to take root, a black Toyota Corolla pulled up next to Val. For a second her brain screamed at her to run, convinced she'd been spotted by a cop in an unmarked police car, until she saw Stacey in the driver's seat. Val jumped into the passenger's side and breathed a huge sigh of relief.

"God, thank you, Stacey."

She gave Val a curt nod, the chilliness in her demeanor underlining their many unresolved issues, all of which were Val's fault.

Val was about to launch into a long apology when she noticed how very un-Stacey the car looked—empty ashtray, clean dashboard, no junk in the back. "Whose car is this?"

"A friend of mine," Stacey said as she drove.

"Does she know what you're doing with it?"

"Yeah."

"And she's cool with that?"

"She's cool. I'm actually driving to a coffee shop where she'll meet me and give me a ride home. From there you can take the car."

Stacey was making new friends. She deserved them; Val had been a shitty one since this whole mess started.

"Stacey, I'm sorry for everything. I'm sorry I've only been asking you for stuff. I'm sorry I've been keeping you in the dark. I'm sorry I slept with you and then ran away."

Stacey was quiet for a long while. Then she glanced at Val, the coldness in her eyes beginning to thaw. "I'm willing to plead temporary insanity if you are."

"Yes, God yes!" Her voice choked up. "You're my best friend

and I've been treating you like crap and I love you and I'm sorry."

Stacey smiled and put a hand on Val's shoulder. "Girl, you're such a softie."

They both laughed hard at that, the same way they did when they watched a terrible movie together and tried to one-up each other with snarky comments all the way through. Maybe they'd be okay after all.

"Where's Max?" Stacey asked.

"He's trying to track down the accountant who's been helping Barrister steal Lester Carressa's embezzled money."

"I thought Max couldn't remember who the guy was."

"He can't, but…we have clues now."

Stacey lifted an eyebrow. "From *visions*?" She looked curious, like a friend and not a romantic rival. Thank God.

Val shrugged. "We had to. We were getting nowhere without them."

"Was it at least good?"

A slight smile touched Val's lips. "Yeah, it was."

"You don't love him, do you?"

She stared out the window from beneath the hood of her sweatshirt and frowned. "I don't know. I still love Robby." She looked at Stacey. "Can you love two people at once?"

"Yes, you can." Stacey pulled into a mini-mall and parked in front of a glass storefront with a coffeepot-shaped sign hung out front, "The Pothead" emblazoned on it in big looping letters. "This is it. You sure you know what you're doing?"

Val snickered. "Hell no. But it's now or never."

They leaned over and hugged each other tight.

"Please be as careful as possible while confronting a homicidal lunatic," Stacey said. "And don't scratch the car."

"I'll do my best to honor those requests."

Stacey hopped out. Val slid into the driver's seat and waved to her friend as she drove away, hoping it wasn't the last time they'd see each other.

Val doubled back and followed Mercer Street until the white arches of the Pacific Science Center loomed on the horizon. The dashboard clock told her she had about half an hour before the science outreach event was scheduled to start. Select side streets had already been cut off and were thick with foot traffic meandering to the event—bearded hipsters and their kids, Republican parents who supported "change they could believe in." Val surveyed the landscape and pinpointed the spot where the fire would be that she'd run from in her vision. She drove around to the other side of the complex and parked on the street. The more details she changed from her vision, the better chance she had of living. Val checked the revolver one more time, lining up one of the two bullets in the chamber. Then she pulled the sweatshirt's hood down over her face and got out of the car.

Faint rock music wafted from the Science Center, dark green pines peeking into an azure sky while the Space Needle ruled over them all almost directly above her. It was a gorgeous fall day in progress. Her gaze swept over her surroundings and homed in on potential threats: a small group of excited college students; a middle-aged couple walking their sweater-clad pug; a couple of police officers down the street giving directions to a woman and her young daughter. For the moment she'd gone unnoticed. Please let it stay that way, at least until she found Delilah.

Adopting a casual slouch, Val crossed the road and began to walk up a soft grassy slope. She was halfway up the hill when a concussive force slammed into her from behind, knocking her forward onto her knees. The explosion roared through her ears for a terrifying second, replaced a moment later with a cacophony of car alarms and shrieks of horror. She looked back and gawked at the husk of Stacey's friend's car engulfed in flames, a black ring scarring the pavement around the explosion's epicenter—the trunk.

"Holy shit," she muttered. "Holy sh—"

An elderly man rolled around on the ground close to the remains of the car. Val scrambled to her feet and took a step toward him, then stopped when she spotted the direction-giving police officers sprinting to his aid. She looked around her and saw onlookers either panicked or in shock. Every cop within a ten-mile radius, plus the entire Seattle Fire Department, would be there in less than five minutes.

Run.

Val turned away from the chaos and ran.

Chapter Twenty-nine

Max nudged Val's gun in his waistband until it stopped digging into one of the bruises on his back. He didn't like guns, had never felt comfortable with one. Maybe it was the frequent urge to put the barrel in his mouth and pull the trigger that turned him off. He distracted himself by studying the crumpled stationery papers covered with numbers from his vision as he waited in the passenger's seat of Kitty's car—at least, he thought it was her car. Didn't seem like her to stack the dashboard with bobble heads and pile the backseat with junk, but he'd never been in her car so he wouldn't know for sure. He certainly didn't expect her to pick him up wearing cargo pants and a hemp-woven sweater, a knit cap wedged over her lustrous blond hair.

"Why are you wearing that?" Max finally asked after they'd been sitting in silence for ten minutes, parked two blocks away from the intersection of Main and Third Streets. She'd been his assistant for over a year, and he'd never seen her in anything besides short skirts and halter tops, or nothing at all. "Are you on your way to a Lilith Fair revival or something?"

"I'm meeting a friend after this," she said in a silky voice at odds with her earthy outfit. "We're getting coffee, then going hiking."

"I'm sorry if I screwed up your plans."

Her lips curled into a sly smile. "As long as that twenty percent raise is forthcoming, it's fine."

"I can only guarantee you a raise if I live, and then don't go to jail."

"That means it's in my best interests to help you."

"Yes, I...suppose so." His chances of success were small; it was in her best interests to extricate herself from the situation, but she kept helping him anyway. She didn't actually care about him, did she?

"Are you still getting paid from my account?" he asked.

"No, your assets have been frozen."

He sighed. "Shit."

"Also, you've been voted off the Carressa Industries board of directors, almost unanimously—Michael Beauford was the only holdout. I think they're working on changing the name of the company, too."

"Well, that's...exactly what I expected." Max shrugged. "We should stop pretending I'll ever be able to pay you for this. Consider yourself a free agent. If anyone fingers you for helping me, I'll say I blackmailed you into it."

"You're so sweet," she said in her usual sphinxlike way where he couldn't tell if she was joking or not. "I'll help you pro bono, then, as your friend."

"I don't have any friends."

"I'll be your first."

Max let out a dry laugh. He couldn't recall how many times they'd had sex on his payroll, and now she cared enough to want to be friends. Maybe they'd grow to love each other in about two hundred years.

Kitty nodded toward his papers. "You get those with her?"

"Yeah."

"Congratulations."

Max rolled his eyes and felt himself stupidly blush. Was she really congratulating him for finally having sex with someone other than her? A lesser man would have been embarrassed by the reference to his pathetic love life, and he...was a lesser man. He refolded the pages and shoved them back in his pocket.

"We have one minute," he said, pointing to the dashboard clock. "Get ready to drive to the intersection."

Kitty started the car, waited thirty seconds, then pulled into traffic. They rolled up to a red light at the intersection of Main and Third as the clock flicked to two thirty-three. Max sat up in his seat and scanned the cars around him until he saw it—the white Ford Taurus, one lane over and two cars down. He opened the car door.

"Good luck," Kitty said.

Max nodded at her. "Thank you, Katherine."

She smiled warmly, though her eyes remained little orbs of blue Arctic ice. Always the sphinx.

He stepped out of Kitty's car and stalked down the side of the road with his head lowered, then cut across two lanes to the Ford. Max opened the passenger's side door, slid into the seat, and shut the door behind him in one smooth motion. The pudgy man behind the wheel snapped his head toward Max and gaped in horror.

"*Georgie*," Max said at the sight of the accountant. The name had popped into his head like a forgotten song. "Your name is George McOwen, but people call you Georgie!"

Georgie grabbed Max's sweater with both hands and yanked Max's face to his. "*They're coming after me!*" Sweat rolled down his red cheeks, his Coke bottle glasses askew. "You have to help me! They're gonna kill me! They're gonna—"

"Stop it!" Max slapped one of Georgie's hands away while the other maintained a death grip on Max's collar. "When you worked for Dean, did he order you to help him embezzle money for my father?"

"They've been watching my house for days. They're just waiting for the right moment to kill me."

A fluffy yellow cat mewled from a crate in the backseat next to a suitcase with clothes bulging out the sides, tossed together for a hasty escape.

Max frowned at Georgie's panicked face. "Then you routed that money back to Dean Price after my father died, didn't you?"

"Why won't they leave me alone?" Georgie cried. He glanced at his cat. "I'm sorry, Bing. I'm sorry I got you into this—"

Max seized Georgie's coat lapels. "Answer me!"

Georgie yelped. "What?"

"Did you embezzle money away from Carressa Industries for my father?"

"Y-yes."

"Using an account in Dean Price's name?"

"Yes."

"Then, after my father died, you began siphoning that money back?"

Georgie's face crumpled and tears leaked out his eyes. "Yes."

A tirade of car horns erupted behind them when the light turned green and the Ford Taurus failed to move.

"Who did you give it to?"

"I don't know," Georgie said, his lips quivering, voice a high-pitched whine. "Dean told me to put it into a bunch of different accounts so I did."

"Shell accounts?"

"Probably, I don't know. I didn't ask questions. Dean told me years ago to create the account and set up the financial architecture so the flow of money couldn't be traced, so I did. Then I heard nothing about it for decades, until last month he told me to bring the money back, so I did it. I just did what I was told!"

Max scowled at Georgie's willful ignorance, though it wasn't surprising given the accountant's complete lack of a spine. So that's how Barrister was funding his campaign—using Lester's embezzled money out of an illegal account in Dean's name and funneling it into shell accounts where it could be "donated" to Norman's political action committee in amounts small enough to avoid drawing the FBI's attention, with Dean's help. Max doubted Norman or Dean would, or could, set up a complicated network of false accounts on their own. Even if either of them had the criminal know-how, there's no way they'd risk a paper trail leading back to them. Norman must have a criminal middleman, maybe the same guy providing the muscle to intimidate Georgie.

"You're going to tell the media what you just told me," Max ordered Georgie.

Georgie's eyes widened so they took up the entire diameter of his Coke bottle lenses. "*What?* No!"

"You conspired with my *defense attorney* to steal my company's money! I would drag you to the police station, but they tried to beat me to death so the media it is. We're going to the Pacific Science Center. Now."

Georgie shook his head. "No, no, no," he chanted.

"Yes. Drive."

Georgie kept shaking his head in silent shock.

Max gritted his teeth and pulled Val's gun from his waistband. He hated having to wave the Glock around, but Georgie wasn't budging without a little motivation. Max took care to aim the barrel away from Georgie. "I said *drive.*"

Georgie's breath caught when he saw the gun, and for a moment he completely froze. Then he burst out the driver's side door and ran for it.

"I'm not gonna shoot you!" Max called after him. "Come back! *Fuck.*"

Max scrambled out the driver's side and took off after Georgie. The accountant sprinted across the road, arms flailing as he moved his thick legs as fast as they'd go. Cars slammed on their brakes and swerved to avoid him. Max chased him, enduring the onslaught of horns and obscenities that followed in Georgie's wake. Whether Georgie's panic made him unusually fast or Max's injuries made him unusually slow—probably both—Max failed to catch him before he ran into a Starbucks. Max burst into the coffee shop a few seconds later to find Georgie ranting at a terrified barista while a stunned crowd waiting for their cups of joe looked on.

"They're trying to kill me! They're trying to—"

"Georgie!" Max said.

Georgie's head snapped toward Max. "He's trying to kill me, too!"

Every pair of eyes cut to Max.

"No," Max said, "I'm not trying to—"

"That's Maxwell Carressa!" someone yelled.

"He's got a gun!" another person said.

The crowd gasped. Max looked down at the gun still in his hand—he'd forgotten he still held it—as people backed away from him, then fought to reach the exits.

"I'm not going to shoot anyone." Max shoved the gun into the back of his pants. "I'm not—"

His words were drowned out as the crowd's haste to escape reached a fevered pitch. Pumpkin spice lattes crashed to the ground, overturned chairs clanged against the tile floor. A hysterical middle-aged woman in a black track suit slammed into Max, knocking him backward. For a second the coffee shop spun around him as his fragile brain struggled to absorb the blow. Max held his head and squeezed his eyes shut until the spinning stopped. When he opened them again, he saw Georgie fighting his way to the side exit. There was no way he was letting that bastard get away again.

Max was hot on Georgie's heels as the accountant stumbled out the door and into the drive-thru lane. Georgie tripped and fell into the road between two cars in line for their afternoon coffee. At last Max got his hands on Georgie. He hauled the panicked man to his feet and slapped him hard in the face. Georgie reeled for a moment, but finally stopped struggling.

Max held tight to Georgie's coat so he couldn't run again. "I'm not gonna kill you!"

Georgie whimpered. "I knew stealing the money was wrong but my mom had credit card bills. Dean said he'd pay them. All I wanted—"

"I don't care! You helped start this mess, and you're going to help me fix it. You—you…" Max lost his train of thought when he noticed the car in front of them—a silver SUV. The driver craned her neck at them, eyes wide and mouth agape.

He remembered the message from his vision: *Silver SUV—stay to the right.*

Max pushed Georgie to the right just as a shot rang out. The SUV's rear window cracked into a spiderweb of shattered glass, its center a bullet hole where Georgie's head had been half a second before. The driver shrieked as she pointed a tiny gun at them, something she probably kept for personal protection. She jumped out of her car and backed away, her face twisted in panic. Max pulled Georgie to the ground with him as she waved her gun wildly in their direction. Georgie screamed when she let off another bullet that went wide and pierced a hole through the drive-thru menu sign.

"I am not a victim!" she shrieked, and sprinted out of sight.

"Holy fucking shit," Max said. He shoved Georgie into the passenger's side of the SUV, then crawled over him into the driver's seat and punched the gas. Great—now he could add carjacking to his list of crimes.

"This isn't happening. Isn't happening…" Georgie muttered.

Max ignored him and cast frantic looks in the rearview mirror, searching for police or any other tail. He glanced at the clock: two forty-one. No time to lose before the Pacific Science Center event began at three.

"We're almost there," he said to himself. "Goddammit, Val, please wait for me, just this once."

Chapter Thirty

Val ran from the fire that engulfed the car she'd arrived in.

Jesus.

Curious bystanders who'd heard the explosion without seeing it began to converge on the scene. The group she recognized from her vision emerged from over the hill on her left.

Don't look back.

The man who'd flagged down the policeman who would shoot her spotted Val running, and followed her with his accusing eyes.

Just keep moving.

She slowed to a trot and tried to look terrified rather than guilty as she hurried away from her potential murderer and toward the Pacific Science Center's tantalizingly close white walls.

She cut to the right off the paved path and made a beeline to the first door she saw into the Center. When Val neared the entrance, she recognized it as the same one she'd used in her vision, from the opposite direction. Beyond lay the storeroom where another murderer waited. Walking past it, she resolved to use the next one she came across until she saw a string of police officers running straight toward her on their way to the scene of the explosion.

"Shit," Val muttered under her breath. Now she had no choice but to use the storeroom entrance, and pray that one bullet was all it took to bring down the psycho within.

As police sirens began to waft through the air, she doubled back and slipped through the unlocked side entrance. She drew her gun and advanced through the storeroom with her back against the wall, alert to any movement, any human-shaped shadow, any noise that wasn't the wailing of emergency vehicles or her pounding heart. A wave of cold relief spread over her when she reached the other side with no sign of her killer. Either she was early, or he was late. It was possible that the explosion happening on the opposite side of where it had originally taken place caused him to alter his plans. In any case, the future was already changed. Maybe this time she would live.

Val ran into the service hallway, silent save for the echo of her footsteps and the muffled sirens outside. She passed pallets stocked with cellophane-wrapped merchandise, just as she'd done in her vision. Breathing hard, her periphery flying past in a blur, she saw the fork in the hallway ahead.

Take a right this time, she told herself. *On the left is the space exhibit maze. That way leads to death.*

Her breath caught when a figure emerged from around the corner in front of her. It grew into a hulk clad in a crisp black suit, a red tie dangling from his neck like a bloody tongue. She stumbled to a halt as Norman Barrister turned down the service hallway toward her. He stopped midstride. His eyes widened as recognition flashed across his face. In his right hand he held a gun.

Shoot him. Shoot him! SHOOT HIM!

Val raised her gun a half second before he raised his. She pulled the trigger and let fly one of her two bullets. It whizzed half an inch past his head and blew a hole in the cement wall behind him.

Shit.

She dove for cover behind a pallet as Barrister let loose a volley of his own bullets while ducking back behind the corner. The echo of gunfire hung in the air after the firing stopped. Val panted where she crouched against the wall. Where the hell had he come from? Maybe the other person like her, the one on his team who could see the future, told him she'd be here. Thank the Lord none of the bullets had connected. Well, maybe one had—she touched her upper arm and saw blood on her fingertips. A scratch compared to what could have been.

"You're like a bitch with a bone, Sergeant." Barrister's voice reached Val from where he stayed out of sight around the corner. "You're just gonna keep chewing until you choke on it."

They were both Army-trained, both in defensive positions, waiting for the other to make a move. Val glanced behind her. She'd never make it back the way she'd come without drawing his fire; it was too far, and there wasn't enough cover. She looked to her left; an alcove with a door at its terminus marked "Wing C" was about a twenty-five-foot sprint away. A wide-open chasm in his line of fire separated her from the alcove. If she could distract him, she might make it.

She tried to steady her voice, eliminate the breathiness that gave away her fear. "At least I'm willing to admit that I like bones." Val searched the cracks between the pallets for a view of him. "How does it feel to be the worst kind of hypocrite, *Colonel*? To hate gay people while being gay yourself, to lecture everyone who will listen about integrity while committing murder and theft for your campaign?"

"You've got some strange ideas," he said, his voice dark and steady. "You're the one who's snapped and come after me. You couldn't hack it in the Army, and now you blame me for your pathetic wreck of a life. Your sister killed herself because she couldn't stand being a slut, right?"

Val's grip tightened on the revolver. Goddamn him. She almost threw back an insult about what a wife-beating bastard he was, but stopped when she realized, if he ended up killing her, he'd know his wife had turned on him. He might then go back and kill Delilah over the betrayal. If Val had to die today, she wouldn't take innocent people down with her.

She finally spotted him through a sliver of space in the pallets. He peeked around the corner for a fraction of a second, then disappeared again.

"I guess you've got no problem sleeping your way up the economic ladder. Spreading your legs for Maxwell Carressa's money must have been easy, with a face like his. You know how many cunts offered themselves to me to secure a promotion or get out of a deployment? Whores, all of them."

Barrister poked his head out to survey Val's position again, then withdrew it. Through the sliver, she trained her gun on that spot.

"Max is going to the media with everything we know," she said. "He's telling them right now how you framed him for murder, how you and Dean stole his father's money to fund your campaign. How you murdered Chet and Robby to keep them from exposing you."

He scoffed. "If that's true, then what are you doing here?"

"I'm offering you a chance to come clean, to salvage whatever human dignity is left in you. It's over."

He laughed. "You do know Maxwell Carressa is guilty, right? No one's going to take his word on anything."

"We've got the accountant who helped you." God, she hoped that was true.

Barrister was silent. He didn't move.

This isn't working, she realized. He wasn't going to back off, and there was no way Val could get to Delilah without a fight.

He's going to kill me, or die trying. And I'm going to do the same to him.

With a laser-like focus, she summoned all her concentration on the spot she knew Barrister would emerge from, her gun steady as a compass needle pointing north. One bullet left—it had to count.

"Why did you kill Robby, huh? Why not kill Chet *before* he met with Robby? Pretty stupid move on your part." *Come get me, you son of a bitch.* "My only awareness of you would've been as the most overrated commander I'd ever had—and as a failed candidate for mayor. Now I won't leave you alone until everyone knows what a piece of human waste you really are."

She saw his black sleeve edge up to the corner, then his foot.

Come on, come on...

The crags of his face appeared. Val pulled the trigger—

An arm like a steel rod hooked around her neck and yanked her backward at the moment the bullet left the chamber. The plastic-wrapped merchandise exploded in front of her as her final bullet shot upward and hit the far wall to the left of Barrister.

Well, that's that, then, she thought as she and her attacker stumbled backward. Now all she had were her bare hands.

She slammed her elbow into her attacker's chest. His grip around her neck slackened and she shoved him away. She spun to face him and recognized her potential rapist and murderer from the storeroom, a thin, Italian-looking guy with oily hair and a shiny suit. Val spotted a Glock in his hand as they faced each other down. She dropped her own gun and lunged for his before he could lift his weapon. Her body crashed into his skeletal frame, her hands latching on to the forearm holding his Glock, keeping it pointed away from her. They spun in a circle like two hawks joined in a death spiral, his liquor-soaked breath heavy in her face as he grunted with effort. Val tried to twist his arm into a submission lock as they struggled chest-to-chest, but the agility with which he'd been able to sneak up on her also allowed him to slip out of her grasp. With a final snarl he shoved her away and backed into the hallway. She stopped short and stayed behind the pallet, unwilling to step into Barrister's line of fire.

The Italian looked from her to the abandoned revolver at her feet. He smirked and flexed the fingers still wrapped around his Glock while Val stared him down. She wouldn't give him the satisfaction of cowering or pleading for her life. She only hoped Max would succeed where she had failed.

"Well, look at this," the Italian said. He raised his gun at her. "Norm, she's out of—"

Two bullets ripped through the Italian's chest. He collapsed, flailing his arms and legs as he gawked at the new holes in his dress shirt leaking crimson gore. Still clutching his gun, he coughed up blood.

"You…idiot…" he gasped in Barrister's direction.

His startled eyes drifted to Val. With nowhere to run, she recoiled as he lifted his gun off the floor with a shaking hand, desperate to take someone else's life as his slipped away. His finger twitched against the trigger, but the life drained from his eyes before he could fire. The Italian's arm fell back to the ground, and he was still as a pool of blood grew around him.

Val sucked in breath for the first time in what felt like an eternity. She huddled in the corner made by the wall and the pallet, totally defenseless.

"One problem solved," she heard Barrister say, "one more to go."

Chapter Thirty-one

Max drove the silver SUV as fast as possible without attracting the attention of the police. He wiped his sweating palms against his pant legs and ordered himself to stay calm. They were almost at the Pacific Science Center. If he could get there before the fire Val saw in her vision started, and before she was spotted by someone on her way to Delilah, *and* if he could force Georgie to confess in front of an audience, then…he didn't know.

The plan was crazy. It wasn't as much a plan as a desperate attempt by two desperate people to reclaim their futures from a fate that'd so far been worse than cruel. If he could finally be free of the invisible strings that had controlled him his entire life, and be with Val without the specter of Robby's unresolved death hanging over them, then the recklessness they'd been forced to embrace would be worth it.

His heart stopped when a police cruiser with its lights flashing screamed up behind them, but it flew past. He glanced in the rearview mirror but didn't spot any other cops or pursuers, thank God. Georgie wept in the passenger's seat, his fat cheeks jiggling with his sobs. Max frowned as pity for the pathetic accountant tempered his anger. He didn't like to see a grown man cry.

"You're going to be okay," Max said to Georgie, aware it was probably a lie. "Once everyone knows the truth, the people who've been chasing you will have no reason to come after you anymore."

"Bing," Georgie cried. "I just left him."

"Who?"

"My cat. I just left him behind in my car. What kind of monster have I become?"

Max repressed an eye roll. "Everyone deserves a second chance, if they're committed to making amends." Max certainly hoped that was true—he wanted a second chance. "How much money did you embezzle away from Carressa Industries for my father anyway?"

Georgie hiccupped, then swallowed hard. "About, uh, a little less than, um, forty million, I think."

"*Forty million dollars?*" Max's anger surged back. "What the hell was he planning to do with that kind of money?"

"I don't know. I never—"

"Yeah, I know, you never asked." He could guess why his father would hoard that much money—it was Lester's escape fund in case Max ever wised up and turned on him, so he could sip daiquiris in the Bahamas instead of facing the consequences of molesting his own son for years to pad his bank account.

Too late, Dad.

Georgie wiped tears from his eyes and looked at Max. "Do you think someone found Bing and—"

"Your goddamn cat is fine. Shut up, please."

Five minutes later the Space Needle dominated the sky directly above them, the Pacific Science Center nestled at its base. A stream of people heading to the event cut across the road at more frequent points as he got closer. Within a block, he saw folks running, talking excitedly with one another, pointing toward the Center. Flashing lights emerged in the distance, around the glow of fire.

Max squeezed the steering wheel until his knuckles turned white. He was too late to reach Val before the fire. Now she was somewhere inside the Center, either fighting for her life, or... He didn't want to think about the other possibilities her first vision had proffered. He needed to ditch Georgie and get in there and help her as soon as possible.

Traffic in front of him stopped as other drivers noticed the disturbance on the far side of the Center and craned their necks to look. Ahead of him, a local news van—probably in the area to cover the science outreach event—sat crooked in the grass where it had rushed to pull over. The camera crew spilled out of the back, untangling wires and snapping pieces of equipment together in a mad scramble to capture the surprise story. A platinum blond news reporter yelled at her colleagues to pick up the pace while she hunched in front of the van's side mirror and applied powder to her face. Her butt partly obscured the logo of the TV station familiar to every Seattle local: KIRO 7 News.

The number 7 is important...

Max hit the gas, dodged the car in front of him, and cut onto the lawn. Georgie yelped and braced himself against the dashboard as they bounced across the grass and slammed to a halt three feet from the news crew. Max jumped out, ran to the passenger's side, and dragged Georgie from the SUV while the crew stared in stunned silence.

"Want a *real* story?" Max said to the wide-eyed reporter while he held a struggling Georgie in place. "Today's your lucky day."

"Are you *Maxwell Carressa*?" the reporter asked like Santa Claus had appeared.

"Yes, and this is the accountant who was colluding with my defense lawyer to steal my company's money."

The blonde—Bridget Pearson, Max recalled from the handful of news broadcasts he'd seen her in—looked back and forth between him and Georgie. "Oh my God. *Oh my God!* Carl, get over here *now*!"

A young man with a giant camera perched on his shoulder rushed forward. Bridget fluffed her hair, snatched a microphone from Carl's hand, and shoved it in Max's face.

"Mr. Carressa, are you saying that your lawyer, Dean Price, who you and your girlfriend killed yesterday, was framing you for your father's murder so that he could steal your money?"

Max eyed the camera, saw the red light that meant it was recording. He frowned; he hated the media. Even before his father's death made national news, the paparazzi harassed him constantly. They'd lurk in the bushes to snap pictures of "Seattle's most reclusive millionaire bachelor" getting into his car or some other banal action that would pop up on the Internet a few hours later. Slow news days often featured an update on his love life. Why anybody cared, he'd never know, though the ever-present nuisance meant he spent a lot of energy avoiding them, in case they stumbled upon one of his real secrets. At least now he finally had a use for the vultures.

"We didn't kill Dean Price," Max said to the camera, "Dean Price killed himself. And for the record, Valentine Shepherd isn't my accomplice. She's innocent of any wrongdoing. People were trying to kill her, and—"

He stopped himself, glanced at the Center. He was wasting time with the cameras when he needed to get in there to help Val. Besides, he should talk to a lawyer—one who wasn't plotting against him ideally—before saying anything more. He'd already delivered Georgie to the media. Mission accomplished. Time to get the hell out of there.

Max shoved Georgie toward Bridget. The accountant stumbled forward and fell to his knees, eyes wide and lips trembling.

"Talk to him," Max said. "His name is George McOwen, and he can tell you all about how he and Dean Price embezzled my company's money."

Georgie shook his head. "They made me do it!" he cried. "I was afraid. I wanted to keep my job and—"

Max didn't stick around for any more of Georgie's blubbering. He turned away and trotted toward the Pacific Science Center's entrance. A mob of cops and firefighters grew each second as waves of emergency vehicles appeared on the scene. If he kept his head down, he could ride the crowd of confused and excited civilians into the Center before the area was locked down.

"Wait!" Bridget called after him. "Everyone still thinks you're a murderer. Don't you want to tell your side of the story?"

"No," he said, and disappeared into the chaos.

Chapter Thirty-two

Val breathed hard where she crouched against the pallet in the service hallway, trapped. Ten feet away, the Italian's body continued to leak blood onto the white-tiled floor, his gun still cupped in his slack hand. She balled her hands into fists and forced herself to rally. There was a way out of this. There was always a way. If she could get to the dead man's gun, she could fight back—

Pallet merchandise ten inches from Val's chest exploded when Barrister shot through her cover. She gasped and hit the floor. Chunks of a destroyed plastic toy dug into her forearms. She needed to move, or die. Her escape was just twenty-five feet away, across the hallway through the door marked "Wing C"—

Another bullet blew through the pallet. It left a divot in the tile where it ricocheted off the ground to her left. He was shooting downward. He knew she was lying on the ground to minimize her profile. He knew all these tactics. Any second he'd realize she was out of bullets rather than panicked. Then he'd just walk up and kill her. But since he hadn't stepped out of his cover, he didn't yet realize she had no ammo…

Val grabbed the discarded revolver from behind her as another bullet ripped through the pallet and took out a chunk of her thigh. She cried out as pain shot up her leg, though thankfully the leg still worked. The pain fueled her anger and fortified her resolve. If he thought she'd roll over without a fight, he was dead wrong. Fuck that bastard. She leaned around the corner with a careless rage, pointed her gun straight at Barrister's exposed torso, and pulled the trigger.

The gambit worked. Barrister ducked behind cover as the revolver's hammer clicked into an empty chamber. She flung the gun down the hallway at his position to buy herself an extra second of confusion. As it sailed through the air, she lunged for the Italian. She heard the revolver hit the floor and slide as her fingers scooped up the dead man's gun. Slipping a little on his blood, she sprinted for the alcove. A bullet whizzed past her head and crashed into the wall behind her just as she crossed the alcove's threshold. She threw open the door to Wing C and rushed inside.

Val pressed her back against the wall next to the door and gasped for breath, her heart pounding like a Tomahawk war drum. He wouldn't follow her, not now that he knew she had a fully loaded gun to ambush him with. He'd try to waylay her at some other point up ahead. Her eyes cast about for any sense of where she was, for an exit sign. The room was dark, illuminated only by emergency lights sparsely dispersed along the periphery. In the corner she saw the silhouette of a giant globe hanging from the ceiling, the rings of Saturn extending from it.

"No!"

She'd stumbled into the closed space exhibit, probably from the opposite side this time. At least she had a weapon now, the Italian's Glock—which just happened to be the same make as her own gun, like in her vision…son of a bitch. Despite all the things she had changed, events were still playing out toward the same conclusion.

A more calculating man would've retreated back to the Center's main hall, found the police, claimed a mad gunwoman was stalking him, and pinned the Italian man's murder on her.

That's what a rational person would've done—not Norman. He was coming to kill her.

She'd be damned if she let that bastard choke her to death. He wouldn't get away with what he'd done, so help her God.

Val followed the wall, hoping it would lead her to the exit like in a traditional maze. But an asteroid display cut her off after a few feet, and she was forced to go deeper into the exhibit. She swerved around models of stars, exoplanets, black holes. Past a panel illustrating the history of the universe. She took a right at a pile of disassembled display parts—and ran into the asteroid display again.

"Goddammit!"

She rushed around the display, turned left, and stumbled to a halt when a replica of the Mars Rover came into view, next to a "Fun Facts about Mars" placard.

Oh no.

She spun around, and of course, just like in her vision, Barrister was there. He clocked her in the face so hard she flew backward and crashed into the wall. Her gun fell out of her hand and disappeared somewhere on the ground. He grabbed her sweatshirt in both hands and threw her against the wall again. Val pounded his chest with her fists and kicked him in the shins, but his massive frame absorbed the blows with more irritation than pain. He lifted her in the air and slammed her into the ground, knocking the wind out of her. Then he wrapped his giant hands around her neck and squeezed.

Val clawed at his hands, but they were like metal vises. She looked away from his grotesque face, warped in homicidal fury, as stars popped in her vision and blackness closed in around the edges.

Please don't let it end like this.

She didn't know who she pleaded to—God, the Fates, whoever pulled the invisible strings of the future, whatever gave her the ability to predict this moment. The woman in white, with a voice like a Baroque sonata.

"You know what you must do, and yet you keep dying."

Her fading gaze settled on the display to her right—a kiosk dedicated to Olympus Mons, the tallest mountain in the solar system.

"Pray at the base of the mountain that touches heaven."

This was it. She pawed at the kiosk, her strength quickly waning. Her hand fell, and she groped around the floor underneath it.

Please. Please.

Then she felt it—the Italian's gun. It must've slid under the kiosk after she'd dropped it. She grasped it with weak fingers and put the barrel to Barrister's head as blackness devoured her world. With all the strength she had left, she pulled the trigger.

Through her sliver of consciousness, a pop. Then the vise around her neck loosened. Val gasped, sucking in precious air. It burned through her bruised throat and flooded her lungs. She blinked as the dark outline of Olympus Mons came into focus again, towering above her. Barrister's heavy, dead body slouched on top of her chest. After pushing him off with shaking arms, her whole body a mass of trembling jelly, she slowly sat up. She touched her throat, felt the raw skin where Norman had nearly crushed her windpipe. Maybe he *had* crushed it; every breath felt like fire, though the pain was a bargain for the sweet air it provided.

She couldn't believe it. She'd lived. She'd changed the future.

Justice for Robby had been delivered. What now for her and Max? Did Delilah still need her help, and would Barrister's wife still come through with evidence to incriminate her husband? How would she explain any of this to the police? Would they still try to kill her? Would Max go to prison for killing his father? All the questions she'd put off thinking about jumped to the forefront of her mind now that Robby and Chet, and Dean to an extent, had finally been avenged. She couldn't think of any answers. The relief of just breathing, of feeling her heart beat, dominated her thoughts.

With great effort she hefted herself to her feet. Val stood still for a moment to ensure her wobbly legs would hold, then shuffled forward to renew her search for the exit with significantly less urgency. She limped on her injured leg, the adrenaline that had compensated for the pain now dissipated. Finally the exit revealed itself behind the Mars section, a simple glowing red sign above a black door that reminded her of the Red Raven's entrance—a doorway into another world.

She pushed open the exit and stepped into a loud room full of anxious people, a stage wedged against the far wall where Barrister was supposed to be addressing his fans about his love for science. The noise from the commotion outside had apparently masked the firefight that'd taken place inside the service hallway.

For a moment no one noticed her, the wanted fugitive, standing there holding a gun, bullet wounds on her arm and leg, fresh bruises marring her face and neck. Then a woman looked at her and shrieked. A shock wave rippled through the crowd as everyone's attention jumped away from the explosion outside and onto Val. People backed away, and a bubble formed around her. From the corner of her eye she saw a flurry of movement. A second later a college-age version of the colonel pushed his way through.

"Where's my father?" Norman Junior demanded.

She opened her mouth and tried to ask him where his mother was, but the words came out as a wheeze through her mangled throat.

Junior narrowed his eyes and stepped toward her with the same arrogant bravado as his father. However Norman had terrorized his wife, his son seemed ready and willing to carry on his violent-asshole legacy. "I'm not afraid of you, bitch—"

Val's mouth curled into a snarl and she raised her fist like she might punch the little fucker's face in. The crowd gasped and the bubble grew wider as Junior recoiled from her and backed away.

Before she could break his nose, a sign above his head caught her eye—"Puget Sound Model and Saltwater Tide Pool," with an arrow pointing to a corridor on her right.

Puget Sound…that's where Max's visions had told him to go. That's where she'd find him—if he was alive. Wherever Delilah was, she was safe from her husband now. Val could track her down and get the evidence she had after making sure Max was okay.

Val lowered her fist, though the invisible cordon around her remained. No one followed her as she limped toward the Puget Sound exhibit, praying she'd find him there.

Chapter Thirty-three

With his baseball cap and hood pulled down over his face, Max followed the crowd of confused event goers looking for shelter into the Center's main entrance. People huddled around the floor-to-ceiling windows, exclaiming into their cell phones and comparing notes—*explosion, car bomb, arson*—and theories—*terrorism, anarchists, teenage prank gone horribly wrong.* Fake dinosaurs roared nearby. No one gave him a second look, because even if someone recognized him, what in the world would Maxwell Carressa be doing there? Thank God for confirmation bias.

Max scanned the signs above him, looking for directions to the space exhibit. He saw a hanging placard with a section whited out, possibly where the space exhibit used to be. Before he set off in that direction, his eyes landed on a different sign: "Puget Sound Model and Saltwater Tide Pool." Puget Sound—that's where his vision wanted him to go…maybe. Without his books for confirmation, it was impossible to know for sure what the numbers tried to tell him. But Val had seen Puget Sound in her vision, too; unlikely to be a coincidence that the Pacific Science Center just happened to have a Puget Sound exhibit. Maybe that one led to the defunct space section. But if he was wrong and the exhibit led nowhere, he'd have wasted precious time that he could've spent saving Val's life…

He was overthinking it. He should trust the visions. Though he hated them, they'd never been wrong. Max took a breath, then weaved through the crowd toward the Puget Sound exhibit.

A rope with a "No Entry" sign in the center cut through the hallway from the main entrance, meant to section off the area for the event. After ensuring no one saw him, he ducked underneath the rope and hurried inside.

The clamor of the main entrance gave way to the soft gurgle of a water filtration system. A diorama of Puget Sound sprawled in the corner of a long, curved room with colorful information booths every couple feet. Cigarette smoke tinged the air.

No sign of Val.

He took two steps into the exhibit's main area, then froze when he heard a lone man's voice around the corner. With a hand on the gun wedged at the small of his back, he inched forward, not daring even to breathe to keep from alerting whoever lurked nearby. Slowly an artificial tide pool emerged from around the corner, a twenty-by-five-foot enclosure on a raised platform with algae-covered Plexiglas walls at waist height. Marine life lounged within the water; filtered air bubbled to its surface. At the edge of the pool, the back of a man's cheap brown suit came into view. He leaned against the pool's edge while he smoked a cigarette and talked on a cell phone.

"I'm here," the man said into the phone. "This is stupid. We should just kill them." He took a drag off his cigarette, then flicked the ashes into the tide pool as he exhaled. "Yeah, yeah. A man can dream, though."

With a shiver, Max recognized the voice of the police officer who'd attacked him in the parking lot—Sten Ander. Though the exact details of what had happened were a blur, hot anger from what he *could* remember prickled across his skin. He pulled out his gun and snuck up behind Sten.

"Are you going to the victory party?" The cop paused while the person on the other end answered. "Just wear a wig. No one will recognize you... Well, I'm going, I don't care what Cassandra says. I'm sure she already knows exactly what I'm gonna do anyway."

Max crept closer, gun pointed at Sten's back.

After another pause, Sten said, "All my pants are party pants, honey. I've got a pair of ass-less chaps I've been saving for just this occasion." He took another puff, flicked ashes into the water, then laughed. "Yeah, well, I hate you, too, baby. May we both eat shit and die." He hung up.

Max rammed the butt of his gun into the back of Sten's head. Sten dropped his phone and staggered forward. Before he could fall, Max grabbed him by his coat collar and shoved his head into the tide pool's water. Sten bucked and thrashed, sending up a storm with his arms.

"How does it feel to be ambushed and helpless, you sick fuck?" Max said through clenched teeth. He braced his forearm on Sten's neck and used his weight to hold the cop's head underwater. Max relished every second of Sten's panic.

If he killed Sten now, he'd be doing the world a favor.

The thought froze him. That's what he'd told himself after he snapped and killed his father—*I rid the world of a monster.* Would he keep succumbing to his anger and murdering people he deemed unworthy of life? How was he any better than them?

Mercy, his vision had implored of him. *Show mercy.*

Max began to ease off Sten's neck when he saw the cop grope for the sidearm strapped against his hip. He seized Sten's trigger finger and yanked it back until he felt it snap. A scream bubbled up from the water. Max took Sten's gun, jerked his head out of the pool, and threw him on the ground. The cop sputtered and gasped, clutching his mangled hand to his chest.

Sten coughed up water. "Oh," he said. "You."

Max shoved Sten's gun into the back of his pants while he pointed his own gun at the prone man. "Where's Val?"

"How should I know? You're the one with magical sex powers."

Max flinched. Great—a psychopath in a position of authority knew one of his deepest secrets. Maybe he should've killed him after all.

"Get up," Max said.

"Why?"

"We're going to find Val."

Sten's eyes widened with fake concern. "But there's a crazy bomber on the loose."

Max kicked Sten in the legs. "*Get up.*"

Sten took his time standing and winced when he touched his

finger, cocked at an unnatural angle. "You sure you wanna be seen leading a cop around at gunpoint?"

"You're not a cop."

"Funny, my badge says I am, though these days I feel more like Cupid."

Max scoffed. "You're dirty as shit. I know you're one of Norman Barrister's lackeys and you murdered people on his command. Not to mention how you tried to beat me to death." He shoved Sten toward the exit. "Move, asshole."

Sten shuffled forward. "I'd ask how you plan to prove any of that," he said over his shoulder, "but I already know you can't. I'll admit to a dirty mind, though. How was the fucking, by the way? I'm dying to know."

Max's finger tensed against the trigger. "Shut up. Move faster."

Sten didn't move any faster. "Did she go down on you? That's her specialty."

"I said shut up."

"Or do that thing where she lets out this sexy high-pitched wheeze—"

"Shut the fuck up!"

Max threw his shoulder into Sten's back. Sten tumbled forward, and would have face-planted into the floor if he hadn't ran straight into Val as she rushed into the exhibit from the opposite direction.

For a couple seconds that felt like an eternity, the two struggled while Max could only watch in horrified silence. Despite his mangled finger, Sten easily gained the upper hand on Val as she reeled from his sudden appearance, her face and neck badly bruised while blood leaked out of wounds on her arm and leg. Sten twisted her wrist, and she grunted in pain as the gun she held—not his father's gun, Max noted with the cold detachment of someone watching a car wreck from the sidewalk—slipped out of her hand and into his. He clamped his arm around her neck and jerked her back flush to his chest. With his uninjured hand, he put the gun to her head.

He glanced at Max's Glock. "Drop it."

Max didn't move. He left his gun trained on Sten, Val his human shield, as his mind worked furiously to come up with any other option. Val tried to speak, but either the chokehold of Sten's arm or the damage done to her neck kept her words from coming out.

"*Drop it*, pretty boy. She won't be so hot with a bullet in her brain."

Val shook her head. Her wide eyes pleaded with him to not give in. Max still didn't move. His body had gone numb. He should have killed Sten when he had the chance. *Goddamn mercy. Why?* Maybe Max could shoot Sten in the head, but he wasn't a good shot, and he couldn't risk hitting Val. He loved her. He couldn't—

"Oh, for fuck's sake." Sten sighed and rolled his eyes. His finger tightened on the trigger, resigned to fire. "Fine—"

"*No!*" Max dropped his gun. "There. Let her go. Please let her go. Arrest me. Kill me. Do whatever you want with me. Just let her go."

Tears filled Val's eyes. Sten laughed.

"Oh, you two!" Sten said. "You make me wanna buy the world

a Coke." He looked at Val, leaned his head into hers as if he was smelling her hair. She cringed as his lips touched her ear. "Don't say I never did anything for ya," he said, then turned the gun on Max.

The bang of a gunshot echoed through the exhibit. A shriek finally clawed its way out of Val's chest. For a moment Max thought Sten had shot the wall behind him. Then he felt a strange pinching sensation in his gut. He looked down, and saw blood. His own blood. He put a hand on the red stain that blossomed at the base of his sweatshirt. Warm liquid flowed through his fingers. Strange, it didn't hurt.

The world tilted on its side, and Max fell to his knees. Sten shoved Val away, then disappeared as she ran to Max. He reached for her as the ceiling slewed toward the floor. Then his head was in her arms, and he was looking up at her as his body went slack. Val's tears rained onto his cheeks, her wet eyes the color of storm clouds on a clear summer day, rolling in from nowhere to stop a couple blissful hikers in their tracks and make them stare.

"Don't move," she said in a hoarse whisper. "I think—I know help is coming. It's coming, Max... *Max*—"

Her words trailed off as Max's eyes closed against his will. Damn, he was going to die—when finally, for the first time in his life, he wanted to live.

Chapter Thirty-four

Val stared dully at the mud-colored liquid in a Styrofoam cup a police officer had placed in front of her—instant coffee with a dash of instant creamer, which tasted instantly like turpentine. She sat alone in an interrogation room, shoulders slumped, hands in her lap, waiting for her lawyer. She picked at the bandage around her sprained wrist and tried to be happy she was still alive.

After she'd been arrested at the Pacific Science Center and Max had been rushed to the hospital, they'd carted her down to the police station and tried to wring her through the third degree before she lawyered up. For once, Sten was nowhere to be found, though she didn't trust anyone in the Seattle PD—any of them could be his accomplice. She'd told her court-appointed counselor everything—everything that didn't make her sound insane anyway, which meant leaving out the visions-of-the-future parts—and then he'd told her to sit tight while he corroborated her story.

She'd spent a restless night in jail, fully expecting to get shivved in the back, startled when she opened her eyes to rising sunlight and her still-beating heart. Now she sat and waited, exhaustion from her ordeal continuing to weigh her down, still expecting a cop to burst through the door and plug her full of lead at any moment.

She jumped when she heard the click of the doorknob, then relaxed a little when her lawyer, Joshua Samson, slipped into the room. The middle-aged man gave her a large smile as he entered, the top of his bald head glinting under the fluorescent lights.

"Good morning, Ms. Shepherd," he said with pep as he took the seat across from her. "How are you—"

"How's Max?" she asked, her voice still hoarse from the previous day's choking.

"Still in the hospital. I can't get any more information than that, I'm sorry. HIPAA and all."

At least he wasn't dead. It would be all over the news by now if he'd died. *Please, God, don't let him be dead.*

"I do have some good news for you, though." Joshua smiled again.

She leaned toward him. "You searched Norman Barrister's financial records and found evidence he was using stolen money from an account in Dean Price's name to fund his campaign?"

"Well…no."

Val sighed and fell back in her chair. "Of course not."

"The cops got a confession out of the accountant," her lawyer said. "He confirms that Dean Price was siphoning money from Carressa Industries into an offshore account. Apparently the other man killed at the scene was helping him—Giovanni Dinapoli was his name. Career criminal with a lengthy record for money laundering, racketeering, identity theft, forgery, sexual assault, and a few other violent crimes to spice things up."

"That's the man Barrister killed," Val said, "probably to cover his tracks, and blame it on me after he killed me. Or maybe Barrister planned to kill me and blame it on Dinapoli, then claim he killed Dinapoli in self-defense." The Italian must have been the one giving Barrister information about the future, the one like Max and Val. He had to be. No one else made sense.

Joshua looked away. "Huh."

Val narrowed her eyes at him. "What do you mean, 'huh'?"

"Well…the initial forensics report from the scene contradicts your version of events."

She raised an eyebrow. "Like how?"

"You say you shot Mr. Barrister, but ballistics reports it was Mr. Dinapoli's gun that killed him, and also shot Mr. Carressa. And it was your gun that killed Mr. Dinapoli."

"*What?* How is that—that's not even possible. Max had my gun."

He shrugged. "I'm telling you what they told me. They also say the car that exploded outside the Center was registered to Mr. Dinapoli."

Val shook her head, speechless. Either the forensics reports were falsified or the scene was altered to match a narrative she didn't understand yet. Why would the cops spend weeks trying to capture or kill her, just to let her off the hook now?

"I also talked to the Barristers' lawyers," he said. "I can't tell you exactly what they said, but I can tell you that they have information that's consistent with the police report." Joshua leaned toward her and talked softly. "What I'm saying is—your version of events is significantly different than everyone else's. So, as your lawyer, I'm suggesting that it's in your best interests to stay quiet about your accusations against Norman Barrister."

She scoffed. "You've got to be fucking kidding me."

"Nobody will believe you, Ms. Shepherd. I'm being totally honest here. Maybe when Mr. Carressa gives his statement if—*when* he recovers, but right now it's your word against everybody else's. People will think you're nuts. You won't come out of this on top."

"But Delilah Barrister asked me to help her. She said she had evidence of Norman's dirty dealings. He was abusive and cheating on her, and she wanted out. What did she say?"

Joshua pressed his lips together and frowned like it pained him to speak. "She wouldn't corroborate your story."

Val grit her teeth. So now that Val had solved Delilah's problem with a bullet to her husband's head, she'd re-erected the perfect housewife façade. Which meant Val could kiss whatever evidence Norman's wife might've had to incriminate Norman goodbye.

"*Goddammit.*" Val slammed her fist on the table, and Joshua jumped. "What about Robby, huh? Barrister killed Robby, or this Dinapoli guy did it for him. How are we going to prove that without connecting Chet to Barrister?"

Joshua shook his head. "I guess you can't."

She stared into the dark depths of her coffee as tears filled her eyes. "Then this was all for nothing," she muttered.

He put a hand on her forearm. "I'm sorry, Ms. Shepherd. I do have more good news, though."

"Yeah, right," she said, wiping her eyes.

"The coroner ruled Dean Price's death a suicide, so neither you nor Mr. Carressa will face charges concerning that."

She shrugged. "At least *one* piece of evidence wasn't tampered with."

"Also, given the fact that Mr. Price conspired to steal money from his client's company, the case against Mr. Carressa is now impossibly tainted. Once he's healthy enough to retain another lawyer, it'll be a slam-dunk to get the charges against him dropped. And the DA knows it. So"—he slapped his palms on the tabletop—"he's not going to press charges against you, either. There's no point if they're almost certain to be dropped. That means you're free to go."

Her mouth fell open. "I can walk out of here right now?"

"Yep." He gave her a triumphant smile. "The Pacific Science Center might bring charges for trespassing, and maybe criminal mischief and evading police, but given the extraordinary circumstances and media attention, I doubt it'll go anywhere. In any case, they're all misdemeanors."

She looked at her lawyer, waiting for him to break into a "Just kidding!" sadistic laugh like Sten would have done. It made no sense. After everything that happened, and everything she knew, they were just going to let her go? Why? *Why*—God, she was so sick of that question. At this rate she'd never know.

Val stood up, limping a little on her injured leg, walked to the interrogation room door, and opened it. Some cops strode by and glanced at her like she was a celebrity in an airport, but no one stopped her. She looked at her lawyer.

"Do I owe you anything?" she asked him.

"A 'thank you' would be nice, but I'm used to being unappreciated," he said with a wink. "Mind the reporters. They're swarming outside."

"Thank you," she said. "I could use a ride to the hospital, if you want some free advertising."

* * *

Val hustled past the flock of reporters camped out in front of the Harborview Medical Center, who swooped in with microphones as soon as they recognized her. Tempting as it was to scream the truth about Norman Barrister while she had everyone's full attention, her lawyer was right—no one would believe her without Max or Delilah to back her up. She needed to touch base with him before she went on the record about anything. If he was all right. If he was awake. Her stomach lurched at the possibility that he wouldn't wake up, that maybe the vision she'd seen of him dying in a hospital bed wasn't due to Sten's beating, but the gunshot wound. She buried the thought as she hurried through the hospital's sliding doors, the clicking of cameras receding behind her.

She tracked Max to the intensive care unit on the second floor. Tired people filled half the waiting room, slouched in stiff-looking chairs. The few that looked up did a double take when they saw her, their eyes cutting back and forth between her and the television that droned in the corner showing news footage of her running into the hospital. She tried to ignore them as she walked to the check-in window.

"I'm looking for Maxwell Carressa," she said to the receptionist on the other side of the thick window. The hint of fear that permeated her voice surprised her. She sounded desperate, and she couldn't filter it out. "I heard he was here."

Recognition flashed across the receptionist's face when she looked up at Val. "That's correct," she said.

"Can I see him?"

The receptionist hesitated, knowing full well who Val was and her connection to Max. "I'm sorry, ma'am," she said softly. "Only primary support caregivers and family members are allowed inside."

"But…he has no family." In truth, Robby's sister, Josephine, was Max's next of kin, though nobody but Max and Val knew that yet.

"I'm his family," a man said behind her.

She turned to face an older gentleman, his craggy face warm and genial despite the expensive business suit he wore.

"I'm the closest thing he's got anyway, as his emergency contact." He cocked an eyebrow at her. "Valentine Shepherd?"

She nodded.

"Michael Beauford, CFO of Carressa Industries." He held out his hand.

She hesitated a moment before shaking it. It was hard to trust anyone anymore.

"I've worked closely with Max for almost a decade. He's a good kid, most of the time."

"Isn't he technically your *boss*?"

Michael laughed. "Not anymore. He was voted off the board after he became Seattle's Most Wanted. Now he's just a regular millionaire schmuck. So, you're his...what? Girlfriend?"

Val opened her mouth, then closed it when she realized she didn't know how to answer. She wasn't really his girlfriend. They hadn't known each other long at all—a blink in time compared to her relationship with Robby. She barely knew Max...That wasn't true. She knew practically everything about him, and he about her. They'd certainly seen, felt, and tasted every part of each other. But what did any of that mean? She cared about Max, maybe more than cared—fleeting feelings that might fade now that the pressure that forced them together had lifted. And what did he feel for her? They'd had sex—great sex, many times—only because they had to, because that's the way their power worked. By itself, it meant nothing.

"I'm not his girlfriend," she finally said. "He hired me to look into his father's death, to prove his innocence. In the process, I stumbled across a plot to steal his money. They tried to kill us, so we ran. I guess...we're friends now."

Michael lifted his eyebrows like he could smell her bullshit. "Okay..."

"How is he?" Desperation tingeing her voice again despite her attempt to keep it out.

"He had a piece of his large intestine removed," Michael said.

Oh God. A lump grew in her throat.

"He's recovering from the surgery now. Saw him about an hour ago. He's still real groggy, kept falling asleep while I was talking to him, but the doctors say he'll make a full recovery."

Val realized she'd been holding her breath. She exhaled as a smile grew on her lips.

"The cops have been waiting around for a chance to question him." He cocked his head toward a couple of plainclothes men Val hadn't pegged as police when she'd entered. Now she noticed their intense glances in her direction as dead giveaways. "Until Max can talk for more than two minutes without passing out, I told them to go to hell."

Val grinned at that. "He needs another lawyer. Can you get that for him?"

"Already done. The cavalry is on its way."

She bit her lip. "Can I see him?"

Michael nodded. "I'll take you inside. He might still be out of it, I'll warn you now."

At the receptionist's desk, he got her a wristband that allowed her entry into the ICU area. Val followed him through sterile white corridors until he reached a nondescript room. He rapped on the door, waited a beat, then opened it.

"Max?" Michael poked his head in. "You're not getting your colostomy bag cleaned right now, are you?"

When there was no answer, he pushed the door open and stepped inside. Val followed close behind. They walked into a room with yellow walls, the morning sun bathing everything in a warm glow through white window curtains. In an adjustable bed flanked by beeping equipment, Max lay in a blue hospital gown with his head turned toward the window. An IV snaked out of his arm and into a drip bag at his side.

"Max?" Michael said.

Slowly Max turned his head to look at them. Seeing him move sent an irrational thrill through her—proof that the entire hospital hadn't conspired to lie to her, like that was possible now.

"Your friend is here," Michael said, stepping aside to reveal Val.

Max looked at her blankly, then smiled when his brain caught up with his eyes. "Hi," he said to her in a weak voice.

She smiled back. "Hi."

After a few seconds of silence where Max and Val stared at each other, Michael cleared his throat. "Okay, well, I'm going to wait outside while you two talk 'business,' as 'friends.'" He waved once and left, shutting the door behind him.

Val pulled up a chair and sat next to the bed. Her gaze traced his cracked lips, sallow skin, black and blue cheeks, and heavy eyes. Despite it all, as when they'd been in bed together, he looked content. Happy, even.

"How are you?" she asked.

"I didn't die," he said, his voice little more than a whisper. "You didn't die, either. That's a lot better than I thought we'd do."

"That is amazing." *And suspicious.* "I sort of told Michael that you hired me to look into your father's death and exonerate you, so you might want to stick to that story."

"Sure. It's not so far from the truth. You did find out who killed my father."

"Yeah, about that—my lawyer was pretty confident the DA's

Shana Figueroa

office will drop the murder charges against you. Dean blew up their case." Val grinned. "So when you get released from the hospital, you'll probably be able to go home."

"Oh." He frowned and looked away.

Damn him, he still wanted to confess. "I'll help you get settled while you recuperate." She touched his hand, and he looked at her again. "I think you've suffered enough, Max."

He searched her eyes with his, then lifted his arm and brushed his fingertips against her bruised cheek. "Where's Norman?"

"Dead."

"Good."

Val cupped Max's hand in hers, turned her head, and kissed his palm. The smile returned to his face. She laid her head on his chest, closed her eyes, and listened to his heart, loving every beat. Loving *him*.

Chapter Thirty-five

The savory smells of eggs and bacon permeated the diner as the late breakfast crowd began to filter out. Val sat in a booth tucked away in the corner, out of sight of any news reporters that might be lurking nearby, and sifted through a stack of folders. Her cell phone beeped.

Tell me what the pancakes taste like, Max texted her.

She patted the half-eaten buttermilk slab with her fork and licked the syrup off the prongs. *Sweet maple on top of blueberry goo, melted butter seeped into the bread. YUMMMM*, she texted back.

A minute later, her phone beeped again: *Damn you.*

She responded: *Don't ask if u don't want 2 know.*

I thought I could handle it. I was wrong.

She chuckled, then forced herself to push the phone away. If she didn't stop texting with him, she'd never get any work done. Val picked through the folders, each one a new case for Valentine Investigations. Since word had gotten out that she'd "cracked the Carressa case," all the clients that had jumped ship during her time on the lam came running back, plus a flood of new ones. Business had never been so busy, though she spent most of her days at the hospital with Max, keeping him company while he healed. If he got the all-clear from his doctors, he could finally check out that afternoon and go home. Maybe eat some solid foods.

The familiar beep sounded from her phone again, enticing her like the rattle of a box of Meow Mix to a hungry cat. Val tapped a folder she'd laid open and tried to read Stacey's hand-written notes above an e-mail chain, but she couldn't stop eyeing her phone. She bit her lip, then snatched up the cell and read the text: *I hate green jello. I will never eat it again. NEVER.*

Val wrote back: *And chocolate pudding.*

No, I could never hate chocolate pudding. A moment later, he texted: *Get me out of here.*

A warm smile spread across her lips. She would read through a couple more cases, finish her coffee, then head back to the hospital.

Eh, what the hell—she'd already looked through five of them; she could look at the rest later. And the coffee wasn't great anyway. Val closed the folder, put it back on top of the stack, and fished money out of her pocket to pay the bill and go.

As she waited for the server to bring her change, Val's gaze fell on the television suspended above the take-out counter, its volume muted. Delilah Barrister stood in front of a podium before a slew of reporters, her face a mask of anguish despite perfectly coifed hair and makeup. Norman Junior stood close behind her—Derek, the text at the bottom of the screen read. He scrunched his face in an unconvincing version of "concerned" while he held his mother's shoulders and stared blankly off-camera. "Live—Delilah and Derek Barrister Speak Publicly for the First Time Since Norman Barrister's Death," the headline read.

"Giovanni Dinapoli had been terrorizing us for months," the closed captioning on the TV spelled out as Delilah talked. His mug shot floated into the corner of the screen. Strange, Delilah had never mentioned Dinapoli to Val. "He threatened my life and my son's life if Norman didn't pay him. Norman wanted to go to the police, but I convinced him not to, for the sake of our family." She wept as Derek patted her shoulder.

Val narrowed her eyes at the television. Was that true? Why hadn't she told Val about the extortion? Sure, Delilah obsessed over appearances and was willing to lie through her teeth and leave Val dangling in the wind to maintain her perfect housewife image, but it still seemed like a fairly major detail to leave out if she truly feared for her life. Without taking her eyes off the TV, Val slurped down coffee. Her mouth had gone dry. Something didn't add up here.

Delilah composed herself and went on. "In the end, my husband did the right thing and confronted Mr. Dinapoli. He stood up for our family and it cost him his life. My husband is a hero."

The camera panned out to show members of the Seattle Police Department nodding behind her. And holy shit, there was Sten. Val choked and wiped her mouth with the back of her hand. He stood behind Delilah and to her right, his hand wrapped in a bandage, faded bruises still coloring his face around the giant mustache. He nodded enthusiastically along with everyone else.

What the hell was he doing there? If Barrister had owned the police, and Sten worked for Barrister, did Sten now work for Barrister's widow? Val didn't totally understand how the transfer of illegal power worked, but she doubted allegiances would shift that easily.

Unless they hadn't actually shifted.

No. *No.* It wasn't possible. She wouldn't even entertain the idea she'd been played that badly. There was absolutely no way Sten had been working for Delilah all along, that she was the one who could see the future, that she'd told Barrister about Lester Carressa's impending death and maneuvered Sten against Val and Max.

No way Delilah had tricked Val into coming to the Pacific Science Center, knowing she'd run into Barrister, knowing she'd kill him.

A wave of nausea hit her. Ridiculous. Paranoia clouded her thoughts again. She needed to get a grip on reality, and get the hell out of there before she puked all over the table. Hands shaking, Val began throwing the folders back in her tote. She stopped when she noticed a stack of mail wedged in the middle, a manila envelope with no return address among the bills. These must be the e-mails Delilah had promised, the ones that incriminated her husband. Breathing a sigh of relief, Val pulled out the large piece of mail and ripped it open. Barrister's wife had come through after all.

Val dumped the envelope's contents on the table. They were indeed e-mails, thank God. She read the first one, only two lines, from someone named "Fortuna" to an unknown recipient:

> I've told dearest he needs to take care of R. That should bring
> M and V together, as you've requested.

What the hell was this? She looked at the date—five days before Robby died. R, M, and V…No. She pushed it aside and read the next one, from Fortuna again, written three days after Robby died:

> R gone. M and V made contact.

Then the next one, written by Fortuna six days after Robby died:

> M and V together. Our asset made sure they'd stay that way for
> a while. Everything going according to plan. Stop worrying. You
> rely too much on your Alpha.

"No," Val whispered. Goddamn her. *Goddamn her!* Covered in a cold sweat, Val splayed the rest of the e-mails across the table in a manic attempt to read them all at once. Each was short, one to three lines long, primarily from Fortuna to an anonymous account. They all said some version of the same thing: *Get rid of R. Get M and V together. Keep M and V together.*

Val struggled to keep down her breakfast. Robby *did* die because of her. Someone desperately wanted her and Max to be together, and they'd enlisted Delilah, aka Fortuna, to make it happen. But why did it matter? Why were they important?

She got her answer from one of the last e-mails, dated three days ago:

They're in love, as I foretold it—me, not your Alpha. Remember that. A child is certain, no matter what happens now. I expect the support you promised per our deal. The wheels of political progress need greasing.

It wasn't Max and Val that were important—it was their off-spring. These anonymous people wanted to steal their future child, the beautiful boy or girl she'd seen in her visions. God no. *Hell no.* She backhanded the e-mail away as if she could reach through the page and slap Delilah herself. That's when she saw the paper underneath, the last in the collection Delilah had sent, not an e-mail but a blank page with a single handwritten note:

Thank you for killing my idiot husband.

She sat frozen, her mind reeling. The waitress wandered by and asked if she'd like a coffee refill for the road; it was all Val could do to shake her head in response. She could take all these e-mails to the FBI, or even the media, but how would she explain them? It made no sense without disclosing the whole future-seeing aspect of it, and nobody would believe that. Even Delilah's personal message to Val, as damning as it seemed, meant nothing without the context behind it, and that bitch knew it. Whether or not Barrister had truly been abusive, Delilah was no victim. She and Barrister were two fucked-up peas in a pod. Delilah had sent her this glut of information solely to torture her. And it had worked.

Her eyes wandered back to the TV, where the squeaky-clean public version of Delilah Barrister, mourning yet stoic widow, still addressed an audience of reporters at the press conference.

"I've talked about this at great length with my family, and we think the best way to honor Norman's memory is to continue his fight for this city and state that he loved. Therefore, I will be taking my husband's place in the run for mayor."

The closed captioning noted excited gasps from the audience.

Delilah looked at the camera. "I ask that everyone that would have voted for my husband, and those that are still undecided, cast your vote for the values and integrity my husband gave his life for, and for a better future for Seattle and Washington State."

Val remembered her first vision with Max:

I'm standing on the balcony of Max's house, the balcony where he threw his father to his death. The sky is overcast, the water is black. All of the glass is cracked, and trash is strewn everywhere. At my feet I see a weathered newspaper with a headline that reads:

President Barrister Declares War

Before I can check the date or read the article, the brightest light I've ever seen bursts in the sky and mushrooms upward. I hear and feel a rumbling that grows louder, shattering the glass around me, until a shock wave hits and I'm engulfed in flames. I'm screaming as the fire chars the flesh off my body and roasts my bones.

President Barrister—*Delilah* Barrister. For Delilah's help, these anonymous and powerful people had promised her a ticket to the White House. And Val had danced like a fucking puppet to her lies.

Still feeling like she might vomit at any moment, Val gathered the papers back together, dumped them in her bag, and crawled out of the booth. The TV finally cut away from Delilah, onto a different subject: "Secret Sex Tape of Mayor Brest and Unidentified Blond Woman Goes Viral on Internet—Poll Numbers Plunge."

Her cell phone rang on her way out the door. She glanced at it and saw Max's number on the caller ID. Their child couldn't be stolen if they never had one. Tears filled her eyes as she watched it ring, and ring, until it went to voice mail, unanswered.

Epilogue

Kitty drummed her nails on the chair's steel arm as she sat across from Cassandra in the Alpha Seer's Hong Kong office. Per usual, Cassandra was dressed in her white blouse–pencil skirt combo, black hair cascading down her back, while Kitty wore a black pantsuit, her blond hair in a tight bun. She watched as Cassandra drew what looked like plans for a Rube Goldberg machine on a piece of paper, head down in quiet concentration. It was hard to break the habit of waiting for a cue to speak, though Kitty knew there wouldn't be one.

"Delilah is up by six points," Kitty said. "She's almost certain to beat Mayor Brest. The good people of Seattle don't want a mayor who gets his rocks off by wearing diapers and pretending to be a baby. Unfortunately, Delilah also tipped off Valentine to her future Alpha child. She's spooked, and has stopped seeing Max romantically."

No reaction from Cassandra. Made sense, given that the Seer already knew exactly what Kitty would say. Still, Kitty had to say it; otherwise, there would be nothing for Cassandra to look into the future to see—the paradox of remembering the future.

"Seems to me Delilah hasn't lived up to her end of the bargain, if she told Northwalk she'd get Max and Valentine together and then split them up again—"

"Do not kill Delilah," Cassandra said in her breathy British accent, not looking up from her drawing. "She will be dealt with. In time."

Kitty tensed against her will. Often it seemed as if Cassandra could read her mind, though she knew the Seer couldn't. She and Sten would be dead by now if Cassandra or any other member of Northwalk knew their thoughts. *We should just kill them*, Sten had said. She would if she could. How do you kill someone with perfect recall of the future? The fact that Northwalk still employed them meant they'd never succeed, or Cassandra hadn't seen fit to warn anyone for reasons only she knew. Though if Kitty had learned anything from a lifetime of manipulating the future at Northwalk's bidding, it was that anything was possible. Patience was key.

"You must ask," Cassandra said.

Kitty composed herself, relaxed. "How do you want me to get Max and Valentine together again?"

Cassandra finally looked up from her drawing, put her pen down, threaded her slender fingers together. "Let the gale raze their affected hearts. Then offer the life boat."

Wait, was what Cassandra meant. That, Kitty could do. She'd been waiting all her life, waiting for the right moment to seize what was hers. It *would* happen, Cassandra's failure to see it be damned.

"There is more," Cassandra said. She never asked questions that weren't rhetorical; she only made statements.

"The doctors tell me they were able to successfully reverse Max's vasectomy during the surgery on his bullet wound. Sten's a good shot."

Cassandra looked at her drawing, tracing the intricate lines with her fingers. Kitty knew it was part of a machine, something Cassandra was bringing into being before its time.

"So many moving stars," Cassandra said. "They bleed into each other." Her ethereal eyes filled with tears that leaked onto the paper. "There shall never be another one."

Kitty had no idea what Cassandra was talking about. The Seer knew things no one else could understand, things no one *should* understand. Being able to see everything until the end of the universe wasn't good for one's sanity. She didn't have much time left before she totally lost it. Northwalk was champing at the bit for Max and Val's Alpha child.

Cassandra looked at Kitty. "Go."

Kitty stood and walked toward the exit.

"End it, Omega," Kitty heard Cassandra say behind her. *Omega*—Cassandra's designation for Valentine Shepherd. "Save us all."

Acknowledgments

I'd like to thank my agent, Carrie Pestritto, for taking a chance on a new author with a very weird idea. I'd also like to thank my excellent editor, Madeleine Colavita, for frustrating the hell out of me by pointing out areas where my manuscript needed work that I was sure were already perfect, then proving me wrong when the final product turned out to be a hundred times better than the original.

I'd like to give a shout-out to my writing group partners in Dayton Write Now who had to suffer through the crappy first drafts of my story: Karen Brandin, Amy Jomantas, and Daphne Burgard. Another big thanks goes to my other awesome writing group, Western Ohio Writers Association, including their fearless leader Gery Deer and his beautiful wife Barbara, and the three sexy amigos: Bill Bicknell, Michael Martin, and Philip A. Lee. Without their #RealTalk and much better grasp of the English language than me, I never would have made it as a serious author, or known the difference between a participle and a gerund (...I still don't, but they remind me!).

Thanks to the men and women of the US Armed Forces for giving me the opportunity to serve and protect my country, as well as a steady paycheck that allowed me to write for the love of it. Specific thanks to my military friends and coworkers who managed to stifle their shock and express support when I told them I wrote romance rather than military sci-fi.

Finally, I'd like to express my extreme gratitude to my family: my mom for encouraging me to follow my dreams; my sister for giving me her love and support; my pugs for being my writing buddies and arm rests; my daughters for tipping the scales of my lifelong memories from mostly bad to mostly good; and my husband for keeping the home fires burning and giving me his unwavering support when each day I went to work, then came home and sat in a corner and plinked away on my laptop.

Much like an Oscar speech, there are dozens of other people who contributed to my success and deserve to be recognized, but at this point I'm being figuratively played off the stage. So if you're one of those people, please accept my apologies, and my thanks!

Please see the next page for a preview of *Retribution*,
the next book in Shana Figueroa's
Valentine Shepherd series!

Chapter One

Valentine Shepherd ran so fast, she felt her heart might explode from the strain. She rounded a corner and sprinted down her Tacoma suburb street, quiet in the late morning when most people were at work. With the mid-July sun hard on her back, she crossed the invisible finish line in front of her house and slowed to a halt, put her hands on her knees, and threw up into the bright green grass. She wiped her mouth with the back of her hand and cast a glance around her neighborhood to ensure no one had seen. No workout felt good enough without a dollop of pain—sore knees, joint aches, pulled muscles, nausea. Going easy on herself meant letting weakness fester, giving her enemies the upper hand. She'd be damned if she let that happen again.

Val walked half a block away from her house to cool down, then turned and walked back. She stopped and stared at a car she didn't recognize, parked on the corner in front of a fire hydrant.

"BFG three thousand fifteen. BFG three thousand fifteen," she said to herself, committing the car's license plate number to memory so she could track down who it belonged to, who

Delilah Barrister had sent to watch her. Then again, why would she bother having someone stake out Val's house? She was a goddamn prophet—like Val, but better. More devious at least. Norman Barrister's widow probably knew what Val was doing every second of every day.

Val shook her head at the mystery car. "Shit," she muttered, turning away from yet another shadow to obsess over.

She stalked back into her house, kicking aside one of Stacey's raincoats splayed on the floor next to the door. She'd need to have another talk with her friend about leaving crap lying around for clients to stumble upon. Very unprofessional for the recently popular Valentine Investigations. Business had been booming since she'd "solved" the mystery of who killed Seattle millionaire Lester Carressa and exonerated his only son and heir to his fortune, Maxwell Carressa, of the crime back in October. They'd even had to turn some clients away. She hated saying no; she was often their last resort for justice. But even with Stacey's help and her own ability to glimpse the future, she was only one person against a world where cruelty and injustice were the norm.

Val rubbed her sweaty face on a dishcloth and threw open her fridge, then shoved aside bundles of kale Stacey bought but would never eat and grabbed a beer from the back. She touched her hot cheek to the cold glass bottle, rubbed the condensation on her skin, and let it trickle down her neck. Then she twisted off the top and took a long drink. The immediate buzz was comforting. Dwelling on things she couldn't change would drive her mad. She should accept it and move on, like Max had done—

A lump grew in her throat. *Don't even start*, she chastised herself. She chugged the rest of her beer. *Don't think about him. He went on with his life. You can, too.* She looked at herself in the gold-burnished decorative mirror—the one she'd put up in the hallway across from the kitchen a million years ago, when she'd lived there happily with Robby and gave a shit about home furnishings. Her strawberry-colored hair hung in a high ponytail glistening with sweat, flushed face dominated by gray eyes the color of steel. She sneered at the woman behind the glass.

"How's being mayor?" she said to her reflection. "Working your way up to governor, still milking your dead husband's glorious legacy?" She stepped closer to the glass, imagining Delilah's premonition of this moment, the good laugh the mayor would have about it. "You know I'll kill you, right? I never thought I was capable of cold-blooded murder, but you've made me reconsider—"

"That's some crazy shit, Shepherd."

Val jumped at the man's voice coming from the living room. She dropped her beer bottle and lunged back into the kitchen. Staying low to the ground behind the counter, she threw open the cabinet door underneath her sink and grabbed the gun she kept there—one of many she hid around the house in case of emergency. She braced her arms on the countertop, gun pointed at the voice. Her eyes narrowed when she recognized Sten Ander, corrupt Seattle PD Vice Squad detective and Delilah's henchman, where he lounged on her sofa with his legs crossed and fingers bridged behind his head.

"Come here to finally kill me?" Val said to Sten, the psychopath who'd tried to murder her and Max on three separate occasions. She hadn't seen Sten since he'd shot Max in the stomach at the Pacific Science Center. He'd shaved off his giant 1980s beat cop mustache; now he looked like a darker, crazier version of Jeremy Renner with a narrower nose and thicker eyebrows.

"Yes, I came to kill you," he said as he bounced his foot in the air. "That's why I'm unarmed—to show off my head-exploding psychic powers." He stared at her and scrunched his face in mock concentration, then relaxed and sighed. "Damn. I was sure that would work."

Fucking Sten. She'd never met a person so full of shit, and she'd met a *lot* of shitbags in her line of work.

Val kept her gun trained on him. "What do you want, Sten?"

"I came to deliver a message."

"So spit it out."

"See, here's the thing. It's kind of complicated. I think—"

"Oh, for God's sake." Val lowered her gun, turned away from him, and opened the fridge. She pulled out another beer. "If you're gonna start with the bullshitting, I'd rather you just kill me." She popped off the cap and took a long swig.

"*I think*, before I give you the message, we should talk about your budding drinking problem. You'll never score another rich boyfriend as a paranoid drunk."

Val slammed her bottle down on the countertop. *Fucking Sten* and his mind games. "You wanna talk?" She stomped around the partition and shoved her gun in Sten's face. "Let's talk."

He looked down the barrel of her Glock and lifted an eyebrow, more surprised than scared.

"Tell me why you're working for Delilah."

"'Working' is a strong word. 'Indentured' is more accurate."

"Why?"

Sten sighed, and for half a second his laidback-asshole demeanor betrayed a hint of sadness. "Because I owe a debt I can never pay back."

Val gritted her teeth. "What does that mean?" She grabbed the lapel of his cheap suit coat and yelled into his face, "*What the fuck does that mean?* Why does everyone have to talk in goddamn riddles?"

"That's the condensed version," he said, "The full story would take all day, maybe all week…" Sten trailed off as his eyes drifted down to her wet cleavage, bulging out the top of her sports bra.

Of course he'd be thinking about sex as she assaulted him. Or maybe he just pretended. He'd throw up any distraction to avoid telling her the truth about whatever game he and his coconspirators played. She could play games, too.

About the Author

Shana Figueroa is a published author who specializes in romance and humor, with occasional sojourns into horror, sci-fi, and literary fiction.

She lives in Massachusetts with her husband, two young daughters, and two old pugs. She enjoys reading, writing (obviously), martial arts, video games, and SCIENCE—it's poetry in motion! By day, she serves her country in the US Air Force as an aerospace engineer. By night, she hunkers down in a corner and cranks out the crazy stories lurking in her head.

She took Toni Morrison's advice and started writing the books she wanted to read. Hopefully you'll want to read them, too!

Learn more at:

ShanaFigueroa.com

Twitter @Shana_Figueroa

Facebook.com/Shana.Figueroa.9